The WHITE Hour

THE
WHITE
HOUR

NEIL GUNN

RICHARD DREW PUBLISHING
Glasgow

First published 1950 by Faber and Faber Ltd.

This edition first published 1990 by
Richard Drew Publishing Ltd.
6 Clairmont Gardens
Glasgow G3 7LW

© Foreword Dairmid Gunn 1990

The publisher acknowledges the financial assistance of the
Scottish Arts Council in the publication of this book

British Library Cataloguing in Publication Data
Gunn, Neil M. (Neil Miller), 1891-1973
  The white hour : and other stories.
  I. Title
  823.912 [F]

ISBN 0-86267-279-1

Printed and bound in Great Britain by
Cox & Wyman Ltd., Reading

Foreword

Although best known as one of Scotland's most revered and popular authors of this century, Neil Gunn began his creative life as a short story writer. As early as 1929, one year after the publication of his first novel, *The Grey Coast*, a collection of short stories made their appearance under the title, *Hidden Doors*. Over twenty years were to elapse before the second collection of short stories, *The White Hour*, was to be published. During these years Gunn wrote fifteen novels, several short plays, an authoritative book on whisky and its significance in Scotland, an autobiographical odyssey, *Off in a Boat*, and a series of meditative essays brought together in one book, *Highland Pack*. Both *Off in a Boat* and *Highland Pack* have been published in the Scottish Collection.

The White Hour was conceived at a difficult time for the author. From 1938 to 1949 Neil Gunn and his wife had lived in a farmhouse on the slopes of a Highland glen linking the county town of Ross and Cromarty, Dingwall, to the small village of Strathpeffer. It had been an idyllic spot for a reflective writer with its magnificent view of the mountains in the West and easy access to hill and moor to the North. There Gunn had spent his most creative period, writing many novels, including his great masterpiece, *The Silver Darlings*. There he had written four of the novels already published in the Scottish Collection series — *Second Sight*, *The Shadow*, *The Silver Bough* and *The Lost Chart*. The move from this retreat had been involuntary, the result of the ending of a rental agreement. A peaceful and creative period had ended and a more uncertain and demanding time begun.

A new house had to be bought without the support of the proceeds of a house sale. The house chosen was attractively situated on the western side of the Cromarty Firth between Dingwall and the village of Evanton, but there were drawbacks. The house was wedged between the sea and the main road leading to the North. Gunn felt hemmed in and cut off from the land, and customary walks had to be taken along the long garden by the firth, quarterdeck style.

It was during this unsettled period, described so succinctly by Gunn's biographers as one of "marking time", that the author turned to journalism to augment his income. The American market was lucrative and American agents appreciative. It was a psychological boost for Gunn, which led him to collect his later short stories, along with some of those that had appeared in the 1929 collection, and make a book of them. In 1950 *The White Hour* appeared in the bookshops to remind his wide circle of admirers that he could write short stories and write them well.

The title is subtly chosen. Although the story in the collection by that name concerns an old woman's premonition of death, any sense of fear experienced by her is subtly tempered by the knowledge that her life will continue after death through her attractive granddaughter. The white light is softened. White, of course, has many connotations.

In Russia's northern city of Leningrad the White Nights are those summer nights when it scarcely becomes dark and during which a mystical half light prevails. It is neither night nor day and there is an absence of clear definition. It is perhaps no coincidence that a short story called *Half Light* appears in this collection. The hero of the story, an educated man, returns to his native community, loses his destructive logical objectiveness — the black and white syndrome — and identifies himself with the surrounding elemental forces — particularly the sea. Critics might say that this short story is only too reminiscent of the Celtic Twilight school. There is certainly a hint of that school in the work, but there is also in it a grim realism that is the hallmark of another great literary tradition. Gunn's success lies in his ability to harmonise the dissonant strains within Scottish literature associated with the schools that have been described as "Kailyard", "realist" and "Celtic Twilight".

The White Hour is the harvest of a long period of creative writing and thinking. Every variety of short story is represented from those dependent on colour and mood to those centred on a plot with cumulative action. There is the simple folk tale, *Henry Drake goes Home* and the horrifying account of unbridled scientific experiment in *Dance of the Atoms*. The rural idyll, *The Blaeberries,* is in sharp contrast to the horror of *The Clock* and *Symbolical.* Neil Gunn gives this simple explanation of the stories in *The White Hour*. "That they all had the same begetter will doubtless worry the pure ctitic, but a man takes his short stories how and where he finds them — in contradiction perhaps to the novel which might be conceived of as taking to a wife." Despite their variety the short stories are connected by an unbroken thread of perception. It takes the form of a psychological element within the psyche of certain characters that makes them receptive to the two worlds of actuality and imagination. In the 'half light' there has to be a merging of the opposites.

Dairmid Gunn

Contents

THE CHARIOT   *page* 11
WHISTLE FOR BRIDGE   28
HILL FEVER   33
THE OLD MAN   40
PAPER BOATS   51
SYMBOLICAL   58
BLAEBERRIES   65
THE TAX-GATHERER   69
THE WHITE HOUR   80
THE TREE   86
ON THE STONE   104
THE BLACK WOOLLEN GLOVES   118
DANCE OF THE ATOMS   128
LOVE'S DIALECTIC   143
THE MIRROR   158
THE LISTENER'S TALE   167
THE CLOCK   177
SUCH STUFF AS DREAMS   185
PURE CHANCE   192
DOWN TO THE SEA   214
THE GHOST'S STORY   222
MONTROSE RIDES BY   231

CONTENTS

HENRY DRAKE GOES HOME   *page* 242

THE TELEGRAM   251

HALF-LIGHT   257

THE MOOR   274

Note

The majority of these stories appeared in the *Scots Magazine* over a period of many years; others in *Chambers's Journal*, the *Cornhill*, *Dublin Magazine*, *Scotland's Magazine*, *Scottish Field*, *Spectator*; a few have been taken from a collection called *Hidden Doors* (1929) now long out of print. Acknowledgments are gladly made. Some that might have been included are omitted because at least their substance was incorporated in novels. Minor revisions have been made.

The Chariot

"You think I'm on the mend, Doctor?"

"You just take care of yourself and keep on as you're doing." The doctor nodded agreeably. "Don't get up. Give the old organ a chance. It'll do its best for you."

"I feel a bit easier." The eyes in the spare face had a glassy sheen and looked at the doctor as if they would look through him.

With his characteristic tender gesture, the doctor laid the old man's wrist on the coverlet. "There now!" he said, getting up off the bed. "I'll look in to see you again soon."

The old man removed his eyes. They were inclined to fix in a stare.

As the doctor closed the door behind him, the patient's housekeeper came from the kitchen and asked in a hushed voice, "How is he?"

"He feels a bit easier," said the doctor. "But you mustn't let him get up or exert himself in any way."

"All right, Doctor. He's not so difficult now. He was asking for you last night."

"I'll be out again soon. There's not a great deal I can do for him. He just has to rest."

"When will you be? He'll be asking me."

"Let me see," said the doctor, lifting his eyes from the anxious face, with the wisps of grey hair beneath the open-work dust-cap it always wore in the morning. "Not to-morrow —nor, perhaps, next day—but certainly the day after."

"You couldn't make it the day after to-morrow?"

The doctor thought for a moment. "Very well," he said.

"Thank you, Doctor." She nodded with relief. "I'll tell him that."

As the doctor left the house and walked quickly out to his car, he heard smothered laughter coming from the shop, which stood a few yards up the main road. The village consisted of a loose cluster of about a score of dwellings, but the countryside around was dotted with croft houses and the little fields were clearly defined, the potatoes a mass of flower and the corn just ready to turn. It was a lovely day, and the laughter from the shop was the hidden heart of it.

The doctor smiled to himself as he got under the driving-wheel. It was easy to diagnose the laughter. He took out his cigarette-case; there was only one in it, so he slipped from the car and went up to the shop.

They were all caught red-handed in their mirth—Bobbie, the lovely flashing Johanna with her finger-tips on the counter, the old woman with the basket, a couple of young women and a boy. The laughter was sliced off. But Johanna's eyes held a certain mantling challenge as she waited for the doctor's order.

No one spoke until the doctor had got his cigarettes and was turning away; then the old woman, in a restrained, sober voice, asked, "How is Mr. Macready to-day?"

"Not so bad. It's a fine day."

"Yes, it's a beautiful day, Doctor."

"Thank you," said the doctor, and threw Johanna a glance. She smiled out of a face vivid with life, not exactly a bold smile, but with the unconscious challenge in it which a man feels.

If it is unconscious! thought the doctor, who believed that what Johanna needed was someone a dozen years older than herself.

All at once he felt relieved, almost happy. The truth was he did not like the old man. He had the curious feeling for a doctor of almost having to force himself to call. Accordingly, he made sure that he fulfilled his professional duty. In the past, Donald Macready had made sure that he did no more than that. "I'm feeling much better, Doctor. I don't think you need call again." As direct as that, the old devil! He was not going to pay for an extra visit if it could be avoided. The doctor remembered how angry this had made him the first time.

But things were a bit different now. It seemed to have dawned on Donald at last that the chariot might be drawing near. He looked to-day as if he had heard it. The sound must have been a pretty bleak one, for visits now were what he wanted.

The doctor's humour took an edge as he reflected what a miser the old man had been. Not that it mattered much in itself, a man's being a miser. If one got fun out of that, why not? It was when this miserliness crushed the fun out of others that the thing became accursed, made you feel bitter against it, and vindictive. He had robbed the countryside, got the poor people in his debt and fleeced them—not dramatically, but in that hellish little by little, that slow grinding that never let up. And it was so easy to do, because they were an improvident lot, leaving to-morrow to take care of itself, hoping for twin lambs, a good fishing, a bumper crop, believing even that the weather would change and be fine at the right time. Yet somehow a people who, in a certain mood, went to your heart.

Anyway, they could laugh—even if they felt guilty with illness so near! The hidden laughter of relief.

And Johanna, Donald's niece and heiress, would fairly make the money spin. Thousands and thousands—some said over fifty thousand. A catch for some bright youth! Though Johanna was all there, and a real good business girl. But how she would do it in style, upright, with her pointed breasts, when she started, when she was challenged! She would all right!

The doctor smiled, for Donald's visit had been the last and he was on his way home. With luck, there would be a round of golf in the evening, so he could let his mind free, even with Johanna!

Though it was interesting to speculate just what Donald must have thought this last year or two as he privately contemplated the passing of the vast horde he had accumulated, with such fisted hardness, over a lifetime, to the flashing Johanna.

The doctor's eyelids crinkled in a measuring humour. But no, there would have been nothing of that dubious warmth in their relationship. On the contrary, he had seen him "short" with the girl. Just as he was with wild flowers that made the grass rank. Weeds. The bluebottle that distracted you by buzzing on the window. The doctor made quite sure of this. He nodded, certain.

What, then? Just the one thing: that Donald so lived—had so lived—that his life of the moment, his money-making life, could not end. Without thinking about it at all, he had felt himself immortal. He had taken the girl to his shop and house because she was of his blood, because he therefore need not pay her a real wage, and because, being of his blood, he could presumably rely on her against the outside world. He would, in fact, have a vague grudge against her. Not because she was not his own child—he had never had time to marry, and in any case would probably have been harsher to her had she been his daughter—but because she was young, not sufficiently absorbed by the business; because she was not—himself.

But it didn't matter. He could tolerate her all right, for at any moment he could send her packing. He had the power, the money, and death was so remote that the thought of it could not touch him.

It was not quite so remote now!

Two days later, as the doctor approached the house, he wondered if he should suggest a heart specialist from Glasgow. After all, the old fellow had the cash and should at least be given the opportunity to use it, for his peace of mind if nothing else. The doctor's lashes flickered in their dry humour as he saw for a clear moment the two planes of his own mind: the professional plane where he would do everything possible to help his patient and that other human plane from which he observed what was happening with an insight so absolute that it was arid. As this insight had been growing in him, he dismissed it. He would suggest that the specialist should charter a plane. It would be expensive, and would take up so much less of the specialist's time that the unnecessary visit could to that degree be given some face. After all, if his patient wanted it . . .

To keep his eyes from the house he let them rove over the countryside. It was another lovely day, when growing things matured or flowered, with a warmth that ran through the air in a delicate fragrance. Like something long lost from the human condition, this fragrance touched the doctor for a moment.

The eyes were on him from the instant the door opened, but the body was still as a log, as a dead body laid out. The doctor sat cheerily down on the edge of the bed and looked at him, steadily, and the old man waited, not inconvenienced by the inscrutable professional look, but on the contrary seeming to drink it in, with a relief that could almost be seen.

"Just about the same, Doctor." He moved his head, began trying to describe pains he had had, placed his hand on his breast. The doctor nodded, and the old man sighed.

"They're looking after you all right?"

The eyes regarded the doctor, with their thin, glassy light, as if they did not understand. The doctor repeated his question. The eyes turned from the doctor's face to the window. "Yes," he muttered with indifference. "They" were clearly of no interest to him, were already dismissed.

The doctor caught the wrist gently, and while he felt the pulse, the old man lowered his lids and breathed heavily with a mournful sound of ease.

"Yes," said the doctor at last, nodding as he laid down the wrist, and again he looked steadily at the face. "So you're not feeling too grand to-day?"

"Just about the same."

"It's a slow business. You must reconcile yourself to that."

"Yes. So long as I'll get better?" It was only faintly a question.

"Oh, we'll see to that." The doctor began talking about food and bodily conditions, and had a look at the tongue. Then in the same conversational tone he said, "Perhaps you would like to have another opinion?"

There was a pause as the eyes stared, it seemed uncomprehendingly, at the doctor.

"I mean the opinion of another doctor—a specialist. I could arrange it for you, if you think it might make you feel easier."

"No. Oh no." The words sounded automatic. But the doctor, who was now watching the face acutely from behind his pleasantness, saw something wary in the expression, almost frightened, and decided that the old man was not quite so low as he had thought. The old Adam was still there!

But when the doctor was sent for specially the following morning, he decided that a night's reflection had prepared the old man to slacken the purse strings. And now he almost regretted having mentioned the matter of another opinion. The truth was he disliked all that the old man stood for, and did not give a hang for his money or how he spent it. His own account would not include a halfpenny more than the normal charge, whether the old man were dead or alive. If he had to ring up a Glasgow specialist he would take care to give him his very frank opinion of the case—as well as the old man's circumstances. What then happened could happen, but it was so much extra work, unnecessary, and he was busy enough.

"Well," he said cheerfully as he entered the sick room, "what's all the trouble this morning?"

Something like a smile came to the gaunt features, and as they were not used to smiling, the expression was curiously repellant, particularly as the eyes, in their tendency to stare, took on that glassy light from the window. "I hope I did not take you away, but I was thinking over what you said about another doctor. Would you like me to have one?"

"That's for you to say. If there's anyone you would like, I could arrange it."

"Do you think it necessary?"

"Frankly, no. But that's only my opinion."

He sighed. "That's all right then. I did not wish to trouble you. But if you wanted another doctor, you could have one. I was frightened you might think I didn't want you to have one."

"Don't you want one, then?"

"Not if you don't yourself, Doctor. I'm satisfied."

"You're quite sure?"

The eyes looked at him, and for a moment there was an odd, indescribable tension that the doctor could not fathom but that made him feel uncomfortable.

"Quite sure," said Donald.

"In that case, it's all right," said the doctor, getting off the bed. "We'll look after you as best we can."

It was no good talking to the housekeeper, whose mind had been devilled out of her, so he went up to the shop. Bobbie was opening a wooden box, and Johanna greeted him with her full-open sky-blue eyes. He took some money out of his pocket and she placed his brand of cigarettes on the counter. He glanced at Bobbie, and she said: "Bobbie, you might see about that box in the yard." She was a sensible girl, and the lad went. "How is he this morning?" she asked.

"Pretty much the same—although he seems changed a bit. Anything happened to him?"

"No. Not that I know of."

"Did he mention anything to you, or the housekeeper, about getting another opinion, medical opinion?"

"No." Her fair brows gathered in a small pucker, imperious, concerned for the doctor, as she gazed full into his eyes.

"That's all right, then. To ease his mind, I said to him last night that I could arrange for another opinion if he liked. That's what I thought he wanted me for."

"Was it?"

"No. At least he said he didn't want another opinion if I didn't want one. I couldn't quite make him out."

"I don't think", she said, turning her face to the window with its laden shelves, "that—it would be a question of expense. I—hardly think so."

That was frank and clever of her. She surprised the look of admiration in his eyes, and, with a thoughtful smile at the packet in his hand, he extracted a cigarette and lit it.

"I just wondered," he said easily.

"I think it is because", and she looked away again, "he has faith in you."

"You think so? That's odd, because we haven't been too friendly."

"Perhaps that's why."

He glanced at her quickly.

"How do you mean?"

"Because he saw you were independent."

He considered her face as he did a patient's, but with the smile of tribute lighting up his brown eyes. "Now that *is* clever of you."

She moved at haphazard, trying to keep back the blush, but

it deepened steadily. He regarded the window; then, taking out his silver cigarette-case, began to fill it. "All the same, I wonder?" and he looked up sideways with the friendliest smile.

"I know he does," she answered, twisting the end of string that overflowed from its tin canister round a forefinger, head up, annoyed with herself. She dropped the string. "He thinks he can trust you."

"You think that?"

"He thinks it."

He laughed. "You're fairly bright this morning."

"How is he, really?"

"Pretty bad, actually. Anything might happen—fairly soon. I wanted to say as much to you."

"Oh." Her expression sobered and she grew quite still. In the silence they heard footsteps approaching the door.

"I'll keep my eye on him—and let you know."

"I wish you would," she said impulsively, hardly looking at him.

"Don't worry about it," he suggested, calming her. The customer, a woman, entered behind him. "I'll look along to-morrow morning."

"Thank you."

As he drove on to his next patient, he could not help smiling at Johanna's penetration. Acute of her—whether true or not. And for a little while he could not be bothered probing the truth for thinking of Johanna. It was pleasant to smile and feel amused in this careless way. Fresh and new. Another lovely day. The weather would probably break down just when the corn was ready for cutting. There was humour in that, too, the strange, inscrutable humour that hung over the sunlit land.

Perhaps the old man did respect him? One did respect one's enemy if he was firm and of a piece. His vision narrowed, focusing the old man's mind. He began to feel himself inside the old man's skin. Quite suddenly intuition revealed the pattern with all the certainty of a direct sensation. His foot eased on the throttle to let the car go slow. But he could not readily focus thought, so he stopped the car by the roadside and, under the influence of a fine excitement, automatically lit a cigarette.

She was quite right. Money was not the trouble. Very simply what was happening to Donald was this: all his life his relationships had been to things, to cash. But he had now heard the chariot, and the chariot had no relationship to cash—very, very definitely. The doctor's eyes narrowed. Donald now was wanting relationship to life, to another life, instinctively feeling that that would keep away the terror, the lonely terror, of the chariot. In that stark desert loneliness, where the money-hunt had taken him, *money was of no use*.

The doctor nodded and smiled with one corner of his mouth. He's going to use me now! He's terrified! His humour grew so bleak that a withering came to his own face. Suddenly he started up the car and set off at speed.

When, next morning, he sat down on the edge of the patient's bed and pleasantly began asking the usual questions, he was ready to confirm his psychological diagnosis. And from every slightest movement, or intonation, or facial expression, what the previous day had been incalculable was now clear. The old man was not so much greedy for life as greedy for the doctor's life. And the doctor led him on, as though some ultimate subtlety in himself, fine as a knife-edge, had to be satisfied or assuaged. He reverted again to the getting of a second opinion, but this time directly named a consultant in Glasgow. Of course, the chartering of an aeroplane, not to mention a fast car and so on, would be very expensive. But if his patient thought it was worth it . . .

All this easeful play, wherein the two planes of the doctor's mind got dubiously intermixed, did establish a certain curious nemesis. The old man at last, at the end, could not trust anyone outside. Did not want anyone from outside—if he could put his full trust in the doctor. And for this trust he pleaded, yet not openly, for he had his own character, moulded by past custom.

"Well, I'm pretty busy just now, but I'll look in to-morrow morning."

"*Any* time you're passing, Doctor. I'll be glad to see you."

"Very good." He smiled to his patient and went out.

But there was a taste in his mouth, and when he saw a customer going towards the shop he got into his car and drove off. As he drove off, he thought he ought to have gone to the shop and spoken to Johanna. He wondered if he would stop the car and go back. But the car went on, driving itself with a mechanical persistence that his mind, in its peculiar humour, observed.

The next day, affairs went a stage further. For the first time the old man showed signs of wanting to talk. The doctor decided that this was merely a device to detain him. But presently he saw it was more than that. For in the old man's talk about his affairs there was no genuine interest in how they were getting on.

"You needn't worry," the doctor had said, heading him off. "Johanna is a very capable girl. Things are safe with her."

But he was not worrying about Johanna. He wanted to talk about his business because he wanted to talk about his life. Out of a slightly morbid curiosity the doctor listened for a time. "It's been a hard life, and many folk were against me . . ." But there was a limit to what he could listen to, so he got off the bed, pleasantly. For he could not hurt the old man, could not mortally offend him.

He wants to make me his confessor next! he thought, as he went outside and glanced towards the shop. He had better see Johanna, if he was to avoid thinking as much about her as he had done last night.

There were customers in, but Johanna must have seen him through the window, for she met him at the door and they walked down the few yards to the car.

"You were quite right," he said, as they stood by the car. "I didn't look in to tell you that yesterday because I saw you had customers. But you were right—about the money."

"I thought I was. He was always wondering when you were coming, and was inclined to blame us when you didn't turn up."

"I suppose he blamed me, too?"

"He did—to begin with. Not now."

"Look here," he said spontaneously, "what about leaving that old shop now and running off with me to town for a cup of coffee?"

She glanced at him, smiling, and looked away. "I should love it."

"Well?"

She dismissed the play. "Perhaps you'll let me know how he is to-morrow?"

"So you won't come? All right. I'll remember that—until to-morrow!" Then as he went into the car he beckoned with his head. She turned away, and because there was a small flush on her face she hurried.

That brightened her up! he thought. All the same, his offer *had* been spontaneous. He had better watch himself! There wasn't a cell in her body that wasn't alive. She was certainly a lovely creature, with something genuinely shy behind that country flash of boldness. Or was he imagining it? He knew he wasn't. She needed her share of self-protection against the country lads, who in their natural improvidence made love naturally. He laughed.

But there was an extraordinary persistence of life in Donald, and the doctor grew to hate the sight of the house. He was finding it more and more difficult to indulge the old man mentally. He would listen, but he was evasive, and after a time headed him off. The reaction of dislike for the old man that this produced hung about his own mouth, his mind, in an inverted distaste for himself. When he felt the patient trying to justify his way of life in an oblique effort to draw understanding, sympathy, his whole body would in an instant quicken with a sort of cold fury that was yet almost passionless, while he smiled and countered with a play of easy optimism. "Time enough to worry—you're not dead yet!" The glassy eyes would look at him.

All this began to have its effect on the doctor, curiously darkening life for spells. Then he decided that it was beginning to have its effect on Johanna. The vivid spontaneous quality, that is the core of life, was netted in its shadow. The doctor could see, in his mind, Johanna moving about in this shadow, her face petulant, dreary with a sort of ill-temper that remained suspended, directionless, in a sordid world.

This, perhaps, was allowing intuition too much rope. But there were ways of testing it, and though Johanna had a degree of loyalty to her uncle which he admired, her reticence and a certain moody, troubled look, however momentary, were all the more expressive on that account. It really was extraordinary how pervasive the old man's mind had become. One could almost imagine it in the cow that, with swollen sides, still kept tearing at the grass in the ditch as she was driven home.

Within ten days the relationship between Johanna and the doctor took a definite change. It entered into a sunless phase, which the bright sun in the lovely ripening weather mocked at with its hidden thought. But though Johanna thus lost her flashing challenge, she somehow came still nearer to the doctor, as two human beings might draw together who had to find their way out of a wood or a wilderness.

It was not that the old man was the ogre in the wood, the invisible devil in the wilderness. But there was enough of that in it to invade the professional plane, to stiffen the doctor against yielding to the potency of the old man's character and influence. And the power of that character he had ample time to think over and to assess, until it assumed, by its terrifying persistence in time, every day, every hour, year after year, a more destroying potency than that of any ogre or invisible devil. It checked here, it checked there, little by little, in this and that, until it baffled and frustrated and subdued. Johanna's flashing challenge had been the rebellion of youth outside the ogre's immediate presence. But now Johanna, having been joined by the doctor, heard the chariot and became aware of the sunless wood.

And Donald would not have been beaten by them had his attention not been divided by the approach of the chariot, which had precisely his own power of persistence.

Ah, more than his own. And as at last he began to realise this, he seemed to withdraw from the doctor and enter on the next terrible phase, the unhuman phase.

The doctor's intuition became extremely acute, and when he thought of that battle—no, not a battle, but a state of endurance cold and tough as stone—between approaching death and the waiting old man, he got out of its filtered loneliness a bitter savour. He went over some of the meaner thing Donald had done, and got the impression again of a whole life devoted to money-making, money-hoarding. He couldn't take his money with him now! By God he couldn't! The doctor caught a glimpse of something horribly spiteful and malignant in money, and something of what he saw was caught in his own smile.

His patient's face took on the likeness of stone. He ceased to speak about himself. To the doctor, however, there was in the hollows and bone ridges, in the withdrawn expression, a pathos that affected him, in an unexpected moment of feeling, with a sense of colossal guilt. Not so much his own guilt, as the guilt of all mankind, an incredible and pathetic conspiracy in guilt.

This was carrying the myth too far, he decided, and went up and saw Johanna. Her flame was oddly subdued these days, but, for some reason, he felt its warmth all the more. She looked as if she were trapped and did not know where to turn; or had things to say and could not say them.

And now he found he could not say much to her himself. It certainly had become quite impossible to invite her light-heartedly to the town.

"I don't think it will be very long now," he said, almost casually, as he lit a cigarette.

The skin of her face became transfused with blood, but no longer in a blush, in a strange congestion of feeling rather, that appealed to him profoundly as though, by an act, he could dissipate its moodiness and release the pure light.

To defeat the heavy pulse that began to beat in him, he said, "Don't worry. I'll see that everything is all right."

The suggestion of sympathy in his voice did not help her, and she turned her eyes to the window, stiffening her face against an emotional surge. The eyes were blue wells of living light.

"What about a run into town?" he said lightly, smiling. The sudden words were little more than a perverse hardening against the moment.

She turned from him. He heard Bobbie's footsteps in the back shop and went out.

The smile stayed on his face, as if concerned with something, thoughtfully, ironically, at a distance; but when his lips got a little dry he drew up. Could thought of the old man's death have got her into that state? Partly, of course—but certainly only partly. He looked about the countryside as he automatically felt for his cigarette-case. Odd! he decided, the smiling gleam in his eyes not altogether dry. Very odd! Then, about to tap his cigarette on the silver case, he paused, and stared into the sunlight that lay on the ripe fields. The sunlight smiled back in its evasive, knowing way. It knew all about it all! In an instant his body ran hot, and Johanna came walking, as it were, towards him, out of the potato fields and the ripe corn, along the land under the blue sky.

His hands were a trifle shaky as he drove on, and he drew the cigarette smoke deep into his lungs, thought shut off.

That evening on a sudden impulse or intuition he went out to see the old man. Johanna and Bobbie were helping to unload a lorry beside the shop. As he got out he saluted them and turned down to the house. He read the housekeeper's face, saw its relief, its sudden resignation, and he knew that that face would have made no mistake.

The old man's eyes slowly turned on him, coldly, distant. The bone ridges and the flesh had caught the final stillness of stone, the everlasting stillness. From the doctor the eyes asked nothing; in their own need they lifted from the face and stared at the ceiling.

Never had the doctor seen such utter bleakness. He sat on the bed and stared at the face. There was nothing to be said.

Then, just before the end, there was an inward movement, a stirring of the mind, an appalling comprehension of the past by the spirit; the doctor felt it in himself with extraordinary power. The loneliness, the bleakness, were intensified a thousandfold; were apprehended now as never before, apprehended finally and beyond all possibility of change. As if the stone face had been struck, the mouth opened in a guttering "Ah-h-h".

The doctor shuddered, got up off the bed, and closed the eyes.

Presently he went out to break the news to Johanna. The lorry was driving off and she came to meet him, her eyes reading his message as she approached. He took her hand and with a smile placed it in the crook of his arm. "Keep your spirit up," he said.

She bit on her lip, but went with him down to the house.

From the kitchen they heard the housekeeper's moaning

voice. About the only abandonment left to her was indulgence in sorrow.

"Like to see him?" he asked suddenly, smiling in his light, friendly way. She would have to see him some time, for it was the country custom. She did not know what to do, and not knowing why he did this himself, he opened the door and ushered her into the room where the stone face lay under the ceiling.

She looked at it, and then, as if hit by some primeval terror, turned blindly away, choking.

"It's all right, Johanna," he said, detaining her with an arm. He spoke softly. His arm firmed. He put his other arm round her and she struggled against him as if to walk through him.

But he held her and spoke her name twice softly, his voice searching her out, searching out her face, searching out her face until he found it, and her arms gripped him as the last and only thing in life to which they could hold, gripped blindly and held to him and dwelt in him.

And the mood that had been growing within him these last years, the half-friendly but arid insight, the deadly insight, was dissolved, and life ran in a wild warm tide.

Whistle For Bridge

Donald's father was responsible for English in a large secondary school in a Scots industrial town, a slight fair man who at irregular intervals told the barber he would have nothing on his hair. When walking through a field he would sometimes take his son's hand, for he always appeared cool and unhurried and was rather given to staring through pale blue eyes.

This particular summer, Donald, who was nine years old, had quite a lot of freedom, for in the Highland town to which they had come for the vacation, his father had run into an old college acquaintance named Murray, who taught science but whose passion was for what he called analytic psychology. It was, for example, quite a simple affair for Murray to explain specifically why Shelley came to write the singular things he did write. Donald's father thought that what Shelley wrote had also a certain interest in or for itself. "I know," said Murray, "and I'll tell you exactly why you think so." In no time they were having great talks, wandering about or sitting on a wall or a bank. Actually, however, Donald's father mostly listened, and when he did not quite agree said "Um", while his eyes gazed remotely over a meadow.

It was out of such subtle indications of resistance that Murray first got his theory. In acute ways he pursued it, for he was a bright, intelligent analyst, until the truth seemed to lie veiled before him like a hidden vice. His old college friend was a secret poet!

So young Donald left them on a seat by a cemetery and wandered along a path that passed near a farm cottage beside which two men were quarrelling. "You can whistle for it," said one. "By God," said the other, following him, "I'll make you whistle out of the crooked side of your mouth." They disappeared behind the steading.

The path at last climbed up a steep wooded bank and Donald found himself by a slow-winding waterway. It was lovely and quiet here. The banks on each side were golden with broom and whin taller and thicker than ever Donald had seen. There was a scent that came up to him and went away in a mysterious fashion. The scent, although elusive, had yet a thickness in it that might have choked him if it had stayed. He pursued it tentatively in a world that had waked out of a drowsy afternoon and become watchful. The water was clear and still. There was not a human being anywhere. The birds sang in notes loud and challenging. The colour of the scent was yellow. And the thousands of golden flowers, all packed together like swarming bees, dazzled the eyes. Donald listened and became watchful, too, and faintly dazed about the forehead.

He might have hummed to himself and run away back; but he didn't, though he was now excited with the fear of something about to happen to him. And then as he stepped carefully along his heart gave a leap. Through the clear water towards him came a great grey-backed salmon. It swam slowly with a lazy movement of the whole body. It had a white patch on its side and on the top of its head. He saw its eyes, and its mouth kept opening whitely as if it had a half-crown in it. Donald could not move because he was rigid with fear of this beast that was not a beast but an apparition. Its nose touched the stones blindly beneath his feet; its back fin cut the water; it wriggled clumsily, disturbing the water to a faint panic, and set off again.

But Donald could not set off blindly. The bank held him,

as curiosity holds fear by cramping it. He saw the moving angle in the water. The nose of the angle touched the other side. There was a disturbance on the surface. But the beast did not start back again. It hung about that off side, quietly engaged on its strange business. What could that business be? What awful secret thing was it doing? If Donald could have tiptoed over a bridge, he would have . . . Swallowing his heart out of his throat and panting a little, he looked about him. Rising out of the golden broom beside him was a black board with great white letters:

WHISTLE

FOR

BRIDGE

Donald stared at the board.

But in a little while he assured himself that the board could hardly be enchanted because it was too real. It just meant to whistle for the bridge. Yet he was frightened to whistle for it, as any grown person might very well be frightened to create something out of nothing. For already he knew how the bridge would come. It would spring out of the thick bushes beyond the gorse on the other side and curve in a great dark arch over to his side. But the temptation was terrible. It nearly made him sick with excitement. And at first he was safe enough because his lips were so dry that they could make no sound. Then his lips moistened themselves, and he had to become extremely careful, so that, to begin with, he made only the very tiniest whistles. The whistles grew bigger, and at last in a splendid frenzy he whistled all he could. Nothing happened. Not a thing. He whistled again. And again. No arch invaded the sky. He was safe! Until in a flash he knew he was wrong: he had to whistle out of the crooked side of his mouth. The crooked side was for him the right side. Try as he might, the right side would produce nothing but breath. Quite by accident, however, the left side of his mouth gave a low mysterious whistle, and at once the earth responded in a hissing sound.

The sound was well down, but it was coming up—and up—it was coming upon him from behind. . . .

It was a steamer, with a slim bow cocked up on the water. She had grey coils of rope and black buoys on her deck. A man stood near the little wheel-house, broad-shouldered as a whaler. He saw the white scared face by the board and smiled and pulled a string. At once there was a hollow, shattering whistle that went on as if it were never more to stop. It stopped, and the man, who had the face of all the kind sailors in the world, waved to the boy and, pulling the string again, made an extra playful little cough of a whistle all for his benefit.

As the vessel disappeared round the bend, the man looked back. Then the place was emptier than it had been in the beginning, and the boy started running back to find his father.

One of the two men who had been quarrelling was now with a young woman who, as Donald passed, said in a strange, challenging voice, "He may whistle for it, but he'll get it some day." His father and Murray were no longer by the cemetery. At last he saw them away across a field, and by the time he overtook them they were walking along a road. They were still talking, or at least Murray was, when he came up with them. As he felt his father look at him, warmth came into his face, he did not know why. But his father said nothing.

Murray's talk was full of intricate and difficult words so that one could shelter behind them, though his little hard laugh occasionally was disturbing. They came to a low bridge over water.

"This," said his father to him, "is the Caledonian Canal."

"Boats go right through it," explained Murray, "from Inverness to the West Coast."

Donald recognised the water. "But the bridge——"

"They whistle for it," said Murray, "and the two men turn that handle and the bridge opens."

Revelation caught Donald in a flash of light and he went hot with secret shame.

"What did you think?" asked Murray, eyeing him.

Donald brought to his face the calm, far-eyed expression of his father, and said, "I was just wondering." His father took his hand.

Hill Fever

At midnight the light goes grey. This grey has the deadness of grey grass; very still and curving with the near breasts of the hills—so near that they are at hand, wherever the eyes rest—and the fingers touch.

At first it is like tracking silence to its lair. Iain Og, to give him his boyhood name again, felt indeed that he had trapped it. Here at last all sound had died and was resumed again into the womb of negation.

At first. Then the silence rose up out of that negation and opened like a flower on a movie screen, silently. The petals were the surrounding peaks set in a whorl, row behind row. Standing on the crest above the high hut was like standing on the sterile centre of the flower of the world's death.

Which was a trifle grandiloquent once the mind, grown cunning, had harried the romantic need for vast contrasts and come deep upon that odd, if final, duality of life and death. Odd, because it stares, or sets the eyes staring—at the near hillside, for example, as it comes down, and slowly up under the fingers. The fingers pierce softly the black peaty earth with its oily ooze and, withdrawing, create their own gentle slimy suck of negation. The suck attracts; absorbs fascination, or horror, into mindlessness.

But opposite, where the breast swells slowly up, the same earth gathers invisible tension. Perhaps it merely cannot be held under the eye like the deathly ooze at the finger-tips. At such a thought the grey air takes on a curious quality, not glimmering so much as watchful or expectant. The silence grows exquisitely thin and taut. The skin grows taut and cold. The roots of the grass and the heath under the brown skin of the slope are invisibly alive. There is a tense twining stress. The mind can sustain in balance no more than a certain weight. The least thing added, even of awareness, makes it topple over like a wave. The hillside opens and out of it in green froth come the fairies. The breast of the earth for the fairies.

Analysis of this kind can have a morbid air. Iain Og himself would have mistrusted the something that crawls in it, like worms in earth, a fortnight ago, when he married his equally young wife (who was a sport and a hill-climber) and brought her here to a just sufficiently commodious fishing hut for the honeymoon. But now he found not the least thing morbid in it. On the contrary, it was all charged with a rare mirth, bridging the gap between black negation under the fingers and that breast opposite.

Indeed it enriched him. He had never felt so full of the very sap of life. It was a health shot through with sunlight. This health could fold over on itself and peer out from the folds like a laughing sprite. Or walk in easy swinging poise, conscious of the toes. All of which, being a trifle undignified, must be suppressed. Hence the mirth, with its glancing, measuring, and even veiled eyes.

Last night, when he had been out in the boat alone and, doubled up over a big trout, had cast his quick smile around, he had seen his wife come ghost-like down to the water's edge. Without straightening himself, he stealthily watched her, until her voice came over the water, calling his name once.

He took the hook out and knocked the head against a wooden edge. The soft slippery body slid from his hand into the shallow bailer. Then he leaned over the boatside. The water was warmer than his hands and his fingers worked in it, each fist cleaning itself.

"John!"

He shook the water from his hands, but did not answer. Not answering was like the holding of a joke in poise. It was detachment from her in a warm assurance. He held the cast of flies against the sky, unravelled it, hooked the tail fly, and reeled in the slack. He liked the sound of the reel at night. He often played with it. Now it was an answer to her. With the point of the rod swaying over the stern, he rowed slowly to her feet.

"Why didn't you answer me?"

He sat smiling up at her quizzically. It had been a hot day. She was in white, and the fold over of the linen left her throat and opening breast shadowy. She looked very cool, even more detached than his admiration.

"Why don't you speak?"

It was idiotic not to speak. Her tone was cool, hardly aggrieved. "I got a beauty," he said, and lifted the wide bailer on to the seat. The spotted pound trout he caressed into show position.

"But we cannot eat any more trout," she said. "Do you know the time?"

"What?"

"It's midnight."

"Midsummer midnight." He looked around. "Edith, do you know, you looked beautiful as a ghost."

There was silence.

"Are you coming or not?"

He stepped ashore, gave a throaty "Heave-ho!" then turned, still smiling. She pushed his face away with her open hand. He kissed its cold palm, used a swift endearing term and watched the effect. Then he laughed out loud. He could have eaten her, and she knew it.

But she was not just in the mood for being eaten. She had hung a whole hour with her pride before going to call him.

At eleven o'clock she had said, I will not go, no matter how long he takes. Then she had thought, I will go to bed. But to go to bed before him would be too absurd. In no time she was working up a resentment. She was being neglected. Oh Lord, that feminine thing—being neglected! She laughed at herself. No, thank goodness, it was not that. But—there was something —the least bit selfish in this queer sort of mindless way of his with the things about him. And it was growing . . . every day. . . . There she was again! She blew out the candle, laid aside her novel, and went to call him.

They walked back to the hut. He was silent. She resented this. Out of her resentment rose a sense of tension that became acute. In no time she felt hysterical. This was humiliating and utterly unlike her. It was getting worse. All her body grew stiff. Her head was so high that her feet stumbled. When he caught her she screeched. But he fought against her breakaway, and in the end she sobbed into his neck.

She said brokenly, "I'm very sorry," but she wasn't. She had really no shame at all. She did not care how she behaved. For the moment had given her an awful revelation of the depth of her love. Awful, terrifying. Its light had caught them, the two of them, on a waste. She clung to him.

"I'm very sorry." She felt his hands. His delicacy in love-making had day by day got a perfection that made her soul ache.

By the time they got back to the hut her stiffness was broken, her body rich, her eyes and lips wet and glistening in the beauty that rain brings out. She did not look at him much. She was half languid in her movements. But in the tiny kitchen when they hit into each other, a waiting humour in her seemed ready to spill. He set the embers of the peat on edge and blew them to a flame; hung a kettle and blew again until his eyes watered. "Poof!" he said, backing away by the stern. She launched a wallop at the stern and sat on it. For one shattering moment she wondered if her recklessness had blundered. The stern collapsed and she landed beside him on the floor. "Edith!" he said, in that intimate way that made her blind her eyes against his throat.

The kettle sang. They made tea. She had never, never in her life, been so feminine and irrational. She felt the wild glow in her skin, felt its colour and his eyes, and catching his eyes her mouth twisted at them.

He went out. It was bedtime. When he was ready to go in again, he paused and looked slowly about him. Then he went up the slope behind the hut until he reached its crest. He sat down, his mind quite vacant. He did not know why he had come up. Time went on. He could not go down. Edith would be wondering. The vision of Edith in her nightdress was so perfect that he smiled to her in adoration. That she might be puzzled again faintly amused him. He was sure of her as of the sun's rising. The grey was lightening; it was catching at last the inner glimmer. The coming of the sun from the abyss. The air sighed in a chill shiver. The first, the austere breath, of morning. This austerity was love's poise. His mind in its still rapture pierced all this and he saw what it was he had come to this place blindly to seek. Race, as it were, passed under his feet. Love, alone, eats itself to lust and grows rank.

He saw her against the hut. Her calling voice was thin and ragged. He could not answer. She came up slowly. He knew the pain in that uncertain coming, but could not help her. She dragged her feet towards him.

"Edith, come here," he said quietly.

She stood two paces from him. He got up and went to her. She did nothing, could say nothing, she who had hated and could have struck him at the foot of that hill.

His tone was even and friendly out of the grey light. It drained her of all feeling. Her mind emptied. Her body grew cold and stiff.

37

"Look there," he said, and pointed to a thin light projected upon the sloping crests of a mountain range. "You can see now that the earth is a ball. You can see the light thrown on it out of space. I never saw that planetary light before. Eerie, isn't it?"

She shuddered.

"Are you cold?" He put his arms about her. His voice broke in a laugh by her ear. She looked beaten.

That was last night.

And now this afternoon they lay on the slope by the hut after a long tramp. He had been kind and friendly all day, almost sensitive and shy; she had been cool and normal. One of these long silences, through which the memory of last night was ever threatening to break, held them to a stillness increasingly expectant. When it was pierced by an incredible "Cooee!" he swung over on his side as if he had been speared.

He spoke swiftly. "By God, they haven't seen us!" He was on hands and knees. The fierceness of his face amused her. "Come on!" He made sure she was crawling after him and then he moved rapidly.

"I just couldn't stand them!" he said as at last he lay over.

"Why?"

"I don't know. I loathe the thought of people. And Dick is an ass! Oh God, I couldn't stand them! Really, Edith, this is our show. They had no right to come. We should never have told them. Damn them! if we lose this—we cannot lose this. Don't you know what's been happening to us? We'll never—*never*—live like this again. We'll be trapped. Heaven above, listen . . . !" It came from him in a spate. He bridged the dualities. He lifted her to the grey light and the planetary light. His utmost incoherence had for her an awful clarity. She saw the last level of his mind—spread open to her feet. Her eyes dilated.

When the voice cried from the ridge above she gripped at her breast.

It was Dick. His back to them, he was calling to his companion. They came laughing down together.

True, Iain Og looked a bit surly over the handshakings, but Dick rallied the young dog: "I do believe Jock's embarrassed!"

Mabel chuckled at their embarrassment. "When you waved your hankie, Edith, as you crawled away behind Jock, we nearly died laughing. Follow my leader!"

Iain looked at Edith. So she had waved her hankie to them, after his back was turned. Only a moment their eyes held, then Iain turned away. Edith went pale and sick-looking. Mabel, more amused than ever, prattled on.

The Old Man

He was the Old Man of the gipsy tribe, and his work consisted entirely in settling the disputes of the upcoming generations. Any evening—or morning, for that matter—he could be found sitting on a dry log smoking his pipe and looking meditatively and pleasantly at whatever was or was not before him.

His advice was most frequently sought after a Saturday's bout of methylated-spirit drinking, mixed fights, and a night or two in the cells. His dispensing of justice followed the invariable practice of never inflicting any penalty beyond his own speech. And his speech rarely began until they had talked themselves hoarse and sometimes into a fight on the spot.

But when he began speaking, he kept going. No mere verbal interruption, however explosive, stopped him. And he talked "like a book". It was even said that he had read old books in his young days, just because he was descended from a ditchside poet who had lived in the year one. More than once opposing sides had combined to call him a windbag and other uncomplimentary terms, and had retired, in new-found harmony, shouting at him as he still went on talking. But such derision would be short-lived. Presently they would splutter and laugh among themselves and say, "Did anyone ever hear such an ould fool?" If the money could run to it, they would bring him a sup of whisky, or a finger of black twist tobacco.

For long enough the camp would be a scene of harmonious endeavour, bounded on the right by horse-dealing and on the left by begging.

However, every now and then he had to arbitrate on difficult matters. A single person would come with a deep personal grievance, touching theft, or hatred. It was not always easy. As each and all came voluntarily, they felt entitled to the advice or backing they specially desired.

But sometimes a man came when his mind was a dark whirl, and then he would not put his point, but talk round about it or remain gloomily silent. This was the most difficult case of all. It gave the Old Man scope. Dan's was a case of this sort.

The snout of his cap well down over his left eye, Dan looked gloomy and raven-dark. His petulant mouth, too, was bitter. When he spat explosively, he turned his nose away at once from the spit as from his own thought or the other fellow's argument. He had white teeth, a brown rich skin, and was just turned thirty. In the way he would often not look at you there was something of a spoilt boy or a warped criminal.

The Old Man said nothing.

In the silence, Dan wriggled and kicked the rotten end of the log, not hard, but persistently.

"I feel every kick in me," said the Old Man at last.

"Ye won't feel it much longer," said Dan. "I'm for off."

"Indeed," said the Old Man politely. "Are you going soon?"

"I'm going at once," said Dan savagely, and he stopped kicking and looked away.

"If you have now finished what you are going to say and want my opinion on it, I'll give it to you."

"What d'ye think ye're talking about?" asked Dan with brutal sarcasm.

"It's a very difficult situation," nodded the Old Man, "very difficult. But it has this to it that it is not new. Accordingly, I can make a few remarks on it in a general way to begin with, for I have found that nearly every trouble in life lifts like a mist once the understanding understands and shines into it."

"Horn spoons!" said Dan.

"Take a case, for example, of a man and his wife. They fall out."

"Who fell out?"

"They fall out more than once. Until the time comes when they are in a continuous state of having fallen out. It is one of the queerest states in the world, that, and one of the most critical. Now the word critical has two meanings. For instance, take the rotten old swing-bridge down there before it broke under you last week. When you were on the middle of it, it was in a critical condition, and—listen, now—you were critical of it being in that critical condition."

"Are ye trying to make fun of me, or what?" asked Dan threateningly.

"So it is with marriage. The two supports of the bridge, as you would say, are in a critical condition, and so are critical one to another. The female support or wife will become critical of the male support or husband. As he moves about in his bad nature, she will see all the nasty things in him that she missed before. She will see first of all that he is ill-tempered, and then she will see that he is mean-spirited, and then she will see that he notices little things like any miser, and then she will see that he is a bully, and finally she will see that he is cruel. Everything, in fact, that she thought he hadn't got, she now sees he has got. She thought him always a good cut above other men. Now she sees that he is below them, for they are manly to their wives, whatever else. When she grows ashamed of him in company——"

"What the blazes——"

"Hsh," said the Old Man. "There's your wife coming round the quarry."

At that, Dan's expression grew so vindictive that it was clear he would gladly have smitten the Old Man out of existence if he could have done it in time. He spat, stubbornly held his ground, and did not look round. When next he gathered sense in the Old Man's words, they were flowing: ". . . so he becomes critical of her. He had thought her a good-looker, and he wonders to himself bitterly where his eyes could have been. He had thought she had spirit and was full of fun, and now she goes about more silent than a funeral, with an expression of misery that if you could get it in a bottle would do for rennet. He bawls at her and she does not answer, and that is enough to drive a lively man to murder. And then she will say something that is worse than saying nothing. When he cannot eat from anger, the small noises she will be making eating steadily like a blind cow will make him want to vomit, and then he gets up and kicks the bottom out of the stool he was sitting on."

"Who the hell told ye I kicked the bottom——"

"Then he begins to notice . . ."

"Will ye listen to me?"

". . . little things that he would be ashamed to tell anyone he noticed. But I can explain that better if, first of all, I compare this wife of his with a young woman he saw singing a ballad song at the horse fair at Knockfalish. The sound of her voice would draw the heart out of you, and she had a shy dark eye more impudent than a bad woman's kiss. When you would be standing there looking at her, you would think to yourself that the whole world could roar to hell in the glory of a dozen or maybe thirteen fights, if——"

"Will ye stop yer gab?" roared Dan, and he caught the Old Man by the whiskers.

THE OLD MAN

"Well," said the Old Man calmly, "have you thought of your complaint yet?"

"Complaint!" When Dan got back his breath, he laughed—and roared, "Has my wife been talking to you?"

"No. She is the kind who would never talk to me."

Dan glared at him and threw his whiskers aside. "Begod, ye're right there. What the hell then have ye been talking about?"

"I have just been filling in time till you could put words on your complaint. And surely the relations between a man and a woman are interesting at any time. For the first time in six months my egg was boiled hard as a stone this morning, and I can only take it soft."

Dan gave a roar of laughter, and took off his bonnet and put it on again. "You, who haven't done a stroke of work in twenty years! You, whose wife has never stopped working for ye in twenty years! You're the one to know about marriage!"

"Well, don't you think I am?" asked the Old Man.

"Ye ould hairy amadan, you!" cried Dan, swaying on his feet. "This is as good as a fair!"

"As I was saying——"

"Oh, shut yer mouth," said Dan, "and tell me this." And when he had stopped the Old Man, he bellowed derisively, "D'ye mean to tell me that that is the way of it between people and them married?"

"That is the way," said the Old Man.

"Between all people?"

"Between all people, everywhere, high and low. To every married couple, from the king and the queen on their thrones to the horse-dealers at Knockfalish Fair, a time comes when that is the way, for better or for worse, for longer or for shorter."

"And who told you about kings and queens? Eh?"

"In the old histories of our country . . ."

"Stop now, will you? Stop!"

". . . the ancient kings and queens would be quarrelling in a way that was known to every story-teller that slept in a ditch. Moreover they——"

"I believe ye there," said Dan. "I've heard the stories myself." He marvelled for a short time, his eyes in a bright humour; then he forcibly stopped the Old Man once more.

"Tell me this," he said, looking at him narrowly, so that he should not escape him. "Tell me this. How d'ye know the exact things they would be thinking of one another? Tell me, now. Come on!"

"How should I know but out of the wide experience I have gained from life? Do you think when I am sitting here alone that I am doing nothing at all? Is it for the like of you——"

But Dan got him stopped by shouting into his ear, "If it is the same with everyone, then it must have been the same with yourself?"

"Manifestly," said the Old Man.

At which great word, Dan roared afresh and tweaked the grey beard in sport. "Are ye telling me!" he cried.

The Old Man smoothed his beard calmly. "I do not like anyone", he said coldly, "to touch my whiskers."

Whereat Dan doubled up.

The Old Man remained silent.

"Is it offended ye are now?" asked Dan, pausing in his laughter to enjoy this new delight.

But presently he said coaxingly, "Ach, now, what are ye offended about? Aren't ye the wisest man in the world? Don't we all know it? Come, now, don't you be offended with me. I'm going away off to the town this night and bedamn if I won't take back as nice a drop in the heel of a flask for you as ever you tasted. Only, tell me this now, and it's all I'll ask. Tell me." His voice lowered confidentially. "When ye were in that state with herself—how did ye get out of it? Wait!

One minute! First of all, was the state ye were in with one another as bad as you have made it out to be? And look!" added Dan threateningly. "If ye tell me a lie I swear on my soul I'll pull the whiskers clean out of you."

"It was worse," said the Old Man calmly. "Much worse."

"Glory be to God," said Dan. "You can go on now."

"And at last," continued the Old Man, moderating his voice as his eye fell on the hump-back of his tent at a little distance, "we came that I could stand it no more. It was the end."

"Good," said Dan. "Go on."

"It was the end. The only thing that was worse than seeing her in my sight was thinking of her out of my sight. And every time I had a look at her out of the corner of my eye, I saw something that made me worse than ever. Sometimes it would be no more than a drop to her nose, or hair sticking out over her ear, or lines in her neck, or a bunch in her clothes, but each small thing would be the last hay seed. Do you know, when I would be going back to her sometimes there would be a reluctance on me like a sick pain. And the way that would make me stop and use words enough to commit my soul, and I would smash my heels in the ground and walk round myself in a small circle . . ."

"Whist!" said Dan, taking a turn round about himself. "That will do for that." He was lost in wonder for a minute and then gave a small chuckle.

". . . so there we were in the wood . . ."

"What wood was that?" asked Dan. "Begin that bit again, will you?"

". . . and the words spoken. I walked away from her. She said nothing. She did not ask me to stay. She did not plead. It was all over. It was finished. Before you can say words of parting like that you have to work yourself into a great rage. I had worked myself so high that a fear got hold of me that she might do harm to herself. For it is never the women who threaten to take their own lives who do take them. It's always the quiet women who have never said cheep."

"Are ye telling me that?"

"Yes. You watch them, Dan. Watch the quiet women."

"Go on," said Dan, thoughtfully.

"It may be difficult for me now to get you to understand, for in that wood a queer thing happened to me. Thinking, as I told you, that she might do harm to herself, I stopped in my tracks, and turned, and went back quietly to the wood. I stole from tree to tree until at last I saw her again, all alone by herself, in that quiet place, with the trees like gallows, where she could do to herself what she might be in the mind to do and no one to say her no."

"And what was she doing?" asked Dan.

"She was gathering sticks," said the Old Man.

"Gathering . . ." A gust of laughter choked the words in his mouth. Twice he looked at the solemn Old Man and twice he laughed. Then he asked. "What did ye do?"

"I sat down and watched her. She went slowly from tree to tree gathering the sticks. She broke them, as she gathered them, into lengths, and made a heap of them. And it was while she was doing this with no one to see her in that lonely wood but my own eyes—it was while she was doing this that the true vision of her came to me. I saw her like the mother of generations, the gatherer and the provider; and I thought to myself that this is the greatness of great women, that this is what remains when all the tempers and vanities of great fools of men have passed on the wind."

"Did ye now? God, and weren't you the great ass! You'll be telling me you wept next."

"I wept," said the Old Man.

"Jehosaphat!" said Dan, and his breath went from him. It came back in a gulp of derision at this old fool of a woman before him. "And to think that we would be wasting time on getting advice from the like of that!"

But the Old Man protected his beard with a smoothing hand. "Time is never wasted," said he.

"Isn't it now? And what advice d'ye think you have been giving me?"

"If I haven't been giving you advice," said the Old Man, "I have been giving your wife time."

"What's that you say? Giving her time for what?"

"When she passed out by a little while ago, going towards the Quiet Wood, I noticed that she had a rope hidden on her. I noticed it because of an end which hung in sight with a loop on it."

"What . . . ?"

"What would she be wanting with a rope and a tree and her married to a fine man like you? It is very difficult for me to answer you that, Dan, but, as I told you before, she is a quiet woman."

Dan swole up with the wrath that was in him, and drew back his fist to clout the Old Man a blow that would finish him. But the other fist, intending to push the Old Man straight, tipped him heels up over the log. After Dan had said a few words, he began to hurry towards the Quiet Wood.

He was in time, thank God! for she had not yet got the rope fixed. From behind the trunk of a tree he watched her, and had great trouble to keep himself from laughing, for she had tied a small stone to one end of the rope and was trying to throw the stone up over a branch; and not only that, but as any fool could see, the branch was rotten!

The shapes she made at throwing the stone convulsed him, for he could have shot it from his thumb-nail; but she was persistent, never losing her temper; she was like doom; and when, at the fourth throw, she got it over, Dan stopped laughing. She lowered the stone down towards her. She's got it now! he thought. But she was in no hurry. She took her breath for a little, standing quite still; then she stirred and looked up at the branch. Would it be strong enough? She tried it; she tugged at it; she tested it with her full weight from a little jump. Crack! and the branch, snapping, fell on top of her fallen body.

Dan fell too and stuffed his mouth. The fun of it was too much for him. And when she sat up and began rubbing her head like a clown in a circus, he turned on his belly, rooting in the friendly earth. "Are ye seein' her?" he asked the earth. "Whist! for God's sake!"

When he looked again she was on her feet, dragging the branch over to a big stone. And then he perceived the reason and purpose of all her acts. She was not hanging herself at all: she was gathering sticks!

He was speechless for a long time, seeing only what a fool he had been, what an ass. The ass swole up and went stalking through all the air to heaven. He clenched his fists in wrath, he began to laugh at himself in derision, in unholy mirth, and then just to laugh inwardly.

At last she had so great a bundle tied round with the rope that she couldn't lift it to her back. He watched her, like a man with a bet on a horse, but she couldn't do it.

"Blast ye!" he said, for his mind had put his money on her.

But was she beaten? She dragged the pile to the top of a little bank and got below it. Straining heavily at the neck, she heaved upward, steadied herself and her bundle a moment, then, bent double, began to stagger away. The end of a stick, jutting from the bundle, grazed a tree and swung her round, and the bundle fell. She looked at it dumbly, then began dragging it back to the little bank.

The sight of her doing this was more than flesh and blood could stand. He jumped up and strode down upon her. "What in the name of little frogs are ye thinking ye're trying to do?

Is it ye have lost your senses entirely? If the thing was too heavy for you, couldn't ye take a stick or two out?"

Her young face looked grey and ancient. There was a dumb misery upon her like the weight of all the world.

"Can't you speak?" he shouted.

"I am tired, Dan," she said. The last shred of fight had gone from her voice. It sounded small and thin, and haunting as a child's.

"Mother of God!" he cried harshly and pulled her against him so that she might not see whatever happened to his eyes, for a wild gush of feeling had started up behind them.

Paper Boats

The two boys fashioned their paper boats with great care. One boy was fair and sturdy and he made folds and bends with the precision of a carpenter. The other boy was dark and so intent on making as good a boat as his companion that he was excited and every now and then stole glances. Clearly this dark boy, whose name was Hugh, was never intended for a carpenter. His fingers were thinner and more nervous, his ruling thumb less firm than George's. His body, too, was more slender, even if it seemed full of an eager fire. It was as though this fire was more potent than the power in his fingers, and his glances were at once jealous and despairing. In his eagerness he completed his boat and cried exultantly:

"I'm finished first!"

George paid no direct attention because he was making a perfect boat and knew that crowing over time was just weakness. He only made a slight sound in his nose as he cocked his head to one side and examined his work, but not loud enough to distract himself. Deliberately he became slower than ever and surer.

Hugh watched him with increasing vexation. He shouldn't have rushed his own one so much. He saw where certain folds did not meet and began pushing them together. But he succeeded only in crumpling the paper, and no matter how he tried to smooth the crumple he failed, so that the last state was noticeably worse than the first.

At last George finished his boat and holding it out on his

palm regarded it with great admiration. "There you are!" he said.

It was so perfectly made that Hugh cried loudly but at the same time carelessly, "Mine's just as good!"

George looked at it—and smiled mockingly. "See that—and that: they should be together. And look at the bulge there! It's crooked. That's no use."

"It's use enough," cried Hugh heatedly. "Wait till you see her in the water."

"All right," said George. "You wait." And they ran to the small mound of sand that was by the cooperage wall near the harbour weather-glass. This glass, in its deep case, still recorded the weather, as it did when there was a harbour master to set it and fishermen to trouble it with anxious eyes. The two boys had the dying creek to themselves. The tide was full in and the fine Saturday morning sun made wheels of light on the water. A gull or two, crying as if they had lost something, heeled over. The boys ballasted their paper boats with sand and stuck a gull's feather upright in the fold amidships. Then they turned towards the stone pier, carrying their craft with eager care.

A breach in the front of the pier allowed them to scramble down over huge slabs to the sea edge.

"You haven't enough sand in yours," said George.

"Haven't I?" challenged Hugh, glancing quickly into his rival's hold. "You wait!"

"You always need plenty of ballast if a boat's going to hold to the wind."

"Do you think I didn't know that?" asked Hugh. "Ho! ho! What wind's in it to-day? Circumstances alter cases."

George snorted. Hugh felt pleased with himself over his blind hit about the weather and became more excited than ever.

"Even if there's no wind on the shore, a gale can be blowing outside."

"If you think I didn't know that," said Hugh, "you can tell it to your grannie."

"Are you ready?" asked George grimly.

"I am," said Hugh.

"Go!" said George.

And they both pushed their boats upon the sea.

George pushed his carefully, but Hugh in order to gain all possible headway thrust his rather forcibly so that the ballast shifted slightly aft; thus George's boat rode perfectly the water while Hugh's stern was too deep.

When George laughed at this, Hugh felt himself grow hot with anger. He wished ardently that his boat would beat George's out into the open sea. He would have given everything he possessed at that moment, including the world, if only his craft would outpace her opponent. For he knew in his heart that she couldn't do it, just as in his heart he knew that he could never draw a straight line like George, that he couldn't press down a crease with his thumb in the flawless manner. George's thumb made a steady unfaltering hiss all along the paper. The paper lay down before it like a cringing dog.

There was a fitful air of wind from the land, but not enough near the pier to stain the water. Thus the two boats for a time scarcely moved at all. Yet it was noticeable that Hugh's boat kept her head to the sea whereas George's boat on an even keel did not know what to do. She seemed to have no spirit of her own and her dead perfection floated listlessly broadside on.

"Mine's gaining!" cried Hugh. The great rock behind the pier echoed his cry, all the way up to its grassy scalp.

"You wait!" said George.

"She's gaining steadily," cried Hugh, and laughed shrilly. His eyes were on fire. The bow of his boat, cocked up, swung a little from side to side, as if it had just been troubled by a real breath. The stern by being low in the water at once steadied and helped this action. The little craft was oddly alive as though it delighted in its imperfection.

George regarded his own craft with hopeful grimness.

"Wait till she gets the wind proper," he said.

By the time they were four yards from the pier Hugh's boat was leading by no more than a foot. George's had straightened up and was overhauling her. They both rose and fell on the slow glistening undulations. George's boat would have overtaken the other but getting an extra little puff of air turned broadside on again and began moving aimlessly across the harbour mouth.

Although the bow of Hugh's boat swung dangerously, it steadied—on the open sea.

For the first time real hope entered into Hugh. He saw with elation that his boat was going to beat George's. All that she had to do was to keep her head to the open sea. He had not expected this. He had been prepared for defeat. For George was better with his hands. He knew that, even if he would never give in to it; and he would never give in to it because the fire in his mind was irked by straight lines. His mind had steeled itself to defeat—and here was victory.

The open sea! His heart sang.

George was annoyed. His boat had no sense in her at all. But if only she would get the right sort of wind. . . . There she was, straightening up again.

Hugh laughed derisively. "She's yards behind already," he cried.

"You wait!" said George.

At that moment a large stone fell between the boats with a mighty splash.

The boys stumbled back against a slab, their hearts in their mouths. Up on the grassy scalp of the rock, they saw three young men laughing in the excitement of their sudden game.

Stones began to fall thick and fast.

"Stop it!" yelled George, whose temper was getting the better of him.

"Stop it!" yelled Hugh also.

"Keep back!" shouted one of the young men, and signalled warningly with an arm.

The stones landed very near the boats and frequently between them so that George's boat began to wash inshore again in a helpless way. Once a stone very nearly got it and it shipped sparks of water from the jabble. It looked completely beaten, the most lifeless thing anyone could see.

"Stop it!" yelled George. "Ye great fools!"

But Hugh's boat, helped outward by the wash from the stones and now far enough from the shelter of the pier to catch what wind was going, was making steadily to sea. As though she were escaping them, the young men on the cliff-top made up their minds to get her and ignored George's boat altogether.

Excitement got such a hold of Hugh that he could not speak. As each stone splashed and missed, he drew breath—waiting for the next. He cast an agonising glance at the cliff-top. But there was no mercy there. Then a stone, cutting under her, made her jump.

A laugh came down and a voice: "That was near her!"

"Watch this!" shouted a second voice.

"This'll settle her!" said a third.

Hugh began to gather a thrilling confidence. Some of their stones were already falling short. She still had her head to the sea, her feather upright, her passage perilous but steady. Already, indeed, she was beginning to look small, removed from them, as if the great glistening sea had taken her for its own. Pride came into his confidence and the spirit of daring of his forefathers.

Only one thrower now could come within a yard of her. The stones slackened.

George's voice came suddenly from Hugh's back:

"They can't reach her. Watch this!"

Hugh wheeled round as George threw. His stone was the length but a yard wide.

"You stop it!" shouted Hugh.

George bent, looking for another suitable stone.

"Stop it, do you hear?"

George straightened himself. "Who'll make me stop it?"

"I will!" said Hugh, a pale flame in his face as he squared up to George.

"Oh, you will!" said George.

"Yes, I will!"

"Oh, I see," said George, opening his mouth and adding "huh!". Then he began looking in cracks of the masonry for a stone. He found one and weighed it on his palm. "Too light," he muttered.

But Hugh knew it was not too light.

A voice yelled from above: "Here, stop that, boys!"

They looked up.

"Go on, now," and a threatening head jerked, "clear out!"

George made a mocking mouth. "I'll see you again about this," he said, as if baffled for the time being, and slouched off trying to whistle.

Like three gods the young men passed beyond the crest of the cliffs, laughing.

Hugh, left alone, found himself breathing hard in and out as if he had really had a fight. Then a great tingling delight came upon him. His heart spilled over. He wanted to do swift violent acts with arms and body; acts of defiance and dancing.

His eyes sought his boat eagerly but now could not find her. She had sailed away into the sea. She was out of sight, going away, away. . . . A tremendous emotion of wonder and triumph overcame him. But then in a moment he saw her. She wasn't really far out, after all. But this, somehow, did not disappoint him; on the contrary it gave him an awesome conception of the size of the sea.

For a long time he played the game of lifting his eyes from the boat and then trying to find her again.

A time came when he could not find her any more. Staring at the glistening undulating sea he found himself listening, holding his breath. All the world grew silent as though a shining finger had been laid on it. Hugh got up and went away, smiling secretly to himself.

Symbolical

His eyes were always full of light. Even before his porridge in the morning, when his thinning hair was spoked in wheels and his eyebrows puckered above the blue, was the light there. And it always had the air of seeing things and having sudden thoughts about them, novel thoughts. Yet in the crofting district of Torbuie the number of things to be seen was strictly limited, and these blue eyes had rested on them daily for over fifty years.

Perhaps, before eyes can look always on the same things and still live, they must be endowed with a second vision. Certainly Hendry Macfie had a way of using words like "queer", "God", "diabolical", following a level twinkling pause, that gave the impression of a disturbing penetration into something beyond, of which the physical object seen was but the shadow. Occasionally, too, with a rather concrete humour. The festering sore on the tinker's horse, for example, might cause a normal eye pain and horror, which it would instantly leap beyond to the representative of the S.S.P.C.A., but "Job must have had great sores on him," reflected Hendry afterwards in the evening's quiet, "when they would be scooping the smelling matter out of them with potsherds . . . like bits of broken flooerpots." The eyes twinkled; the words hung up in the silence their appalling vision, to recur at odd moments, never thereafter entirely to be forgotten.

But his lasting byname of "Symbolical" came to him on a late March morning when the tragedy he stumbled upon uprose as the symbol or vision of all their lives. There had been snow overnight and the white mantle that met the blue eyes through the small kitchen window visibly arrested them in astonishment. His brother's wife, stirring the porridge in the iron pot, answered his exclamations with a laconic, "Ay, there's been four inches fully."

"Where's John?" he asked.

"He's seeing to the lambs."

"The lambs!" he repeated, and gazed on the snow with more astonishment than ever.

Though he would sit up to all hours, Hendry was not an early riser. As a worker he was erratic rather than steady and, perhaps because of his wispish build, gave the impression of trifling with a fork rather than getting his back into it. Often, indeed, the fork and the stony ground would combine to an obduracy against him and would jerk him off his balance, as though they were throwing him aside. On the windy uprise of the croft Hendry might be seen now and then thus niggling at the ground like an overgrown crow. "He's maybe worth his meat," said brother John on one of the rare sardonic moments when he offered an opinion about anything.

Now John could be heard at the door kicking the snow from his boots. He entered solidly, his face whipped red, his cheekbones prominent, his eyes dull.

"Are they all right?" asked his wife.

"Ay."

"Where are they?" asked Hendry.

John turned a slow eye that passed across Hendry's face to the mantelpiece. "Where I left them," he said.

"It came very sudden," murmured Hendry. "Who would have thought?"

There were people who could waste time thinking about how a thing like snow could come—with turnips to be cut, fodder to be brought to the byre, potatoes to be taken from the pit; with the whole day to be filled up one way or another—and there, outside, the snow, covering the grass that had been making a start. Like as not he, John, would have to buy oilcake again; and he hadn't the money to buy oilcake again.

Liz dished the porridge. They ate it in silence. As he pushed his plate back, John said:

"There's no smoke from Geordie Acharn's."

Liz looked at him.

"Is that so?" asked Hendry.

John got up and took his pipe from the mantelpiece.

"Maybe it's too early for them," pursued Hendry, his eyebrows puckering. "They wouldn't get up so early with the snow in it."

Liz muttered after a little, "I thought it was coming on him heavy last night."

"Uh," said John.

"Yes. I could see it in his eyes. He looked as if he might be wandering." She stared vacantly at the window. "Christina herself had it heavy in her chest." She turned and lifted the porridge pot off the crook. What was left in it was thickening and would be warm for the hens. They were on the top of their laying, and if she could keep them at it, this setback in the weather might raise the price a penny or twopence.

"The flu is getting very common nowadays," said Hendry. "This snow won't be a good thing for the ould folk."

"You can cut some neeps when you go out," said John.

"I was thinking", said Liz, "that it would be neighbourly if he walked up to see how they were." She paused with the pot swinging from a bared forearm. "You can say to Christina that I'll take a turn up after denner to see her."

"All right," nodded Hendry.

There was something new about the snow, and strange. Its whiteness was surprising. He went over the knees in the obliterated ditch at the end of the field and paused to look at the hole his boot had made. It was a queer thing to have snow at this time of the year when one came to think about it. His eyes travelled up the slopes until they saw the smokeless chimney of Geordie Acharn's cottage showing above the crest of the last dip in the land before it flattened out finally to the great gaunt moor that swept all the way to the Pentland Firth.

It was off the moor the small wind came and it was at once searching and invigorating. Hendry braced his chest and blew noisily through tight lips. The snow was bright and lay on everything. It must have drifted strongly at one stage. In the lee of the low stone dike there wasn't much, but on the weather side it curved almost to the top—a beautiful curve, showing particularly at the slap in the dike. Hendry admired it and broke the edge of the curve with his boot. Then he looked at the flaw. In that perfect curve there was the flaw-mark of his boot. Queer thing.

After a little time he paused to look down the slopes that finished a mile away against the uprising floor of the sea. The croft houses were tiny oases that seemed to cling to the earth a little more closely than usual, as though they were huddling under the flattening snow on their roofs. Here and there a black dot of a figure moved on the white waste. They would be out looking for the lambs, likely. There had been the cold feel of snow in the air for a day or two back, but what with the birds singing and an odd primrose in the shelter of a ditch, no one really believed it would come to snow like this. And now it had come like a clap. That was often the way. His eyes glistened humorously, as though it were an interesting way. . . . Except for the lambs and the old folk.

As he went on he thought it queer of God, after all, to send snow at lambing time. It was difficult to think what could be in God's head to let Him do that. Perhaps He had something in the back of His mind. . . . Or perhaps God didn't pay any attention to its coming at all. Yet God was bound to know

61

about it. Queer of God, that. And the old folk, with the flu. They died. Perhaps Geordie Acharn was dead.

He looked up and could now see the curve of the roof. It was pure white and extraordinarily still. The chimney was stiff and cold. What if he was dead? What if they were both lying dead in the house? He kept his eyes on the house until he saw it all. It looked like a dead house.

No life moved anywhere about it. Its two small windows were tenantless eyes, one each side of the closed door. It looked at him unseeingly, very still. The draped whiteness of the snow had something terrifying about it that he had never noticed in snow before. And suddenly the windows were looking at him with eyes that did not belong to Geordie Acharn and his sister Christina.

The small walled enclosure in front of the house came into view and in the shelter of the near side of it was a ewe with a newly-born lamb. Unconsciously he slanted his course a little towards this manifestation of life. The warmth of the ewe had melted a round patch of snow, leaving ragged edges discoloured, and in one place sodden red. The lamb swayed insecurely on its stilts and the mother licked the stains and pains of birth away. He looked over the enclosure at the house and after a little moved round towards the front door.

There were footsteps going from the front door. The sight half reassured him. He suppressed a sudden inclination to knock, a thing which was not done, and, raising the latch, put his head in at the door and listened. There was no sound of anyone moving. He coughed, and after a moment said, "Are ye there?" His own voice surprised him. It was little more than a whisper. He thought he heard a spasmodic breathing but could not be sure, so much was his own breathing choking him and his heart beating. Then he distinctly heard something in the kitchen where Christina slept in the boxed-in bed, and, tapping gently the snow from his boots, he entered quietly, head craning forward, eyes round and popping out of his head in a scared way.

The first thing he saw was Christina's eyes. They flared at him wildly from the edge of the bed. Her dank grey hair tangled her brows. She brought up a shaking hand and pushed it back. The excitement seemed too much for her and she had a coughing convulsion which was almost noiseless, so exhausted she was and so choked her chest. He went to her side at once, saying, "What is it, Christina?" He stooped to listen, but it was some time before she whispered: "He's out! He's out!"

"Out, is he?" he answered, lifting his head and looking at her.

She looked back at him, and before her burning eyes he tried to appear thoughtful and nodded his head; then stooped to her whispering lips again.

". . . was wandering . . . and early in the morning . . . went out . . . I . . . fell . . ."

"That's all right," he nodded. "He's maybe back without you hearing him. I'll go and see." He smiled.

In the short passageway between the two rooms of the cottage he paused to get his wind. Then he pushed open the door of Geordie's room and slowly peered in. "Are ye there, Geordie?" he whispered. When at last he entered he found the bedclothes tossed about and Geordie's clothes on a chair but not Geordie himself.

The bright snow dazed him as he came out. There were footsteps—going the one way . . . And the imprints were small and indecisive and anything but what would be made by an iron-shod heel. He followed by the side of them to the byre where they turned in and turned out again, going on round the corner out of sight towards the moor behind.

He went into the byre. The cow turned her head and lowed through her nostrils at him, the chain round her neck rattling and her great round eyes dumb and shining. "Are ye there,

Geordie?" he called to the dark shadows. It was as though he had never heard the loud sound of his own voice before. Quickly but quietly he drew the door shut and stood with his back to it, staring. Then, a little bit away from the footprints, he moved to the byre corner in a hesitant, furtive way.

As he rounded the corner, the death-cold breath of the great white moor touched his heated face, but his eyes, jumping hither and thither, saw nothing—nothing but the little dry-stone dikes, built of the rounded stones Geordie had dug out of the tough heather roots in his ceaseless work of reclamation. For, apart from an arable strip of an acre in the dip where the cottage stood, Geordie had won the rest of his croft from the moor itself with no help but that of a spade and pickaxe. He had been endless years at it, and the sheltering dikes with their countless stones ran this way and that like a heroic signature at the foot of the grim scroll of the moor.

His body gone strangely light, Hendry followed the footprints beyond the last dike. There he came on Geordie sitting in the yard of furrow he had cleared, frozen stiff, his hands knotted to the spade which was upholding him, his lean hairy shanks incongruously exposed and blue, his eyes wide in a fixed stare at the inimical expanse as though they could not get over some final knowledge that had been vouchsafed them. Instinctively lifting his eyes to follow the stare, Hendry had the sensation of that deathly moor heaving and billowing down on him like a sea.

Blaeberries

He was thinning turnips when she passed along the sheep-path that ran between the fael dike at the bottom of the field and the edge of the cliffs. Thus from her waist to her uncovered head her desirability was cut like a cameo against the grey floor of the sea, though he did not lift his head to look. By the time the path had taken her out of sight, he had hoed ten yards without stopping his hoe a moment. When she had disappeared altogether he did look up—to find the thin dark veil that her passing had left on the face of the sea. When his head drooped again and he considered the last ten yards of his work, his lips tightened. The mathematical precision of it was beyond all praise.

In the next ten yards, however, his hoe stumbled once. A further twenty yards, and he found his muscles uncertain and jumpy, as though suffering from reaction after strain. By the time he came to the end of the long row, he was fumbling in and out the green line like a beginner. He put in the next half-hour doggedly, and then it was six o'clock.

Down by the cliff-heads at night he sat, looking on the grey floor that rose so steeply to the horizon. A curlew passed under the stars, fluting forlornly. A peewit swung up from the earth with a swift vehemence, its silken wings and two-winged cry roused in persistent protest. The long tremulous calling of the curlew belongs to the impersonal reaches between earth and star, and its forlorn wave dies out into infinite space. The peewit's cry is an insistent, passionate cry, anxious, of the earth.

BLAEBERRIES

In his listening to the echoes of the curlew's call, his lips tightened. Something wild, clean, unearthly, in that call. For her image was like the peewit's cry in that it had the same vibrant colour to it and urgency—yet not like it at all in the way of earthly care and anxiety. Her earthliness was provoking and red-lipped and untasted, like wine and honey breathed upon; yet like nothing earthly either because of that veiled light in the eyes with its understandings, its reticences, its inscrutabilities.

For an hour the logical working of his mind was beyond all praise. No image of her could intrude wholly. Below, the grey sea washing the feet of the rocks, washing the eternal grey feet; overhead, the curlew calling to the utmost reach of the night; off the sea, the wind cooling his face, set so stonily to horizons. His body was a cool external shiver—a cool clean sheath. That for the first hour.

In the second hour his mind stumbled once, so that she entered by a simple trick. She became a figure in desert places; she became a night-wrapped figure of lost dim moorland places; loose-haired, slim-swaying, like a nymph or prophetess. The loneliness in him cried out and strove towards her loneliness; strove vehemently; but as he yet caught up with her and stretched out his hand, she turned—and lo! the dimness of mystery about her face was instantly changed to the old light, and her smile, gleaming critically from slanting eyes, stopped him more effectively than would any sword. The trick of it went through him in a hot flush, so that all his strength was turned to water and shamefacedness. . . . His body stirred there on the cliffhead and his heel ground an unconscious oath into the soft turf, while his soul cried upon the night words to which there was no more meaning than to the crying of the curlew.

From the third hour she possessed him wholly, so that curlew and peewit and sea and cliff were but the stage machinery against her playing. She gave him the mystical wine and honey, and she gave him the image of red lips like yielding ripe fruit. And he drank and filled himself, a debauchery of shadows and transparencies and treacheries, till, on a moment, his body cried urgently for substance and his mouth for crushing resistances. His eyes rose flashing—to the nothingness of the grey sea.

His head drooped between his knees, and the cool wind came from the sea, passing round him and over him and swaying gently the tall grasses—a night-expanse of heedless, passionless, immemorial things, in which his doubled-up body might easily pass for a grey boulder.

The turnips swelled to a plump girth, the year waxed mellow and luscious. He came upon her of a sudden on an evening of small rain like a mist. It was the rain that draws out and holds fragrance of flower and fruit and gives to the bloom of a cheek the petal smoothness of a rose. She was eating blaeberries.

Her lips were stained purple, her fingers were stained purple, and there were purple stains here and there on her face besides—a ripe black purple. Tiny raindrops clung to strands of her hair, a wild diffusion of light and colour played on her features, and concentrated light and colour flashed in her eyes.

He stood stuck fast, with no power in him to move any way at all. The skin on his face was drawn taut and pale, and his eyes were on her like the eyes of a trapped animal. The first sign of the breathless intensity of his living was a slight quivering at the nostrils; but by that time she had taken in the knowledge of many things.

Plainly they could not stand like that for ever. She smiles, with an exquisite diffidence, and holds out a hand, in the palm of which lies a little heap of berries. He stumbles foolishly among the blaeberry bushes, and as he comes by the hand, stretches out fingers to partake. Whereupon the incalculable impulse which no woman can command runs swiftly down her arm and jerks her hand upwards above his hand—leaving the berries poised daringly midway between his groping fist and his mouth. His mouth! His heart drums in his ears as his head stoops to the stained fingers and the berries. But it is not for nothing that these same fingers—and lips—are stained, with the small rain a fragrant moistening of the petals; not for nothing that instead of picking and eating single berry by single berry, she gathers a whole handful over against one crushing, ecstatic mouthful. While yet his lips are three inches from her palm and opening in expectancy, a second tremor passes along her arm, a wild, mad impulse this, excited by she knows not what of uncertainties and expectancies; yet knowing, too— even to the verge of tiptoe hysteria over man's unbearable slownesses.

And in an instant through the three inches she has smashed hand and berries full against his mouth; and there and then in the blaeberry patch and in the small rain, she is swept off her tiptoes and the unbearable agony of expectancy is crushed like the berries.

The Tax-gatherer

"Blast it," he muttered angrily. "Where is the accursed place?"

He looked at the map again spread before him on the steering-wheel. Yes, it should be just here. There was the cross-roads. He threw a glance round the glass of his small saloon car and saw a man's head bobbing beyond the hedge. At once he got out and walked along the side of the road.

"Excuse me," he cried. The face looked at him over the hedge. "Excuse me, but can you tell me where Mrs. Martha Williamson stays?"

"Mrs. Who?"

"Mrs. Martha Williamson."

"No," said the face slowly, and moved away. He followed it for a few paces to a gap in the hedge. "No," said the man again, and turned to call a spaniel out of the turnips. He had a gun under his arm and was obviously a gamekeeper.

"Well, she lives about here, at Ivy Cottage."

"Ivy Cottage? Do you mean the tinkers?" And the game-keeper regarded him thoughtfully.

"Yes. I suppose so."

"I see," said the gamekeeper, looking away. "Turn up to your right at the cross-roads there and you'll see it standing back from the road."

He thanked the gamekeeper and set off, walking quickly so that he needn't think too much about his task, for it was new to him.

When he saw the cottage, over amongst some bushes with a rank growth of nettles at one end, he thought it a miserable place, but when he came close to the peeling limewash, the torn-down ivy, the sagging roof, the broken stone doorstep thick with trampled mud, he saw that it was a wretched hovel.

The door stood half-open, stuck. He knocked on it and listened to the acute silence. He knocked again firmly and thought he heard thin whisperings. He did not like the hushed fear in the sounds, and was just about to knock peremptorily when there was a shuffling, and, quietly as an apparition, a woman was there.

She stood twisted, lax, a slim, rather tall figure, with a face the colour of the old limewash. She clung to the edge of the door in a manner unhumanly pathetic, and looked at him out of dark, soft eyes.

"Are you Mrs. Williamson?"

After a moment she said, "Yes."

"Well, I've come about that dog. Have you taken out the licence yet?"

"No."

"Well, it's like this," he said, glancing away from her. "We don't want to get you into trouble. But the police reported to us that you had the dog. Now, you can't have a dog without paying a licence. You know that. So, in all the circumstances, the authorities decided that if you paid a compromise fine of seven-and-six, and took out the licence, no more would be said about it. You would not be taken to court." He looked at her again, and saw no less than five small heads poking round her ragged dark skirt. "We don't want you to get into trouble," he said. "But you've got to pay by Friday—or you'll be summonsed. There's no way out."

She did not speak, stood there unmoving, clinging to the door, a feminine creature waiting dumbly for the blow.

"Have you a husband?" he asked.

"Yes," she said, after a moment.

"Where is he?"

"I don't know," she answered, in her soft, hopeless voice. He wanted to ask her if he had left her for good, but could not, and this irritated him, so he said calmly, "Well, that's the position, as you know. I was passing, and, seeing we had got no word of your payment, I thought I'd drop in and warn you. We don't want to take you to court. So my advice to you is to pay up—and at once, or it will be too late."

She did not answer. As he was about to turn away the dregs of his irritation got the better of him. "Why on earth did you want to keep the dog, anyway?"

"We tried to put him away, but he wouldn't go," she said.

His brows gathered. "Oh, well, it's up to you," he replied coldly, and he turned and strode back to his car. Slamming the door after him, he gripped the wheel, but could not, at the last instant, press the self-starter. He swore to himself in a furious rage. Damn it all, what concern was it of his? None at all. As a public official he had to do his job. It was nothing to him. If a person wanted to enjoy the luxury of keeping a dog, he or she had to pay for it. That's all. And he looked for the self-starter, but, with his finger on the button, again could not press it. He twisted in his seat. Fifteen bob! he thought. Go back and slip her fifteen bob? Am I mad? He pressed the self-starter and set the engine off in an unnecessary roar. As he turned at the cross-roads he hesitated before shoving the gear lever into first, then shoved it and set off. If a fellow was to start paying public fines where would it end? Sentimental? Absolutely.

By the following Tuesday it was clear she had not paid.

"The case will go on," said his chief in the office.

"It's a hard case," he answered. "She won't be able to pay." His voice was calm and official.

"She'll have to pay—one way or the other," answered his chief, with the usual trace of official satire in his voice.

"She's got a lot of kids," said the young man.

"Has she?" said the chief. "Perhaps she could not help having them—but the dog is another matter." He smiled, and glanced at the young man, who awkwardly smiled back.

There was nothing unkindly in the chief's attitude, merely a complete absence of feeling. He was dealing with "a file", and had no sympathy for anyone who tried to evade the law. He prosecuted with lucid care, and back in his office smiled with satisfaction when he got a conviction. For to fail in getting a conviction was to be inept in his duty. Those above him frowned upon such ineptitude.

All the same, the young man felt miserable. If he hadn't gone to the cottage it would have been all right. But the chief had had no unnecessary desire for a court case—particularly one of those hard cases that might get into the press. Not that that mattered really, for the law had to be carried out. Than false sentiment against the law of the land there could, properly regarded, be nothing more reprehensible—because it was so easy to indulge.

"By the way," said the chief, as he was turning away, "I see the dog has been shot. You didn't mention that?"

"No. I——" He had forgotten to ask the woman if the dog was still with her. "I—as a matter of fact, I didn't think about it, seeing it was a police report, and therefore no evidence from us needed."

"Quite so," said his chief reticently, as he turned to his file.

"Who shot it?" the young man could not help asking.

"A gamekeeper, apparently."

The young man withdrew, bit on his embarrassment at evoking the chief's "reticence", and thought of the gamekeeper who might believe that if the dog was shot nothing more could be done about the case. As if the liability would thereby be wiped out! As if it would make the slightest difference to the case!

In his own room he remembered the gamekeeper and his curious look. Decent of him all the same to have tried to help. If the children's faces had been sallow and hollow from underfeeding, what could the dog have got? Nothing, unless——The thought dawned: the gamekeeper had probably shot the brute without being asked. Poaching rabbits and game? Perhaps the mainstay of the family? He laughed in his nostrils. When you're down you're right down, down and out. Absolutely. With a final snort of satire, he took some papers from the "pending" cover and tried to concentrate on an old woman's application for a pension. It seemed quite straightforward, though he would have to investigate her circumstances. Then he saw the children's faces again.

He had hardly been conscious of looking at them at the time. In fact, after that first glance of surprise he had very definitely not looked at them. The oldest was a girl of nine or ten, thin and watery, fragile, with her mother's incredible pallor and black eyes. The stare from those considering eyes, blank and dumb, and yet wary. They didn't appeal: trust could not touch them; they waited, just waited, for—the only hope—something less than the worst.

And the little fellow of seven or eight—sandy hair, inflamed eyelids, and that something about the expression, the thick, half-open mouth, suggesting the mental deficient. Obviously from the father's side, physically. The father had deserted them. Was perhaps in quod somewhere else, for they had only recently returned from their travels to the cottage. How did they manage even to live in it without being turned out? But the police would have that in hand as well! There was something too soft about the woman. She would never face up to her husband. When he was drunk, her softness would irritate him; he would clout her one. She was feckless. Her body had slumped into a pliant line, utterly hopeless, against the door. All at once he saw the line as graceful, and this unexpected vision added the last touch to derision.

The young man had observed in his life already that if his mind was keen on some subject he would come across references to it in the oddest places, in books dealing with quite other matters, from the most unlikely people. But this, carefully considered, was not altogether fortuitous. For example, when the old woman who had applied for the Old Age Pension asked him if he would have a cup of tea, he hesitated, not because he particularly wanted to have a cup of tea, but because he vaguely wanted to speak to her about the ways of tinkers, for Ivy Cottage was little more than a mile away.

His hesitation, however, the hesitation of an important official who had arrived in a motor car and upon whom the granting of her pension depended (as she thought), excited her so much that before she quite knew what she was doing she was on her knees before the fire, flapping the dull peat embers with her apron, for she did not like, in front of him, to bend her old grey head and blow the embers to a flame. As he was watching her she suddenly stopped flapping, with an expression of almost ludicrous dismay, and mumbled something about not having meant to do that. At once he was interested, for clearly there was something involved beyond mere politeness. The old folk in this northern land, he had found, were usually very polite, and he liked their ways and curious beliefs. The fact that they had a Gaelic language of their own attracted him, for he was himself a student of French, and, he believed, somewhat of an authority on Balzac.

Fortunately for the old lady, a sprightly tongue of flame ran up the dry peat at that moment, and she swung the kettle over it. "Now it won't be long," she said, carefully backing up the flame with more peat.

She was a quick-witted, bright-eyed old woman, and as she hurried to and fro getting the tea things on the table they chatted pleasantly. Presently, when she seated herself and began to pour the tea, he asked her in the friendliest way why she had stopped flapping her apron.

She glanced at him and then said, "Och, just an old woman's way."

But he would not have that, and rallied her. "Come, now, there was something more to it than that."

And at last she said: "It's just an old story in this part of the world and likely it will not be true. But I will tell it to you, seeing you say you like stories of the kind, but you will have to take it as you get it, for that's the way I got it myself, more years ago now than I can remember. It is a story about our Lord at the time of His crucifixion. You will remember that when our Lord was being crucified they nailed Him to the Cross. But before they could do that they needed the nails, and the nails were not in it. So they tried to get the nails made, but no one would make them. They asked the Roman soldiers to make them, but they would not. Perhaps it was not their business to make the nails. Anyway, they would not make them. So they asked the Jews to make the nails, but they would not make them either. No, they would not make them. No one would make the nails that were needed to crucify our Lord. And when they were stuck now, and did not know what to do, who should they see coming along but a tinker with his little leather apron on him. So they asked him if he would make the nails. And he said yes, he would make them. And to make the nails he needed a fire. So a fire was made, but it would not go very well, so he bent down in front of it and flapped it with his leather apron. In that way the fire went and the nails were made. And so it came about that the tinkers became wanderers, and were never liked by the people of the world anywhere. And that's the story."

THE TAX-GATHERER

When at last he drove away from the old woman's house he came to the cross-roads and, a few yards beyond, drew up. This is the place, he thought, and he felt it about him, gripped the wheel hard, and sat still. Irritation began to get the better of him. Anyone could see he was a fool. He got out and stretched his legs and lit a cigarette. There was no one in the turnip field, no one anywhere. All at once he walked back quickly to the cross-roads, turned right, and again saw the cottage. It was looking at him with a still, lopsided, idiotic expression. His flesh quickened and drew taut in cool anger. He threw the cigarette away, emptied his mind, and came to the door, which was exactly as it had been before, half open and stuck.

When he had knocked once, and no one answered, he felt like retreating, so he knocked very loudly the second time, and the woman materialised. There was no other word for it. There she was, with the graceful twist in her dejected body, attached to the edge of the door. Was she expecting the blow? Was there something not so much antagonistic as withdrawn, prepared to endure, in the pathos of her attitude? She knew how to wait, in any case.

"I see you didn't pay," he said.

She did not answer. She could not have been more than thirty.

"Well, you have got to appear before the court now," he asserted, and added, with a lighthearted brutality, "or the police will come and fetch you. Hadn't you the money to pay?" And he looked at her.

"No," she said, looking back at him.

"So you hadn't the money," he said, glancing away with the smile of official satire. "And what are you going to do now—go to prison?"

The children were poking their heads round her skirts again. Their fragility appeared extreme, possibly because they were unwashed. Obviously they were famished.

She did not answer.

"Look here," he said, "this is no business of mine." He took out his pocket-book. His hands shook as he extracted a pound note. "Here's something for you. That'll pay for everything. The only thing I want you *never* to do is to mention that I gave it to you. Do you understand?"

She could not answer for looking at the pound note. If he had been afraid of a rush of gratitude he might have saved himself the worry. She took it stupidly and glanced at him as if there might be a trick in all this somewhere. Then he saw a stirring in her eyes, a woman's divination of character, a slow welling of understanding in the black deeps. It was pathetic.

"That's all right," he said, and turned away as if she had thanked him.

When he got back into his car he felt better. That was all over, anyway. She was just stupid, a weak, stupid woman who had got trodden down. Tough luck on her. But she certainly wouldn't give him away. Perhaps he ought to have emphasised that part of it more? By God, I would never live it down in the office! Never! He began to laugh as he bowled along. He felt he could trust her. She was not the sort to give anything away. Too frightened. Experience had taught her how to hold her tongue before the all-important males of the world—not to mention the all-important females! She knew the old conspiracy all right and then some! His mirth increased. That he had felt he could not afford the pound—a pound is a pound, by heavens!—added now to the fun of the whole affair.

He did not go to court. After all, he might feel embarrassed; and the silly woman might, if she saw him, turn to him or depend on him or something. Moreover, he did not know how these affairs were conducted. So far it had not been his business. Besides, he disliked the whole idea of court proceedings. Time enough for that when he *had* to turn up.

Before lunch the chief came into his room for some papers.

The young man repressed his excitement, for he had been wondering how the case had gone, having, only a few minutes before, remembered the possibility of court expenses. He could not bring himself to ask the result, but the chief, as he was going out, paused and said: "That woman from Ivy Cottage, the dog case, she was convicted."

"Oh. I'm glad you got the case through."

"Yes. A silly woman. The bench was very considerate in the circumstances. Didn't put on any extra fine. No expenses. Take out the licence and pay the seven-and-six compromise fine—or five days. She was asked if she could pay. She said no. So they gave her time to pay."

The young man regarded the point of his pen. "So she's off again," he said, with official humour.

"No. She elected to go to prison. She put the bench rather in a difficulty, but she was obdurate."

"You mean—they've put her in prison?"

"Presumably. There was no other course at the time."

"But the children—what'll happen to them?"

"No doubt the police will give the facts to the Inspector of Poor. It's up to the local authorities now. We wash our hands of it. If people will keep dogs they must know what to expect!" He smiled drily and withdrew.

The young man sat back in his chair and licked his dry lips. She had cheated him. She had . . . she preferred . . . let him think. Clearly the pound mattered more than the five days. His money she would have left with the eldest girl, or some of it, with instructions what to buy and how to feed the children. She would have said to the eldest girl, "I'll be away for a few days, but don't worry, I'll be back. And meantime . . ."

But no, she would tell the eldest everything, by the pressure of instinct, of reality. That would bring the eldest into it; make her feel responsible for the young ones. And food . . . food . . . the overriding avid interest in food. Food—it was everything. The picture formed in his mind of the mother taking leave of her children.

It was pretty hellish, really. By God, he thought, we're as hard as nails. He threw his pen down, shoved his chair back, and strolled to the window.

The people passed on the pavement, each for himself or herself, upright, straight as nails, straight as spikes.

He turned from them, looked at his watch, feeling weary and gloomy, and decided he might as well go home for lunch, though it was not yet ten minutes to one. Automatically taking the white towel from its nail on the far side of the cupboard, he went out to wash his hands.

The White Hour

He paused by the water-barrel in a momentary listening, while a little white flame crept in about his eyes; then he took the last step to the back door and lifted the latch.

There were two or three paces of a gloomy passage-way to the kitchen and from the gloom he saw the spectral head of the old woman above her dark clothes. From the stiff wooden chair her body leant a little to the flickering fire, but her face was turned from it to the window. The quiet, early-evening light from the window fell with such a radiance on her face that the young man felt the uncanniness of it.

"Well, Granny!" he cried cheerfully, passing the top end of the boxed-in bed into the kitchen itself. A cold, healthy breeze rustled from him, and as he rubbed his hands before the flickering blaze, he laughed.

"Is it yourself!" she cried, with a start. Her welcoming voice was so quavering thin that its warmth went to his heart. The kindliness of her was a thing beyond analysis. "Take a chair! Take a chair!" Her body swayed as though it would take it in for him.

Before he had right seated himself, she lifted her voice: "Mary! What's keeping ye through there at all?"

"Coming, Granny!"

In the little silence that followed, the old woman saw Mary looking at herself in the glass, with her fingers doing this and that; but the young man could not see anything because of the sound of Mary's voice in his ears.

The chair legs scraped under him.

"Ay, Granny, but you're looking well!" In his mouth the title was one of courtesy.

"Oh, I'm keeping fine! I'm keeping fine!" Thin, bony fingers moved restlessly, caressingly on her lap. "It's not for me to complain." She stirred smilingly.

Then he saw that there was something working on her mind and that he had interrupted it in coming in.

"One feels the cold a little at times, what with the nights drawing in as they are."

"Yes, indeed," she said, stirring even more from the thing on her mind. "And sometimes, maybe, I'll be feeling I'm not just too strong. And then—and then I'll be thinking——"

Because of her years, he saw that she could only throw the thing from her mind by telling it.

"You haven't had another turn since, have you, Granny?"

"No. Not that."

She hesitated, but the way he waited held prompting sympathy.

"It was just at this time yesterday," she said at last. "Mary was out somewhere, and I was sitting here by myself. Just about this time, and it won't go out of my head."

At that he looked at her. Her face, he saw, was worn frail and thin as a sea-shell. Its fragility was incredible. An awful, impersonal fragility. Only the eyes belonged to life as he knew it, and even they burned thinly, transparently. It was in the eyes he had always found the resemblance to her grand-daughter, Mary. But these eyes before him had now lost the luminous, welling depth. They had become as thin spirit flames set in the frost-shell of a face.

"It won't go out of my head at all," she went on, drawing strength from him; "and I was thinking about it as you came in. I was thinking about it—and—I was thinking it was coming on me again."

"Was it last night?" he helped gently.

"Ay, it was last night. It was just in the evening about this time. Mary had gone out somewhere, and I was sitting here by myself. The old days had put a spell on me, and I was hearing the patter of little feet running. Then I was a girl myself with the faces of all who are dead and gone laughing and talking, as they would be doing long long ago. They were before me so clearly that there is no telling it. Every one of them by name I had. It was wonderful, so clear it was. . . . I was remembering, too, that first time behind the ould barn at home. I was feeding a lamb out of a bottle and Maurice came round the end of the barn. It came on us there and then, so that we could not speak. . . . There was never a better man to a woman."

In his way, the young man understood this, understood her feelings. It was always the same with the very old, as he had noticed. And by the ould barn there and the lamb—he was seeing the way of it with them so that the surge was in his own throat.

But when she spoke again, such a whispering, frightened note crept in her voice as made his mind start in a small shiver.

"And then—and then the feeling came over me on a sudden that there was Something in the kitchen here—watching me! It was such a terrible, quick feeling that my heart nearly choked me with the sudden fright of it. But when I looked up —there was nothing at all, not a living thing. It's trembling I was in a moment, looking for—for the thing. I thought once it was behind me, so that I could not turn round. But I began to feel it—coming.

"Ah, then—then it was the top of the bed I saw, and the edge of it was looking down at me; leaning over a little it was, and—watching me. And then the table, and the chairs. I looked to the door—the edge of it was pointing straight at me. But the most terrible thing of all was the stillness. I had never heard any stillness like it before—except the stillness of the dead. *And it was more than the stillness of the dead.*"

She paused to gather steadiness in a few quick breaths.

"It was an awful thing, the stillness—with my bits of furniture there watching me like strangers, and waiting, and listening. I looked to the window to see someone passing in the street so that I might cry to them. But the light in the window was white, so white it was that it hurt my eyes to be looking at it. And then it came on me what they were waiting for. Ah, I knew in a moment what it was they were listening for and waiting for to come in—to me. . . . The light from the window was like the light going before a—a Presence."

She just breathed the last word, so that the small shiver went down the young man's spine.

"Old as I am I did not know before that the most terrible of all things to mortal soul is loneliness. There are no words for it. To be left alone, waiting for—that, with not a voice nor a hand, as though you were lost for ever on a great white plain! My heart cried within me for the sound of a neighbour or a child or a beast itself. But it was like as if everything in the world was dead, and me left behind waiting for—that. . . .

"I got to my feet and made as best I could for the front door. I would see someone in the village street. But there was no one in the village street, no living soul, no moving living thing. And down at the foot of the gardens not a tree moved, not a leaf. The trees were grown taller, with a white quietness about them, and a listening and a light among their old leaves. And the tops of them were leaning over a little—*watching me*."

She rocked herself gently.

"I am an old woman who should be prepared, but oh, the awful loneliness, with that terrible white light hurting the balls of my eyes and pressing long white fingers against my forehead. Pushing me back, it was, back. . . . I would not have cared if only some one had been near me. But there was no one, there was no sound. . . . I came back as fast as I could and covered my head and wept."

Mary came in on a quick, light foot and gave a laughing greeting.

"Granny would be telling you of her weakness," she said cheerfully. She flustered about, poking the fire and lifting the kettle.

She had brought a rustle of air with her and a faint fragrance of violets. The fragrance touched the nostrils of the old woman so that she thought of the little green cake of soap Mary would be using at special times. She felt the nearness of their two young strong bodies and her heart kindled a little at the blaze. From the telling of her story there came relief, and the kindliness that was the whole of her welled up.

"Mary——"

"Ay, Granny—I'm just going to fill the kettle. I'll make a nice strong cup."

"Do ye that, Mary."

When the tea was over and the young man might be thinking of going, Mary was out about the back door, washing the cups perhaps. As he got up he was hoping she would not come in. She might come in easily. He had noticed that when the heart is desperately anxious that a woman do some clear simple thing the chances are she will not do it. Mary, however, did not come in, and an unusual thing happened. The white skeleton fingers came out and caught his passing hand, and held it. A terrible fore-knowledge came from the fingers and trickled through his flesh. She did not speak, but the thin flame of her eyes deepened. He needed no word to understand.

The dread thought of it was made bearable because of a final pressure of both her hands. It was the pressure that finishes a heart's telling and another heart's understanding. "In the world there is no girl like her," was her only saying, and with that her hands dropped. He felt the pressure of

84

words in him, but no word came; one might even force a cheery, reassuring laugh, but no laugh stirred in his throat.

He found Mary by the water-barrel. She did not look at him, busy as she was drying the dish-basin. Finally she wrung out the dish-clout, opened it out, flapped it. Then she spread it over two nails by the door.

Before she might turn round, he quickly lifted his eyes from her to the moor. His feelings tangled themselves to a knot in his throat, making his breathing uneven. Something had to be said, and the only natural thing to be said was about the old woman, and the old woman was dying.

"She's—she's——"

"Ay," said Mary, taking the word from him kindly, and staring out over the moor, too.

Her little word suddenly ran with a strange, dark companionableness on the crest of a wave within him. Surging the wave came. He broke the silence by turning his head from the moor and looking at her.

Her eyes shone luminous and soft and of a depth to drown the soul itself. A small crimson flame crept over cheek and neck. Then the wave broke and engulfed them.

The old woman did not see the crushing of the pliant body nor the smothering of the wild kissing, but the companionableness of it was with her in a great sweetness, so that the glazed white light from the window softened to a shadowy beauty.

The Tree

"I've been thinking," said Major Morrison to his gardener, "—been thinking we're a bit too closed in."

"Yes, Major," replied old Cameron slowly, turning his face away and looking vaguely at the trees.

"I think some of them could come down." The humph-humph gruff note was in his voice, his brows were netted a bit, his eyes rather strained.

"Yes," said Cameron. "Were you thinking of any—of any particular tree?"

"Yes," said the Major. "Yes, I was. Uh—I think——" He stopped abruptly. Cameron was still looking away, his expression negative, without any stress. "I think—there's one or two. It's dull. Obstructs the view. I'm going to have them down. Don't you agree?"

"I think it might do no harm."

"Harm? How could it do any harm?" The gruff voice was sarcastically astonished. "I think it would do a damned lot of good. Let in the light a bit. Harm? How do you think it would do any harm? Uh?"

"Oh, it'll do no harm," said Cameron slowly. "Were you thinking of—of any particular——"

"I'll see," said the Major angrily. "I'll go over them and let you know." He walked away.

Cameron heard him mutter to himself. It would be something about "that old fool!" thought Cameron with an ancient humour that touched only his eyes.

THE TREE

"What was he angry about?" asked Cameron's wife, coming over from the end of the gardener's cottage.

"It's that tree again."

"Is he going to cut it, then?"

"I think he had made up his mind to cut it when he started out, but he couldn't just bring himself to it at the last minute."

"Still like that. Poor man."

"He will always argue himself into a temper," said Cameron drily upon the silence.

"Did he say anything to you?"

"It's not me he's saying it to; it's his dead wife." He clicked his long shears and stooped. He was a smallish man with a stone-grey face and warped a bit about the shoulders.

"Couldn't you do something? Couldn't you cut the tree yourself?" suggested his wife, with a rush of vague anxiety. She was a tall, slightly bent, grey-haired woman with a kind face.

"How could I do that?" His lifted look was charged with dry sarcasm.

She turned away, recognising the wisdom in that look, yet knowing, too, that if the tree could be cut down the Major might get some relief.

And yet she wondered if he would. That was the difficulty. She would have egged her husband on and risked their position, if she had been dead sure. In her bones she felt that the tree brought a living warmth to the Major. It brought his wife to him. The tree was like a warm blanket of argument. If it went all of a sudden, his wife might go, and he would have nothing left. After her death he had had things to occupy his mind. But once these things were settled and his newly grown-up family had gone away again, he had been thrown back upon himself—upon his habits and memories. And the centre of his habits and memories was his wife.

It was, in truth, astonishing to so strong a man to discover how empty his world had become, not only in the mental but in the sheer physical sense. It was as if he went out with a long stick and began beating things that somehow were no longer there. The world was a void, without meaning. There was nothing to grip, to order, to push aside. Particularly was there nothing to come up against him, nothing solid, nothing but just damned shadows.

These shadows were the shadows of former arguments, of plans, of disputes about plants and rockeries and trees and paths and the hundred and one things that make up the lively government of a small if ancient estate.

She had been dead about three months and the trees were in heavy leaf. The glory of the rockery was nearly over, but the garden was coming away towards maturity and the forming of fruit. The new strawberry plants had berries of a perfect size and shape. Really wonderful—and the flavour, doubtless, wonderful, too. Only he couldn't quite be sure. The third mouthful had revolted him; the sweetness, too much sugar. Having shoved the sugar from him and taken one neat— he still could not be certain.

A small thing, but it could be very depressing, very maddening, tiresome. Things were without final substance, as if they had lost their reason for existing. She had taken their reason away with her. She had taken the heart out of everything.

Oh, he realised well enough what had happened to him. He had expected to be lonely and find things a trifle pointless. When the danger signal had first been flown, he had in fact got quite a shock. They had still in the normal course of life some twenty active years in front of them, and that death should step in seemed so utterly unreasonable that the idea angered him. As death drew nearer, he began to realise how aimless his life might be without his wife. When death arrived, he wept, his brows ridged darkly, his eyes strained with pain.

But the old lonely world would remain for him to wander in and order. And somehow it hadn't remained.

THE TREE

Here he was actually baffled and groping and unable to make up his mind about cutting a tree!

This tree, a tall birch, slim, yet beautifully proportioned, foliaged in a graceful swaying fashion, was the tree his wife had long wanted to cut down. It blocked up a far view of hills and a middle-distance glimpse of a loch. Her argument had been that they had hundreds of these silver birches, that in fact they had so many trees they were being shut in. She wanted here and there an avenue of escape; a moment of expansiveness for her sight to fly along or perhaps her spirit, though she would not have used a word like spirit to him. She had to be very careful indeed when it came to mention of spiritual or artistic things. Art did not interest him at all, unless it was conventionally unobjectionable, and then only politely. He frowned on her private efforts at painting, not that he really minded—he could even have been vaguely proud of it as an extra sort of irrational feminine grace—but being genuinely fond of his wife, he was jealous of her good name. He would suffer a lot rather than learn the "county" was amused. And none the less because her pedigree was longer than his own, with a few real impoverished titles in it.

For his nature was profoundly conservative. That was why he could not cut down the tree. The trees were his property, many of them twisted and knotted with age. They were rooted, too; rooted. Day after day, generation after generation, they remained in the same place, acknowledging the morning wind or the evening quiet, spring or autumn; green or gold or naked, they were forever permanent.

He genuinely could not understand how his wife could want to cut down this tree. He felt it should be against her very nature, for she professed to love the beauty she found in trees; she painted them. She could exclaim over a tree's perfect proportions. How then could she, without treachery to herself, want to cut down this silver birch? There was a sort of perverse cruelty in it somewhere; either that, or a woman never really did understand—but it was difficult to work out. He was blessed if he could understand it.

Nor could he understand her yet. Though now it was being borne in upon him that there had been far more in her than he had ever quite grasped. For there was nothing clearer than that in going away she had taken the trees with her. And not only the trees, but the garden and the rockery and even the inside of the house, which now had a few hollow sounds with an extra distance between the walls.

And it wasn't much use saying that everything remained exactly as before, for, of course, he knew it did, precisely. Hang it, that was obvious, he was not a fool! Nor was it any use saying that she had taken the spirit out of the trees and plants and things. She hadn't. Oh, God, he knew she hadn't. Why? Because she wouldn't. The realisation of it now came out of him like a shout. She would have done everything for him she could, quietly, her head bent over the rockery, turning round a tree-trunk here, over a shrub there, everywhere, her calm, pleasant face with its concentration, its occasional humour, its sheer sense, and her hair with a touch of that pale gold seen in the birch leaves when they first begin to turn. She would have left everything for him, in healthy fitness, not with any expression of emotion or love, not out of duty, but with an unobtrusive, perfect naturalness. He knew that—as he had never known it before. The trees had not been taken; they had gone with her.

His love for her, thus vague and chaotic, began to gather shape and to grow. At sudden moments of discovery, he would quicken with pride of her. His simple, frank nature was gratified by any words of praise which another might utter: "She was really marvellous—such quiet insight, and—

nothing personal. The simplest folk—extraordinary." He felt like thanking the speaker very much. He generally did: "Very nice of you to say so."

Really he might as well cut that tree down. Of course, nonsense and all that to say it would help his dead wife. Still—it would let in some light. She had been right enough in a way there. Though, after all, how she could actually want to cut down. . . . Still, dammit, there were probably one or two oozing firs that could be well enough out of the way. And, anyhow, he could not go to Cameron and ask for this one only. Would look too much like—Cameron knew all about their arguments.

It was exasperating.

He would not mind cutting the tree for his wife. He was prepared to. Even secretly now might want to. But—the weeks went on. Besides, in any case, to hurry such a thing, as if acting on impulse, emotion. . . .

He so rarely acted on anything else, that exasperation grew. Once he entertained the mad idea of sending Cameron and his wife on a holiday. It rather shook him.

So by the time the trees had attained their heaviest summer foliage, he was completely shut in—and for the first time since the death of his wife he felt stir in him a certain vague satisfaction, a measure of fullness, like the fullness of the foliage.

The trees began to gather about them a new, dark, heavy life. This was something his wife had never known. Or was it life—or death—or what?

He did not speculate. He was covered over. His wife was beyond this, as she had been beyond his near male strength that had always to reach out to take her or to shove her aside.

When the August invitation to the shoot came, he did not reply at once. Of course, he had to go. That was as inevitable as that grouse should be shot. He delayed until he had to wire his arrival. And, surprisingly, he stayed a long time, far longer than he had ever done before. His hosts understood, naturally, that he was postponing the inevitable return to his loneliness and made his stay as pleasant as possible.

But at last the exodus to London compelled his return, and all at once, during preparations for the journey, he became eager and excited to the point of ill-temper. A longish stay at a little wayside station infuriated him. The desire to see his woods was consuming him.

There came the last rise of the road, the dip down and turn round, and there they were.

And then all in a moment he realised that his wife had come back.

Here and there a hanging spray of birch leaves had turned yellow. An odd bracken frond, too. Everywhere could be caught a glimpse of the colour of her hair, and between the trees and down the paths was an openness frank as her face. It was exactly as if from every place he gazed at her presence had just been removed, leaving behind the light of that presence.

It was at once exhilarating and extraordinarily intimate, and was made almost unbearably exciting by throwing into contrast quite involuntarily in his mind the darkness of the closing-in trees before he had gone away. That darkness had been for death. A man shuts himself in, lets the dark trees grow up and over him like the walls of a mausoleum.

Now she was alive again, all through the woods, letting in colour and light. She was doing it herself, as she always had done things, here and there, with bent head or uplifted face.

For the first time in all his mortal career, there came to the Major some conception of the word Resurrection. He had never definitely thought of his wife as lying dead in the earth. To picture her body as rotting away in its black hole was a morbid indecency that could not even involuntarily occur to him. Yet the unadmitted shadow of that picture was now consciously released and dismissed.

And this Resurrection had no religious or church significance at all. It was something entirely personal and unexpected, and so glimmering with light that he did not really entertain it in his thought. It was outside, everywhere, as she herself had usually been. Nothing actually new. Something from *before*, that—well, there it was. As inexplicable as the way in which confidence or delight or belief ever does come to a man.

"Hullo, Cameron!" he shouted.

Cameron emerged from the trees with his scythe. "Welcome back, sir."

"How are things?"

"Fine. I hope you had good sport."

"Yes. Very good. We'll have to get busy tidying up, I see. A whole lot to do, uh? A bit too shut in about that house. We'll be getting lazy if we're not careful!" When he smiled or laughed his expression became very pleasant, almost seemed to flush with colour in a boyish fashion.

Cameron smiled, too. Obviously going out among his fellows, shooting and moor-tramping and that, had worked its healthy wonder on the Major. He was very glad to see it. The Major would become bossy for a bit and then things would settle back comfortably.

"Had you your nephew with you?"

"Yes, Major."

"Enjoy himself?"

"He did, indeed."

"I hope he kept out of mischief!" The Major laughed, for the previous year the young rascal had burst the dam of the duckpond and nearly drowned himself. He had the notion of creating a secondary pond for breeding trout. The Major's wife had had a weakness for the lad, who could work all day quietly by himself in an absorbed fashion. The Major thought he was rather like an eel.

It was really very pleasant to be back. The elderly housekeeper and the two maids were plainly charged with excitement and welcome, as if this were a state occasion and he justified their existence. Very nice of them. Even the younger girl who was given by nature to a warm, stout disorder was all fresh and tidy, with a shine on her face. The tea was refreshing, the linen very white, the blackcurrant jam pretty good. He would have a look around before dark just to see the lie of things. There was a fair amount to think out. Light. Colour. (He could not get these out of his head.) That tree was coming down. And one or two others. Nothing could get at a man unless he opened himself out. Quite suddenly he was overcome with a profound longing for his wife. Tears started to his eyes. He went to his room. He sobbed her name to himself. She was everywhere—and so he realised she was nowhere. And yet she was so near, and he had so much to give her—the trees, the garden, the light, the rockery—everything given over to her with his hands, bearing the weight of them from against his chest—there, Grisil, there! Where are you?

Oh, damn, this was nonsense! A profound stroke of self-pity made him weep again, but quietly, sitting down. Then he wiped his eyes and blinked strongly. Curse it all! He smiled wryly. The weight had been taken from against his chest, however. The light—the light had leaked in.

That tree was coming down.

All along in a sense it had been pigheadedness that had been wrong with him. Had merely felt he didn't want to lose a tree and so had grown obstinate and domineering—in the usual way!

The tree would be a sacrifice.

Nor was there religious significance about the idea of

sacrifice any more than there had been about the notion of resurrection; less, if comparison were possible, because he recognised in the tree-cutting a certain giving way to emotion. It was suddenly as if he laughed, knowing she was behind him. They had often had culminating moments of sheer fun—and not infrequently after vociferous language on his part. For with her steady sort of autumn face she had a way of ignoring or mocking him that was a mad temptation. How furious she had made him sometimes, absolutely furious! Calm and wise, she would go on with her job, not giving in at all, rather short with him if need be, and then her look, smiling, penetrating—Grisil, curse you! the itch for her, the laugh!

He would go out. All at once he was in a hurry, impatient. And though he nursed his impatience by deliberately pausing to examine this or that, it took him a very short time to reach the fatal birch, with not another soul in sight—for he had grown sensitive about being seen gazing at that tree. And it was really a rather fine tree. The sky had grown dull, stormy-looking, full of tailed windclouds; and the trees were not so much swaying as flattening under hand-claps from the sky; flattening and even cowering a little, with a swish and a surge like the sound of sea water—all except this birch, whose every new movement had interest and grace, as if it couldn't help itself, after the fashion of a woman graciously endowed. However the blow came, the resilience and sway-back were unhurried. And the leaves trailed through the wind like fingers through water. Upon the green were two drooping sprays, yellow as if they had been painted. Very charming—and strong, the stem persistent, full of life.

When a man is going to sacrifice, let him be handsome about it. There is little satisfaction in sacrificing the unimportant. The Major became charged at last with something approaching exaltation, and his eye, clarified thereby, observed minute physical things as it had never done before; not merely the shape of the tree as a whole, but individual branches, even individual leaves, the leaf, the branch, the stem. And the clothing of the stem, the silvered bark, the rough excrescences, right down to the disappearance of the main roots into the earth, the earth itself. It was a seeing eye, and such an insignificant matter as a recent surface abrasion not so big as the heel of a boot attracted it in almost startled curiosity. Extraordinary how alert his senses had become! He stooped; a small pad of moss came away in his fingers, revealing a root, as thick as his wrist, neatly and recently cut through!

The shock of this, followed by the pounding of his heart, weakened him physically. He sat down and called upon the Deity in guttural surprise. Then he took His name in vain and went cursing and rooting about that tree like a mad boar.

That only the one root had been severed did not allay his fury; it merely complicated and whipped it, as only a quite senseless thing can.

There came a pause, the slow birth of a black suspicion, followed by a demoniac possession that heaved him to his feet and sent him striding vastly towards the gardener's cottage.

What in the name of the four-headed dogs of hell did this mean?

Cameron's face was the grey boulder in a thunderstorm.

"Speak, curse you! Did you do it?"

"No," spoke Cameron quietly. "I didn't do it."

"What! Who did it then? Who did it?"

The grey stone remained unexpressive; but the Major's eye had not lost its sight. "You know!" he cried. "Out with it! Out with it at once, or——" and he swore by unwritten things that Cameron would be sacked now, on the spot, instantly and for ever.

"It was my nephew," said Cameron.

"Lord!" roared the Major; "that pasty-faced eel!"

Then their eyes met.

"Who," said the Major, voice low-pitched, terribly intense, "who told him—to cut—that?"

"No one living that I know," said Cameron stonily.

There was a long pause. Cameron looked away.

Then his black unreasoning fury got complete control of the Major. Cameron faced him.

"You can sack me if you like——"

"Sack you? I'll murder you!" The large body of the man was trembling convulsively. Cameron saw that he was going to be attacked. He gripped the scythe strongly. His face furrowed. The spirit of the evil wild came glinting out of his eyes. The naked antagonism made murder possible and even desirable. But Cameron's wife threw them back on themselves; shackled them again agonisingly.

Presently the Major could hear her words in his drumming ears. But he did not listen, his hatred was so fierce.

And Cameron had become truculent. He was shouting. "Take your damned scythe! I'm through with you!" His flesh was jumpy. He stamped the earth. He threw the scythe from him and walked away, muttering defiantly and harshly.

"Ah, excuse him, sir; excuse him, Major. He was so sorry, so vexed, when he discovered the boy cutting—cutting—— He was——"

"Shut up!" roared the Major.

"He did not know——"

"If he did not know, who told him?"

Before this cryptic yell, the woman bowed her head.

"You knew I would never cut down that tree for all the powers in heaven or hell. Never! And yet you would drive the boy to cut the roots—the roots! Oh, God, to cut the roots! Such blasted treachery!"

"We didn't——"

"How did he know, then?"

"We don't know——"

"You're lying!" cried the Major.

"Unless he overheard someone——"

"Overheard! Ha, so you were talking!"

"We asked him. He would not tell us. We don't know." She looked at the Major. She was not frightened of him, nor apparently was she afraid of the sack. But there was pain in her face. He saw this pain. It came out to him—with an intolerable understanding. Her eyes were tear-washed. Choking with rage, he turned away.

They would go at once, lock, stock and barrel!

He walked a long way, stumbling over roots, down banks, all round his property, until, in the darkness, he stood before his tree again.

The wind had risen. The branches were threshing, tossing and threshing, in maenad fashion.

He could never cut the tree down now. Never!

The intrusion on his privacy had been unbearable. The eel-faced boy had listened to his aunt and uncle talking. The most secretive and terrible thing in his life was their common talk! Oh, God, it was intolerable! He felt betrayed—betrayed even by his dead wife. She had liked that boy, had called him imaginative and clever. Perhaps, sneaking about the trees, the boy had even overheard himself and his wife having a few words on their favourite topic! And now the eel, in his "imaginative and clever" way, was helping fate—perhaps he had actually thought he was helping him, the Major!

It was too humiliating. Too utterly humiliating. In his travail, his groans mixed with the creakings and flailings of the trees under the dark and ominous sky.

As exhaustion came upon him, carrying tiredness beyond spite, he realised that in some way again he had messed things up. Life happened to him like that. Before his wife died, all his energies somehow had had a direction. Now, damn, everything was empty and meaningless. This afternoon, coming home had been like a reunion; the cutting down of the tree was to let in light. He had felt his life being given a direction once more.

Now his wife was farther away than ever. Dead again in her grave.

He could never cut down the tree. To cut it would have no meaning, would make him out a fool; a giving-in he would never be able to recall without squirming.

It was too late.

All light was lost in the darkness of the sky. And would be lost for ever. In the darkness of trees, shutting in, like walls, like tombs.

He felt lonely and lost, and the ancient instinct rose in him to blame his wife, to accuse her. "Grisil!" he cried, but his voice caught the broken sound of one crying in agony.

He blinked his wet eyes angrily and went stumbling down to his home. He forced the food down his throat. He drank. The rising storm accentuated the quietness of the sitting-room as the hours passed. Once when the window suddenly rattled he got to his feet, and the whisky warmth ebbed from his skin, leaving it icy cold. The idea of someone's being outside the window began to torment him. There were curious noises, whimpering, whining sounds. The whisky was having less than no effect; it was positively sobering him to an uncanny apprehension.

Then he faced it: he was afraid to go to the window.

He went, pulled back the shutters, glared out, and saw a pale face peering from the shrubbery. The face of the boy! The face of the dark eel body, storm-pale, unearthly. It took a few seconds before he recognised a mirrored reflection, outside, of the opaque electric globe in the room.

He banged the shutters violently and went up to bed, full of the relief of blasphemy. But the pale face followed him, and in his dream it wore no opaque mask of any kind.

THE TREE

It was almost as luminous as the ghostly globe of light as it flitted about the roots of the birch tree, burning with an elvish excitement, jerking backward now and then as the grubbing hands tugged. And the tree itself—its swaying branches touched him—the leaves were silk. Rough silk that whisked away from him, ballooned and moulded and draped. And up above—her long hair like yellow feathers. She was the tree—and yet not the tree. And then he understood what was happening. She was taking the shape of the tree, entering into it and bending it over, trying to break it.

The conspiracy between her and the pale face at the roots was perfect. There existed indeed so intense a glee that it became painful. He saw the strain in the high countenance, in the tree-arms, in the mad heave-up and thresh forward to that point of stress that would not break.

The stress entered into himself, but he was imprisoned and could raise neither hand nor cry. Shut into the black wood, entombed in the mausoleum. She was trying to break down the door, to get him out. Her features, forming human size, flashed full of an agony of endeavour, every muscle taut. "Duncan!" Then the upthrusting tree swept her back, and his name fled down the wind.

His cry to her stuck in his throat. His body was powerless as though wrapped in its winding-sheet, yet he knew he was standing on his feet in the dark wood, and in the knowledge was an unclean, shameful impotence. His chest was bursting with an upsurging power. If he could not release it he would swoon and sink into the earth, into death.

Release me! Release me! The silent shout rose in him, surged out of him under terrific pressure, surged with his wife against the tree, surged and sustained the stress—yet!—yet! *Crash!*

With that crash he probably swooned in his sleep, for when he awoke it was daylight.

The storm had been very violent. As he went downstairs

he met the housekeeper who said she had hardly slept from the sound of it. She looked hushed and a trifle scared, as if she had heard unearthly voices in the night.

He smiled, his mind curiously at ease. Before eating, he would have a look round, he said. Green leaves and bits of broken branches were scattered about the lawn. Some of the trees were quite noticeably stripped. The air was fresh, with clouds here and there against the pure field of the sky. The scent of the woods, tinged with earth, was exquisite in the nostrils.

He was in no hurry. But only when he came to the birch tree and found it uprooted did he realise the tension in his breast—by the grateful way it eased. He smiled. It was a lovely morning.

The slightest crisp touch of the exhilaration of autumn. And the scent—invigorating. Lifting his eyes, he beheld far hills, finely outlined in the clear light, and in the middle distance a loch wrinkled its glittering skin. And there, coming up the new avenue, was Cameron, solemn as an old owl! He saw the tree was down. The Major choked back his laugh.

"Well, what is it?"

"It will take us to Saturday to get all our things out of the house," said Cameron quietly.

"Four days! Why so long as that?"

"Because it will take that long," said Cameron.

"Will it? Not if I can help it! And in the first place, anyway, aren't you damned well ashamed of yourself?"

"No," said Cameron.

"You won't apologise?"

"No," said Cameron. "You——"

"Yes?"

"You were as much to blame as I was."

"Oh, was I? Very well, then. I'm prepared to apologise." For the first time Cameron's stony calm lost its certainty.

"No," he muttered. "I don't want——"

"What!" roared the Major. "Do you think I was going to apologise to you?" He laughed. "You fool!"

"I'm not a fool," said Cameron doggedly.

"Aren't you? Really? I think you behaved like a blasted idiot, if you ask me."

Then Cameron looked at him.

"Quite so," nodded the Major. "Two blasted fools, and we'll now have to go and apologise to Mrs. Cameron. Don't you understand how badly you have behaved? Lord, you were nearly as bad as myself. Come on!"

They had often had rows. After them they had liked each other none the less. The Major was in extremely handsome form this morning; full of plans, as they walked along.

He expressed his regrets to Mrs. Cameron. "Your husband is as big a fool as myself. If you forgive us this time, we'll try to do better." There was sincerity behind his smiling fun.

And she accepted his fun graciously and thanked him.

Dammit, he liked the woman, had always liked her. She had a sense of manners. Never overdid such a moment. "That tree", he said, quite involuntarily, "got blown down last night."

She looked at him for an instant and looked away. It was suddenly an intense moment, as if his heart had bared itself. He was just about to laugh, to crash through it, when she said pleasantly to her husband, "Won't that make the tree you wanted for the new rambler? It's long and won't need cutting."

"Yes," said the Major. "Yes," and turned away abruptly. "See you after breakfast," he shouted.

Obviously he was moved from the way he walked. His wife had planted the rambler. He strode at a great pace.

"He would hardly have liked maybe to cut it for firewood," she said quietly.

THE TREE

A smooth peace had come back to Cameron's face. He disliked these quarrels. They made him feel very awkward inside, and because of that roused in him sometimes a devil tough and gnarled as an old root. Peace was what he liked and quietness about the garden and among the trees. He took out his pipe. It was a nice morning. A smile glimmered in his eyes. He turned to his wife and saw slow tears on her quiet, absorbed face.

"What are you crying for?" he asked.

"I don't know," she answered, with profound sadness, and went into the house.

On the Stone

His body was young, prehensile and tough; supple, full of a rolling grace; quick on the toes. He liked a good blow-up when their boat was beating into harbour well-fished; gave some style to the swinging seas. Blue-green eyes flashed in response, quick on his laughter. Sailing a boat or climbing a cliff, he knew the wind or the hand-grip. The old men liked Jeck. He stirred up the drowned serpent in their blood, quickened their glances, brought a forgotten savour into their mouths for the pure comedy of life. They would say anything to tease him, to set him going.

But one evening the comedy was presented so completely that the marvel of it stung them to a momentary silence. The meeting place was always the green in front of the salmon-house, with the sea slapping the shingle where the cobles were hauled up. Tall grey poles stood about the green, usually festooned with grey nets and flat corks, but this evening the nets had just been taken down and the foreman, with one or two of his crew, was in the bothy. After their day's labour, young men and women would gather in about the green, gossip, play sudden chasing games, or dance in the summer dusk if crippled Alastair was there with his melodeon. The older men and the greybeards kept up the stone gables or the wooden sheds with a shoulder or the flat of a back, or even stepped out a pace or two if reminiscence required a mimicry of action. It was a fishing community on a wild northern coast, backed by scattered crofts.

On this particular evening Ellen Macleod was there, and though there was nothing between Jeck and herself except a sort of conflict, yet this conflict frequently produced a clash of wits and a laugh. It could be relied on to add to the fun. She had a gleam in her dark eyes, and a provocative sarcasm could fade on her lips as she looked away. Jeck was slim, but she was full-bodied, smooth over cheek and brow, and at times had a steady holding grace that set a swirl about her like the swirl in a dark pool.

Suddenly a couple of girls started chasing a young fellow round the poles, behind bodies, gripping the bodies as they swung past, shouting and screaming, until in no time there was a tremendous hullabaloo. No one knew what had happened— or cared. But a girl can hardly expect to use even the shyest fellow as a dodging post and get off with it. Jeck, however, was so much a fellow in himself and a fellow for everyone that the shyest girl could use him publicly without implication. And all at once he was aware of Ellen's voice telling him to watch where he was pushing.

"Oh, it's you is it?" said Jeck.

"It is."

"Well, if I was barged into you I couldn't help it, could I? Besides——" he added, his eyes flashing.

"Besides what?"

"Just besides," said Jeck.

Someone laughed. "Give it her, Jeck!"

"I will if she's not careful," said Jeck, smiling, turning away.

Ellen's dark eyes caught their own fire. "I should like to see you try it."

Jeck swung round. "In a minute!" he said.

She regarded him with a mocking but dangerous gleam.

Then all in a moment he was going towards her. Her expression never wavered. On the contrary, it grew more tense; it so dared and repelled him that it was like a whip on his face. But he went on, hardly knowing himself in his action, aware of a monstrous folly. Now she was against him; his arms were round her stiff body; his mouth was swooping down on her lips; felt their cold firmness before she drew back.

The sound of the slap was heard all over the green. He stared at the black fury in her eyes. His face reddened; confused, speechless, he turned away trying to laugh, an awkward hunch to his shoulders. After the silence, men laughed loudly at him, but he had their sympathy. "You're soft to stand that from her!" For there was something vindictive in the way Ellen held her ground before slowly turning away. Clearly the lad had not meant anything special, and after all she had dared him. But the sting of the slap had stung them too. It was exciting. They chuckled against the wall. "Here, Jeck, if I was you——"

But Jeck, as he gathered himself, didn't need any of their advice. "What's one more or less to me?" "One what?" they asked. He laughed now, leaving it to them, leaving Ellen as one of the many.

But when it was quite dark he took to the grassy slopes that crested the sea-cliffs, black anger in his heart, a twisting inner fury that in the instant of hating her called himself an ass. "What an almighty ass!" He smashed an ironshod heel into the turf.

The northern sea boomed hollowly in the caverns, raised its grey face to an obliterating horizon. And it wasn't as if he was a weakling or anything. Sweet heaven, it wasn't. He crushed the bones of his face into the grass. Oh, damn her!

But he saw that it was no good damning her, for the paralysing weakness lay in himself. Whenever he was in her company he felt himself going all unnatural, even physically, in the movement of his limbs, not to mention his tongue and its noises. It was like a secret disease. Oh, it was! And don't talk to him about being soft on her. Muck of that kind. Shut up!

. . . He would make her pay. Oh, he would pay her out! He tore a fistful of turf. And he would do it, showing no more feeling than usual. None. Carrying on as if nothing had happened. . . .

For no one had suspected his weakness; no one except herself. More than once she had secretly mocked him while he was in the awkward throes. He remembered the times, small occasions, in public yet unnoticed by others. For example that day when her father had by great seaman-ship brought home the *White Rose* under sail. He had not known what to say to her there before his own door in the little street. He had made some heavy idiotic joke about her father's hardihood. "He had courage anyway," she replied, her dark eyes smiling. What was there in that? Nothing. Even if she was implying that he, Jeck, hadn't much courage—in other things—what things?—well, she had to make her joke too. Yet it was exactly as if a bomb had exploded inside him. He had gone all to bits, bits that held together miraculously, and marched away, throwing laughing sounds over a shoulder, while inwardly he felt the whole street following him from behind windows with laughing eyes.

Courage to dare her? He wondered, tortured. And even if her words had meant that, would he have had the courage to take the dare. . . . And all at once he realised it was not a question of her at all but himself, of command, control, over himself. Even at the prospect of meeting her, he had always felt that control beginning to slip. Like a young fellow beginning to be sea-sick. As bad as that—and as shameful.

Then on the green there, faced by her challenge, he had for the first time gone on. Suddenly there had been nothing else in the world to do. Even if he had been walking to his death he would have had to go on. And she could have shoved him back in time, could have done something. But she had done nothing. She had waited with perfect control of herself. Then her body, her terrible eyes, her lips—he had felt the cold curves of them running into her teeth.

He lay over and got his teeth in the grass.

For there was a subtler poison still. Between them had always been something hidden or secret, an understanding or knowledge, and he had betrayed it. No, not that; he had betrayed what was delicate and hidden in her; gone up and kissed her like Judas.˙ Before them all. She had stood without moving, knowing he would not dare, knowing he could not. Damn her! he suddenly thought, and lay still again while his mind on its own began searching for some way of triumphing over her, of hurting her cruelly.

The search was difficult, but there was one obvious line of conduct; and that was never deliberately to avoid her presence but on the contrary to swagger into it. She meant nothing to him. If she was sore about the fun on the green and continued to show it, why, it would be worth half a laugh—and, laughing, he would swagger off. He would make her squirm. He would drag the last pennyworth out of that slap. His fingers ripped off a whole divot of thin turf and flung it over the cliff-edge. A rip of laughter went with it. A dangerous sea always inspired him. Why not?

As the boats returned the following morning, there was the customary crowd on the harbour wall. Ellen was waiting for her father as usual. With the boats all fast and the white fish on the quay, the fishermen straightened their backs. Then, the flesh on his bones dissolving, he pretended to see Ellen for the first time and in a cheery half-boisterous voice cried, "Hullo, Ellen!" There was the blind uncertain instant, until— she refused his challenge and he was saved. The way Ellen turned away deliberately as if he weren't there made one or two of his comrades, who remembered the slap, chuckle loudly. But for Jeck in that instant the shadow was lifted from the whole world. Quite involuntarily he laughed. The world was charged with sunlight, crammed with assurance. As he caught a glimpse of the dark flush on Ellen's brow, he stooped to keep himself from laughing too loudly.

Remarkable that so little a thing could produce so vast an effect! Tingling with pleasure, he ignored his father's proffered hand and swung the heavy basket straight to his own shoulders. He joked and laughed with his little brother as he strode home, so like a young sea-god that those meeting him smiled without knowing it before they spoke.

Later, the meaning of it came to him in words: "I've got her now!" So sure was his triumph that vindictiveness hardly salted it. Actually, of course, he meant that he was free of her. He had got her where he could bait her—and laugh.

Utterly delightful was the feeling of freedom this gave him. To treat her in the same way again, a second time, any time he liked—it was enough to urge him on to create the chance, to provide the provocation. And one night at a social gathering, followed by the usual dance, he was positively presented with chances. As he headed into them, his seamanship was inspired. His cunning was a sheer delight to him. A few of them had clubbed together for a bottle of whisky. They had had a round by the high dark church wall and returned to elbow their way breezily through the young crowd at the door, their breath upon the air. "Phew!" said a mouth blowing the whisky smell away. "What are you phewing at?" demanded Jeck, tousling the young hair. This attention from the sea-god was such sweet flattery that the schoolboy wriggled and squared up to fight. But the young men were already glancing over the young women. "There's Janet," said Jeck, "the belle of the ball." As he began making for her through the crush, he roughly if inadvertently shouldered a girl out of the way and turned round to say he was sorry. But it was Ellen and his smile flashed. "Hullo, Ellen!" His hand actually came up and saluted her cheerily as he continued on his course.

Janet was a lovely dancer, fluent as a wave of the sea. He told her so. His breast was filled with pleasure and his tongue with cunning. She told him that she smelt whisky off him and that he should be ashamed of himself. Solemnly he squeezed the breath out of her. "They'll see you!" "Not they—for I'll wait until we're turning—like this," and he squeezed her again. All with an air of calm assurance, lit, however, with an entrancing excitement. She saw it in his eyes. She was very handsome. In the black shadow of the church wall he kissed her. She put her arms round his neck, but would not stay long with him after that.

In this way he regained complete control of himself, and if Ellen occupied his thought almost incessantly it was really only with the joy of having overcome her. He did not mind her being in his head at all, because he could always stand and look at her, and watch her, angered, turn away. All he had to make sure of was that nobody was watching him when he smiled to himself.

It was a grand game. A game for the gods! And when he remembered that the gods were supposed to be jealous of any mortal who aspired to their state, he laughed. When the sea-gods rose against him, he broke their backs with the keel of his boat. Ellen could not fight because it would be against her dignity. Could anything be more perfect, more crammed with fun?

The gods had a look at Ellen. Behind her dark eyes, under her dark hair, lay the round dark pool of her being. It was easy to trouble it, where it lay, invisible.

"Hullo, Ellen!"

She ignored him. He was transported.

Easy to set a swirl in the pool with a forefinger, a swirl like an adder's tail.

"Hullo, Ellen!"

This time she looked at him with an odd troubled light in her eyes. It half-measured, half-mocked him, with something else in it that he instantly feared, then it turned away.

But he wasn't having any of that. Keep her down instantly and at all costs. He laughed. She paid no more attention to him. She walked away.

He saw through her dodge, of course, and this gave him an extra delight, but now the sort of delight that had in it the premonition of a temperature, a fever. When alone, he did not voluntarily recall her; quite involuntarily her eyes looked at him with their mysterious troubled mockery and, while he was trying to fathom them, withdrew.

He began to fear that, as she gained confidence, her power would grow. So counter it he must, without evasion, hitting out at every opportunity. But now a strange self-treachery began to invade him. In this new strife he found he had to resort in thought, in imagination, to violence to overcome her and the violence consisted in crushing her bodily, crushing down on her mouth, until she collapsed into complete subjection. But the imaginative triumph always left his heart beating painfully and his legs unsteady. The mad fever taking possession of him over shadows!

Damnation to that!

So when the evening came that she did not withdraw her look, he faced into her with all his laughing strength.

"Hullo, where are you bound for?"

"Why?" A slow watching satire steadied in her smile.

"Oh, nothing! Nothing at all!"

"Why worry then?"

"I'm not worrying. I was only asking."

"I see."

"Don't be so unfriendly about it."

"Unfriendly?"

"Yes," he said, nodding brightly and smiling all around. Her satire he found positively invigorating, its hidden cause being so intimately known to him.

Then quite suddenly she laughed, a soft delicious chuckle. His startled brows flew together. The flush burned up into his face. The sensation of going to bits attacked him. Fiercely he strove to keep control. His features stiffened in an idiotic grin. She observed them, standing mercilessly still.

"Huh," he remarked. "Hmh."

"Hee-hee," she replied quite solemnly.

He glanced at her in a sudden blind wrath. Her seductive smile withered into contempt before his eyes. Then she turned and left him.

His breathing was tumultuous as he watched her make along the rockhead path. Instinctively he glanced around to see if his folly had been observed. Apparently not. They had happened on each other in the first grassy dip beyond the houses.

His anger goaded him to follow her, to slay her—to crush her anyway. To crush her, crush her, and the worse she liked it the better. Cunningly he spied about him. Not a soul in this first dusk of evening. It was supper time. His mother would be asking where he was.

Nimbly he set off after her, climbing cautiously to each grassy ridge, before slipping over, and down, and up again to the next one, for the green slope above the cliffs went on in a continuous corrugation. She must not know he was following her. Were she suddenly to turn back on the path and look down at him, humiliation would crush him utterly. But if he surprised her, surprised her all alone and far enough from the houses to be completely at his mercy, then she could fight as she liked, look how she liked, she was done for. His anger flushed hotly with a new feeling that made him glance about.

Very warily he stalked her, without sound. When at last she had disappeared, he knew that she must have slipped down into the grassy dip beyond the next ridge. All he had got to do now was to reach that ridge, peer over, and then . . .

His legs began to tremble. The treachery of shyness took possession of him. He stood still.

What could she be doing? Supposing she looked back over the crest at this moment and saw him? . . . Going to bits again! He was harshly, bitterly ashamed of himself; a subject for laughter that would shame him to death. Found following a girl, spying on her. . . .

His swift-searching eyes followed the grassy crest down to the cliff verge. The verge itself was weathered into rock layers, rottenish yellow in colour, but broad enough for his body. These bluffs often took on fantastic shapes. The one he was staring at had a lip beneath a nose. If he crawled onto the lip, the nose would hide him. He might then peer up into the next grassy hollow and see what he would see. After that, he would be in a proper position to go into action.

He found it required a careful wriggle to get his chest off the thin turf and onto the lip of rock. In his passage he actually scraped fine flecks of stone off the lip. Though now he saw that it was a tongue rather than a lip, and that the rock which curved immediately over him was the roof of a mouth rather than a nose. This tongue which he now lay on from chest to thigh was separated by a hand's breadth from the solid rock beneath. To slide off the tongue was to fall about a yard onto a final bluff, like a small chin—beyond which there was a sheer drop of two hundred feet to jagged skerries on which at high tide the seas frothed.

Jeck had such a perfect head for heights that his present position introduced no more than the slightest touch of peril needed to ease his mind. Along with this kind of ease, as always, came the beginning of exhilaration. Then he saw Ellen.

She was sitting in the hollow, just below the path, staring out at sea. Her face was paler than usual and quite expressionless. There were always wind-eddies on these cliff-heads, and now one of them struck her face and threw a tail of hair over her left temple. She never moved. He could see her perfectly, so clearly indeed that he began to feel the pallor on her face. The faint first smother of dusk may merely have emphasised the pallor. All the same it made him uncomfortable. There was hardly any need for her face to look drained as if she had some hidden sorrow! His heart began beating a bit. What on earth was she sitting there like that for? And even while he stared, her head drooped to her knees and the hand that had been on her lap fell over onto the turf.

His eyes were now so wide that when a sudden wind-eddy buffeted them they watered. He wiped them with his knuckles. So queer a tumult beset him that he quite forgot where he was and levered himself upward with such violence that his back hit the arched roof which promptly and heavily thrust him back on the tongue. The thrust was too much for the tongue which broke with a dull rotten thud at the root and canted over upon the rock a hand's breadth beneath. Had the tongue broken of itself there would just have been sufficient incline for it to slip slowly over the cliff. As it was, his left fist got an instant hold beyond the tongue; toes, fingers and knees gripped and pressed; his whole body became a living bar, and so for the moment the broken tongue was kept from sliding over.

The commotion, his own sharp exclamation, caught the girl's attention, for his head was now just visible to her. She got to her feet. He lifted his face from the rock with slow care. It was suffused with dark-red blood and smiled sheepishly.

At once she turned away and went up and out of sight.

He knew he was done for. Whenever his tension relaxed the tongue of rock would slide away with him. He could not have crawled forward even if the tongue had been intact, because just beyond it there had been a small landslide, and in any case it was sheer. To back out was now impossible.

This made him thoughtful, and he found himself astonished that the tongue which must have been all of six or seven inches thick had snapped so easily. Yet he ought to have known it might, for he had discovered often enough how shaly and rotten much of the cliff-head stuff was. But he hadn't stopped to think. It seemed so idiotic to slide away with a bit of rotten rock, so damned stupid. Then a melting flush shot through his breast, for the rock had moved under him. Very slightly. His grip quickened fiercely. After a few moments he began to wonder if the tongue had really moved away—or bedded down.

But he could not hold like this long. He realised that if he were going to try anything at all, swift trick or dodge, he must try it before his strength gave out. Apart from a sickish sensation, he was quite cool. Twisting his head round, he saw that the tip of the tongue lay on the brink of the cliff. A perfect piece of momentary balancing.

Ellen would be going home, very erect, with her pale hostile face. What childish nothings had brought him to this!

All the time, with instinctive cunning, his muscles had been tensioning, flexing, feeling for poise, his toes behind their iron-shod toecaps seeking closely, powerfully, through the turf behind for a crack, a cranny, a hold. Then with exquisite caution his whole body released its downward pressure ever so slightly to thrust backward. The stone moved an inch.

Flattened again, he held the stone. He began to suspect that his jersey had got caught on a jagged edge of the stone. If it had, he was caught exactly like a beast in a trap.

The continued strain had now induced a slight trembling in his muscles. Under its sweat, his face went cold. An eddy of wind struck it. There was no trick or dodge beyond the thrust back. So he must try it again. But not wildly yet, not in a mad heave, for his body was solidly on the sliding rock down to the thighs. He tried. The stone moved. His jersey *was* caught. Instantly out of his throat tore the yell "Help!" Again panic yelled before he got a grip on himself. In the gulping moments of awful silence, of realisation, which followed, he heard Ellen's voice calling him by name from above, sharply, urgently.

His muscles stretched to racking point, he lowered his brows to the stone, breathing heavily. She was coming down behind him, crying his name. "Jeck, what is it?" A hand touched his left boot. "Jeck!"

"Go back!" he cried. "The stone's broken under me. Go back!"

"Jeck!"

He realised her danger. If she clutched his boot, she would be jerked over. He yelled to her to go back. She was in danger already. But she would not go back. Then in a great voice he cried, "Oh, Ellen!"

She answered that cry.

His strength was failing, and he spoke desperate words to her, and she saw how he was placed. But she did not obey the words. For her strong body had grown full of its own resource. Her mind did not break. She saw how the stone was going to take him. Her right hand crept up over the top of his boot, her fingers twined among the leather laces, closed in a grip that could not be broken. Her left hand dug into the grass; her body flattened itself to the earth, taut and heavy, against the coming jerk. Her fingernails broke on rock under the skin of turf, scrabbled at the rock. His boot was moving, she heard his cry through the dark blood in her head. Her left hand, like a claw, ploughed through the shallow turf as her body was snatched to the brink; the fingers slipped into a rock-crack and held; their thin bones were breaking when the jerk slackened and the weight eased. The stone had slid from under him and his hands had come against the chin of rock below, wildly for a moment until they got a purchase, an upward leverage. The stone had lacerated his cheek and blood ran into his right eye. His hands took his weight, but the left was at an awkward angle against the boss of rock. Under the renewed terrific strain his arms quivered treacherously. The stone exploded on the skerries below and gulls wheeled out crying stridently. He had to back upwards on his palms. Suddenly he was aware of Ellen's pull on his boot, weak, but enough to keep him from toppling heels over. The darkness cleared a little, even though the blood-surge in his head thickened noisily. She was holding his boot, tugging it. *Don't pull! hold!* he cried in the desperate silent cry meant for her inner mind. An inch or two, another; with a straighter thrust against the boss, he pushed up a whole foot. She had both his legs weighted now. "Don't pull!" he cried and his voice came through. He was up over the thighs. She had both his feet under her right arm and was clawing upward. He suddenly went with her, backwards on his hands, in over the grass.

They lay side by side like children. She was bleeding from the mouth where the heel of his right boot had kicked her. She was quivering, trembling, but her smile came from the deep pool of her being, quietly up to him from the eternal well. But suddenly she gripped him, held him, gripped him more passionately, crying like a bairn.

The Black Woollen Gloves

The look in his eyes fascinated her. He sat at the opposite side of the reading-room table and a little to her left, so that, with the *Times Educational Supplement* before her, she could covertly watch him. He was reading the *Literary Supplement*—or, rather, had been reading. Whatever the article it had stilled him to absorbed reflection. With the iris gone black in the indifferent lighting, his eyes glowed under dark hair that came over his brows without any parting. His thin pale face had the delicate finish of egg-shell porcelain, dulled a little in grey strength. The pale student, emaciated a trifle, underfed possibly, but burning with inner fires. Her young woman's heart continued its beating.

At last he pushed the *Supplement* away like an empty plate, got up, and walked out of the door. Then the little incident happened that made an instant appeal to her. As he shoved open a leaf of the swing door and passed out some part of his mind must have registered a suspension of rhythm and, just as he was taking the third step down, made him look back—to find the door gaping open. He balanced a moment, then returned and touched the glass panel when immediately it flapped windily into position.

She continued to gaze through the vacant panel. Now why had he done that? Lest they suffer from a draught—where a draught of fresh air would be a godsend? . . . But she did not really question herself. It was enough that she *knew*. His act

118

revealed him to her in a swift intimate way. She got up and went round the table to the *Supplement*.

On Herman Melville. Her brows puckered. She sat down and got lost. Then spreading a vague arm outward in order to lay bare the page, she felt something hairy touch her wrist. Her eyes leapt—and steadied on a pair of black woollen gloves.

Without any process of making up her mind, she picked up the gloves, went hurriedly out through the swing door, down the stairs, and on to the cobbled street. He was gone. A police-man, passing to headquarters next door, looked at her officially. She was new to the town and her scholastic appointment was a respectable one; in fact, her first really responsible Higher Grade post, for she was just twenty-four. She turned from the policeman and began mounting the stone stairs. At the top the swing door welcomed her—open. She looked at it, touched the glass panel, when immediately it flapped windily into posi-tion. A small smile, another moment's hesitation, and she turned and went down the stairs again and out on to the street, carrying the gloves with her.

On the pavement edge opposite the Town Hall, she paused, and for a minute or two surreptitiously watched the faces of passers-by. Then experiencing the woman's discomfort of standing alone in a public place, she went down the narrow street to the great swing bridge over the river. An old man with a grey beard walked up and down in front of his cardboard row of chalk pictures, rubbing his chilled hands. The air was cold and gusty and blew wisps of white hair about his bared head. She clutched the woollen gloves. The tide was in and the water was broad and dark, with the riverside lamps casting golden spears into its trembling sides. She turned back and dropped twopence in the old man's cap. "God's blessing on you!" he said. She hurried from the blessing, hunching her furred shoulders towards her head in a snuggle of secrecy.

THE BLACK WOOLLEN GLOVES

In her little sitting-room she examined the gloves. Cheap, with the right thumb rather crudely darned; long-fingered, thin. Gloves that sheathed a spare hand, a dreamer's hand. She saw again the deep glow in his eyes as he gazed far beyond the realms of the *Supplement*, while she stared at the frugal gloves. The finger waggled emptily, with here a cut on the tip of a forefinger. Long nails, of course.

Normally her fastidious nature would have withdrawn from even touching a stranger's belongings, particularly when found in a public place. The atmosphere of the reading-room was sometimes so thick that it turned her nostrils into deliberate filters. Her complexion was fresh, alive with a warm blood flush, and her eyes glowed darkly. She tried the right glove on, studied the waggling effect, and was about to laugh when her landlady came in. She concealed the glove and asked for a black worsted thread.

Having neatly darned the rent, she once more studied the waggling effect, then turned to her cupboard of books and fished out *Moby Dick*, the only thing of Melville's she had in her irreducible collection of working classics.

But she could find no certain solution of her riddle there. In fact, the more she attempted to work it out the more bogged she got; which proved tantalisingly interesting, there being so many quite fantastic possibilities. She read the chapter on whiteness right through. It gripped her now in a profound way, her intuitions realising themselves in a sort of "translated" vision, uncannily vivid. Her landlady came in with cocoa.

The cocoa was warm and stimulating. She spilt a solid brown drop of it on the abstraction of whiteness . . . and as she eyed this monstrous stain on the ideal, her concern slowly caught a glint of humour and daring. So far she had found this Highland town most respectably unexciting. Some far steeple bell started ringing. She looked at her watch. Ten o'clock. She would have a walk. Why not? She took the gloves with her.

He was standing on the bridge, looking at the black water and the golden spears. Except for one or two hurrying figures, they had it to themselves. Her pulses stirred uncomfortably but deliciously. And just before her hesitating feet reached him, he turned. She felt the flush mounting to her face as she smiled. The flush and the arc-lamp glitter in her excited eyes arrested him for one blank moment—before he mumbled incoherently and strode hurriedly off the pavement, leaving her with her hand extended, clutching the woollen gloves.

She got home somehow, but with no memory of the way she took. It had felt like walking under the black water with the golden spears quivering in her side. As she entered her sitting-room the first thing she saw was the brown cocoa stain on the white cloth.

Something had happened to her so unexampled that Melville's "incantation of whiteness" seemed the light side of an incantation of darkness under which she wanted to bury her head. Nor would humour come to her rescue. He had thought her "one of these"! Soliciting him. . . . Her flesh curdled and cramped. Served her right! Oh, served her right! She ought to have left the gloves where they lay, black gloves, black. . . . But in a swift seriousness she knew that it did not serve her right. It made life mean and suspicious, ugly, horrid. . . . He had recoiled from her. From *her*! . . . She was very wide awake when at last she went to bed, but after an hour she fell through the hypnotism of protest into perfect sleep, and next morning hid away the black gloves and went cheerfully about her business all day.

At tea-time she thought, How upset I was last night! and smiled. But somehow now, with the beginning of night again, the smile lingered and twisted the merest trifle. After all, it was humiliating! . . . Within ten minutes she was in

almost as disturbed a state as she had been the night before.
This was really intolerable! The thought of the black gloves
positively gathered a criminal taint. It was manifestly too late
now to give them up to the librarian. Where had she found
them and when? She could hardly reply that she had kept them
for a night! . . . Well, burn them, why not? That was it—
burn them. But instantly her mind associated the idea with
the latest murder mystery in the press where the murderer
had attempted to burn the dismembered portions of his lady
love. The brown cocoa stain blotted out the last speck of
white.

Of course, really it was all very amusing. Only it was irritating. . . . And so it started all over again.

About the hour when he had left the library the previous
evening, she was on the bridge. Chance was interested (and
perhaps library habits regular) for she saw him coming. Her
warm features stilled to the serenity of ice as she stopped
right in front of him and held out the gloves. "You left these, I
think, on the reading-room table last night." His hand
fumbled and she knew the gloves dropped to the street, but
she walked on evenly as though his unexceptional person had
been less interesting than a dog. She knew, too, as she went on
that he was still standing, lost in a sort of stupor. He had
recognised her all right. Her heart began to beat wildly with
vindictive pleasure, with conscious victory. Perfectly done!
That was that wiped out, thank goodness! She met a fellow
teacher and they got laughing and decided on a couple of
hours in the picture house.

The following night at the same time she found herself
crossing the bridge again. A little stroll before supper. . . .
And there he was—standing as if waiting. Ah! she observed
him pull himself together. As she came nearer she saw that
his pale face was flushed and excessively uncomfortable. She
looked straight at it. The arc-light in his shy eyes made them

glitter. Just as she came abreast he paused and began, "E-excuse——" She looked right through him as though he weren't and continued her even pace—under a suddenly crowing sky. Oh, it was sweet! It was perfect! Not often do we deserve so well of fate! She felt inexpressibly happy.

The following night she was a quarter of an hour late. He was waiting. But at the critical moment he turned to the river. Within the week she was keeping him waiting a full hour. And now it seemed the mere sight of her was enough. He no more made any attempt to speak. Until one evening he was not on the bridge . . . but as she passed by the end pillar she was conscious of a tall figure in shadow. Her heart mounted again.

Then one evening she wasn't going to go out at all. After cocoa, however, she changed her mind. It was so cold for even a dog to wait about. And anyway he couldn't still be waiting. As it chanced they met in front of the chalk pictures, and because her head was a trifle too erect she missed the begging cap and kicked it and the few pennies it contained all about the gutter. With profuse apologies she began hunting assiduously with the white-haired man, who said, being Irish, "God bless you, it doesn't matter at all." She was about his best client.

"Excuse me," said a voice, "there's one under your foot." She jerked her foot away from a spare hand which picked up the copper and dropped it in the cap.

"That's all," said the artist. "Just four of them."

"I'm sorry," she mumbled, "I haven't . . ." She hadn't her handbag.

A shilling dropped in the cap.

"God bless the two av you together!" said the old man.

For some reason the shilling turned her heart to water. It was too much. It wasn't—he couldn't. . . . They were walking side by side with the hot discomfort of the old man's blessing in their ears.

THE BLACK WOOLLEN GLOVES

"I have wanted—wanted to say—that that first night I—
I——" He stopped. She didn't help him any. Her sense of
power suddenly held a cruelty exquisitely surprising. "I
didn't mean—anything," he concluded.

She made a vague uninterested sound.

"I mean—that first night. I wasn't thinking. I couldn't get
over it all night."

The sound firmed to "Oh."

"I was such a fool," he stuttered. "I wasn't thinking. I
mean I was thinking——"

"About Herman Melville." The words slipped out.

"Yes! Yes! Old Melville. Nineteen years all alone—never
did anything. Astonishing! After—after what he had done.
Wasn't it?" He was so shy that his voice had a gulping break
in it.

"I suppose it is," she conceded coldly.

"Yes, wasn't it? Pretty lonely and—and miserable, after
what he had done. Such a waste. Curious that those who might
have understood . . . but I suppose it's always the same. Do
you know Melville?"

"A bit."

They were walking up the riverside, having been deflected
at the bridge-end by a sudden car. The water was dark, but
the farther up they went the more perceptible became its smooth
downward sweep. It gathered all the mysterious, lonely
attributes of water flowing under dark heaven to an eternal
sea. Melville's loneliness was in it, and all the loneliness of
those who traffick in imagination. This lean figure by her side
was in it. And out of its desperation he was struggling to the
exciting warmth and gaiety of walking by her side like a man
clutching at—a straw? She smiled secretively to the water and
let him talk. At the right moment she asked:

"What, then, did you find in the article?"

"It's what I didn't find!" he answered. "Most English

critics never find it, because deep in their minds they mistrust it. It's against their tradition. In spite of themselves they react against it. Carlyle and Melville . . . they admit their greatness and their immense vitality, but they don't admit the greatness of their prose. They detest it."

"Their style?"

"Yes, their style. But it's more than that. It's the old Scots in them. It's fundamental. And it comes out in their English. It's the most fascinating thing in the world." He went on. His mind seemed to be very clear on some traditional idea both subtle and vital, and an underlying warmth communicated itself. There was something so unique and hopeless in his enthusiasm, so visionary, and yet so fine and profitless, that the protective instinct moved in her. And all the time he was talking his shy spirit was gaining confidence. She watched it. It began to laugh here and there. This was so obviously a new experience for it. Then suddenly they came under the shadow of trees where wooded islands lay in the river spanned by white bridges, and abruptly he stopped talking. She laughed, a little low chuckle, as she turned to a handrail and leant on it, above the water.

"I know," he said, "I've been talking too much."

The small current beneath them ran into the main stream and got lost in grey-black undulations like the sleek movements of some fabulous river-monster.

"I've enjoyed it. They don't teach your views of English—at Edinburgh."

"No," he answered, self-conscious again.

Low trees hung over the water, and tall trees behind stretched bare thin fingers to a grey-black sky where here and there a fugitive star gleamed and died.

"Why?" she gleamed.

"I don't know," he answered.

"I'm surprised," she said.

He stirred. "Why are you surprised?" He did not look at her.

She knew what was troubling him, as though she felt her girl's presence trembling to his heart. Now that they were standing still he did not know what to do with himself. And sensitiveness can so quickly withdraw, become remote.

"Surprised?" she echoed. "Because in your mind you are so sure you know!"

"Finally one can be sure of nothing," he said, "except this—that all the fine things are built on nothing."

"Like Scots prose?"

He smiled.

"Or like our being here now," he added.

They were both leaning against the handrail and she felt it tremble. He did not speak. She saw his bare hands clutching the rail. Her mind's eye saw the gloves.

"Obviously your gloves brought us here," she said.

"No—not my gloves."

"But certainly."

"No."

Something about his aloofness was robbing her of that comforting sense of being complete mistress of the situation.

"Have it your own way!" she argued.

He did not answer.

Irrational excitement set up a small vortex inside her breast. There was something extraordinarily evasive about him now like the wind moving about the tall branches. It wasn't fair to her, and less fair to this young moment. Did he mean that what brought them together was something more than—than——Oh, nonsense! Yet she could not turn and go. Nor could she remain silent.

"Oh, well!" she said, and stirred.

"You see, the gloves were nothing."

THE BLACK WOOLLEN GLOVES

"At least they were yours," she argued, and turned to him. Their pale shadowy faces gazed at each other. The dark world swirled in about them. She held her breath.

"They weren't even that," he said. "I, too, saw them on the table, but—they weren't my gloves."

Dance of the Atoms

When the siren hooted outside, Charlie dropped the book he had got lost in and sat listening, his face white and taut, as if the high sound had come from another world; but as it hooted again he leapt to his feet and with a shrill cry of "Wait!" was out the door, along the passage, down the stair-rail on his stomach, and racing full speed along the drive. "Wait!" He was impatient and imperative.

Heath, the cairn terrier, had so well beaten him that he was already on his master's knee, glancing excitedly through the windscreen.

"Well, son; forgotten all about me?"

Charlie did not answer, hardly even looked at his father in his concentrated excitement. The driver's seat had already been vacated. Charlie slammed the door and settled himself, then gathered his brows at the little red light on the instrument-board.

"Sorry!" apologised his father, as he switched off the engine.

Charlie waggled the gear lever, switched on and started up, stretched forward right off the seat until he had pressed the clutch out, put the lever in first and, as he slowly accelerated, let the clutch in and the handbrake off. The car moved forward in an imperceptible and perfect start.

"Sound work!" said his father.

Heath barked. Charlie changed up into second, swung smoothly round on to the gravel in front of the house, changed down to first behind a neat zoom of acceleration, negotiated the off corner of the house, two flower-beds, the trellised arch, and the very awkward garden walk behind the house with its special layout of bulb-beds, crazy paving, and flowering shrubs. Having circled the house he arrived in front of the garage, but with the rear of the car towards the door. All in a minute the gear was in neutral, the handbrake on, and Charlie climbing down from the seat and racing towards the garage door.

"Pretty smart son, this of mine," said Charles senior to the cairn, whose ears he fondled. Brown eyes shining with affection, Heath tried to lick his face, and succeeded, after the remarkable fashion of dogs, in looking humanly foolish. "Pouf!" said Charles generously. He was a large man, well groomed, and full of a smiling fleshy complacence.

Charlie was in his seat again and the gear lever in reverse.

"Ladies and gentlemen," said Charles to Heath, "we are now about to witness the last thrilling act——"

A tiny jerk of the car stopped him. "Ho-ho?" he criticised.

"Ho-ho! to you," said Charlie as, head over shoulder, he smoothly backed the car to a standstill in the small garage.

His father laughed. "Did you jerk her intentionally?"

Charlie was tempted to say "Yes", but the boyish quality of fun had not been developed in him, nor could he tell a direct lie. So he merely continued to be excited and intense. He was over eight years old, and when he was stirred his laughter, instead of being helplessly merry, was fiercely shrill.

His father had scarcely turned the key in the garage door when Charlie had him by the hand, and was pulling him with all his might towards the front entrance of their country house, Heath doing his agile best to add jollity to welcome.

In this strenuous fashion they progressed towards the doorstep upon which Charles saw the welcoming figure of his pale, dark-haired, brown-eyed wife. She was smiling.

"Here!" protested Charles, "this young fellow is getting a bit too strong for me"—he kissed his wife—"he's nearly pulled the arm out of me."

Charlie was still tugging.

"I wish——" said Dorothy, and paused, her thoughtful half-worried smile on her son's head.

He chuckled. "You wish he would! Busy?"

"Drowned. Everybody seems to be coming down at once."

"Here?"

"Don't be an ass. To-morrow afternoon——"

"Come on!" tugged Charlie.

As he allowed himself to be dragged into the hall, Charles kept talking to Dorothy and making little jokes and throwing tags of laughter about. As lord of the manor, he was obviously not displeased by this flattering welcome. From the straining eagerness of his son, he turned to his wife and winked.

"I know," she said with resigned good-nature. "He's been lost there all morning." She sighed.

As Charlie threw the door of his playroom open he told Heath sharply to get out. Heath's ears went down and again his eyes looked human, but now not at all foolish. Charles shook his head at him sadly. "These engineers, y'know," he explained; "very touchy."

"You don't want to come in, Mother?" said Charlie.

She smiled. "Oh, well, if you'd rather not!" Then she turned to her husband. "Lunch in twenty minutes—remember —and no rushing off to wash after the gong."

He chuckled. "All right."

Charlie had the whole intricate railway circuit running very smoothly. Stations, signal-boxes, loop-lines, up-traffic and down-traffic. The recurring trouble of engines getting derailed at the points had been completely overcome. The new siding, however, which had been well discussed, was not completed.

"Of course, I knew it was a ticklish job," said his father. "It will take time. You see——"

"I was reading—that's why," said Charlie as he uncoupled the Flying Scotsman.

"Reading! Ha-ha! Fairy story, was it?"

Charlie looked up at his father with gleaming eyes. The absurd joke about a fairy story did not even touch his thought. "I don't think I want to be an engine-driver any more," he said.

"Hullo! What's gone wrong?"

"I want", said Charlie—and now his excitement could hardly be repressed—"to be a scientist." The gleaming eyes searched his father's face; but the face nodded solemnly.

Thereupon the book was produced. *Shooting Electrons* was its title, and the fly-leaf bore a greeting from Uncle Ned in the Air Force.

"It tells all about what's inside the atom, and it's for boys," said Charlie. "It's very simple. Do you know about all the different kinds of atoms—and how wireless is made?"

"I'm afraid not," said Charles.

"Oh, it's exciting. You see, if you have a thing in the centre and another thing flying round about it then that's one atom. If there's two things flying round it, then it's a different atom. The things that fly round are the electrons, and the thing in the centre is the nucleus. Now when the electrons are flying round and round they knock into other electrons flying round and round, and then—and then——" His voice grew high-pitched; his eyes glittered; the gong reverberated.

"Come on!" said Charles, and together they dashed for the nearest wash-basin.

"Hah-haa?" said Dorothy as they arrived at table breathless. But father and son were full of secret male jubilance. In an excited gesture Charlie splashed his breast with gravy and nearly broke his plate.

"Oh, I wish you could keep calm," said his mother, wiping him.

Over her shoulder Charles winked to his son, and the white face closed its lips tightly.

After lunch, when they were walking together in the garden, Dorothy said, "I'm not too happy about Charlie. I wish he wasn't always so strung up."

"But boys are like that," replied her husband, smiling. He had seen how she had had to control her annoyance at lunch-time, otherwise Charlie would have flown into sharp bits.

"No, they're not," she said. "And you know it. There's something wrong in Charlie—or going wrong. I blame the concentration on mechanical things. And you encourage him in it."

"You think a good fairy tale, perhaps?"

"Please don't chuckle, Charles. I really mean it. I do. I'm serious. I know about the spirit of the age and all that. But at times I am uneasy. I wish he could be warmer, more boyish."

"But he is affectionate. Dash it, you can't have him——"

"He can almost strangle you with affection at times, I know."

Charles looked at her.

"Dorothy, you musn't let your fancy run away with you. Nowadays a boy gets all his fun and excitement out of mechanical things. Even little Charlie there can tell me things in science that I didn't know. All I know really is where money comes from and how it's made." He chuckled again.

This chuckle was the only thing about him that she had never quite got used to. It had an irritating complacency. He was always so reasonable and so sure of himself; everybody else must be wrong.

But that was a small thing at the moment. "Don't imagine", she said, trying to meet his humour, "that I'm jealous because he prefers the company of locomotives and you. Anyone who prefers locomotives and you cannot have much wrong with him. I know. You also imagine I'm probably upset a bit because he isn't dependent enough upon me; starved mother instinct. I wish you wouldn't. I'm merely afraid for his health and his balance. All I want you to do is to make him exercise more. If you could make him do—do foolish, boyish things."

She looked up at her husband. He was smiling.

"You merely think I'm old fashioned?" she said.

He let the chuckle out, glancing at her like a great, sly overgrown boy himself.

He was a loyal and generous husband, who never bothered his head with other women. He had his points. But strangely enough it was the irritating obtuse self-sufficiency in him that frequently was his strongest point of all with her. At a difficult moment, like the present, when she could do nothing about it, she found comfort, a sort of obliterating ease, in giving in to it and letting it envelop her.

She had fought against this many times, but always with completely negative results, apart from the fraying of her own nerves. She had come to realise that when you may not alter what is fundamental in a man, the next best thing to do is to find comfort in giving in to it.

When he saw that she was prepared to be assured, he risked saying, "You mustn't blame him for having some of your own nerves!"

She smiled.

He chuckled, delighted. "And he really has brains. You again! He is going to be a pretty hot-stuff scientist, take my word for it. We're going to be proud of him yet." He nodded confidently. "Science is the coming thing. In the business world, too. I mean, it's *the* thing. Everything else derived from it. I don't want to say anything against your literature or music——"

"But for a healthy boy you think they're pretty poor hobbies?"

When he laughed at her wry mouth, Heath got excited and danced across a newly-planted plot.

"Go it, Heath!" he encouraged the dog as he made circles round his pursuing wife.

It's easy to manage things when you're right—and know how.

And he was certainly right about Charlie's getting pleasure out of his playroom activities. At times the pleasure was so intense that he would cry out to himself and at the things in front of him.

In his book *Shooting Electrons* everything was made delightfully clear and was illustrated with drawings that could make one laugh. The molecule of water, for example, is made up of two atoms of hydrogen and one of oxygen. The oxygen atom is shown like a round white face and the two hydrogen atoms are stuck on it like black ears. Oxygen, of course, is what you breathe and hydrogen is the light gas that lifts balloons. But when two atoms of hydrogen and one of oxygen come together, you get water. Here on this page, again, is an illustration of a motor car in a garage. The engine is running and the dotted line shows the door is closed. Through the exhaust pipe are pouring myriads of atoms of carbon. (Charlie knows what decarbonising an engine means, because he once saw the carbon being scraped off the piston tops.) Well, these carbon atoms coming pouring out through the exhaust tried to join up with the oxygen atoms in the cylinders. Each carbon atom would like to join up with two oxygen ones, and when this happens there is formed the gas that makes ginger beer fizzy. (Charlie likes ginger beer.) But as the supply of oxygen atoms is restricted, some carbon atoms have to be pleased with one oxygen atom, and then the two of them form the deadly gas called carbon monoxide. If a fellow stayed in a closed garage with the engine running he would be dead in no time, because the carbon monoxide would kill him.

While his father and mother were at last deeply and happily engrossed in the layout of new bulb beds (companioned by

Heath, almost equally happy, for now and then Charles threw a stone away absentmindedly), Charlie sat with the book on his knees and stared before him in a pale trance. The marvellousness of the simple but terrific transformation from ginger beer to death overwhelmed him. So highly strung was his mind that it became receptive to the most delicate suggestions from this new atomic world. In fact, when the writer referred to the ceaseless whirling of atoms as "the dance of the atoms", Charlie visualised the dance itself.

But when the wonder of all this had had its innings, the inevitable next stage followed—the desire to act, to experiment, to prove. A craving to make atoms perform, as he could make locomotives and coaches perform, began to get a feverish grip on him. He had never indeed experienced anything quite like the heat of this desire. By night-time it was consuming him.

Moreover, the writer was never tired of showing how always the most thrilling discoveries were made by scientists in their laboratories by pure chance or accident, and often, in fact, when they were looking for something quite different. Then from a simple discovery the whole world benefited, and the scientist became immortal. But he, Charlie, had no test tubes, no batteries, no laboratory, no nothing. The only illustration in the whole book that was not new to him was that of the motor car in the garage.

The following morning his father set off across the fields with him and Heath. Charlie was very pleased to go, because he thought it would be a good chance of talking about the laboratory. Heath could hardly credit his luck and showed it. Charles himself was in good form, both because he enjoyed the country air after the recent hot spell of city life and because he knew Dorothy would be pleased at his taking Charlie away from his mechanics.

And there was the hidden joke, too, in the idea that Charlie *could* be got away from his mechanics! Actually, no doubt, he could have been made as keen on birds and plants as on atoms. And perhaps this might yet be done. But meanwhile a yellow wagtail hovering in sunlight was a dance of atoms; the scent of wild briar a drift of electrons (or was it?).

"Is it, Dad? Or what do you think?"

"I don't know, son, but drift of electrons sounds good to me."

"I'm tired of these trains now."

"I'm sorry to hear that. They were pretty expensive."

"I should like to have a little, just a little laboratory. Would that be expensive? I could keep the trains and make them go, too, if you like."

"But you're too young for a laboratory. Good gracious me! And besides, when you go to school you'll have a laboratory there—a great big one—with all sorts of—of retorts and things in it. You see, you haven't been to school so far because you had that illness when you were six. But you'll go now very likely after this vacation. And *then* you'll have your laboratory."

"But I don't want to go. And I won't have it anyway. Because little boys' schools don't have laboratories."

"Who told you that?"

"Do they?"

"Well——" Charles was stumped.

"They don't. They don't." His voice was growing shrill. "I asked——"

"Heath!" shouted Charles. "Come here!"

The cairn came flat-eared from the warren.

"They don't!" cried Charlie. "Go away, Heath! Go away!" And he kicked the dog that momentarily grovelled in guilt before their feet.

Charles stopped. "Here, son," he said quietly. "You must never do a thing like that."

Charlie's face drew white and taut.

"Say you're sorry to Heath."

The dark eyebrows gathered stormily above the glittering eyes. The teeth were clenched.

Charles saw how hard he was fighting for control.

"Come on, then," he said, and taking the boy's hand he walked on in silence, Heath at their heels.

His son was a dynamic force. Genius in youth was often eccentric. Charles did not want the boy to fly into bits. It was necessary to dominate him, of course, and he would. On this business of the laboratory, for example, he would not give in to him. And meanwhile Dorothy need not see that the paternal authority had been endangered!

And he got over the difficulty very nicely, as it happened. Immediately lunch was finished, Charlie, silent, rose and left the room.

"What went wrong?" asked Dorothy.

Charles chuckled. "He wants a laboratory!"

"A what?"

"A laboratory of his own!" And now it really did sound a splendid joke. Just the sort of grandiose thing a genius would want. Immense, really! The young rascal!

"Look here, Charles. You're not going to indulge him in this?" There was fear in her voice.

"Oh no. I told him that. All the same, he has the ideas. A laboratory of his own—at eight!"

That afternoon the two Nicholsons called for them to take them along to the opening of the new club house.

There was laughter and loud talk. Charlie was sent for and presented.

"Now see you be a good boy till mother comes back," said Dorothy, giving him a kiss.

"'Bye, son!" called Charles, waving a hand with an intimate friendly smile as he stepped after Dorothy into the Nicholsons' car.

They all waved to him.

"Looks as if he was going to run to brains, Charles," said Tom Nicholson.

"Looks like a little imperious aristocrat, *I* think," said Vera his wife.

Charles chuckled. "He's a bit on his dignity because . . ." And then he told them the story about the laboratory. Even Dorothy joined in the laughter. Her husband might be right—as usual. They might yet really be proud of him.

Instinctively she touched wood, and smiled away the horrid involuntary picture she sometimes got of his face—white and intense.

When the sound of their car had died in the distance Charlie turned into the hall. At the foot of the stairs he paused, listening to the muffled sound of a loudspeaker and high, mirthful voices in the kitchen premises. Clearly everyone was having the day off.

In the front rooms of the house was the sensation of emptiness in which tall things could happen; towards evening it was touched with an eerie thrill.

His own room was too small now, too locked in. Besides, he could not go and read in the atom book. That would be intolerable. He had no particular anger against his father. Nor had he pity for himself. He simply felt lonely like the rooms. The intolerance in him did not hate grown-ups; it ignored them. Yet he was haunted by the something tall in them that thwarted him.

He turned from the stairs and went out again at the front door. Heath yapped a welcome at his feet. "Shut up!" he said, startled. Then, as if strolling nowhere in particular, he went very quietly round the corner of the house.

There was the garage exactly as in the illustration—and the car was inside. He saw the key sticking in the lock. No footsteps were following him. He was quite alone.

He turned the key and opened the door. Heath, hoping for the best, was in before he could stop him. Charlie pulled the door behind him and, while he stood listening, found himself gazing at Heath's eyes which shone with expectancy in the gloom.

An odd constriction of pain came on Charlie's heart as if a hand had suddenly gripped it.

In that instant his thought had been given a certain terrible direction. His mouth fell open to let the breath pass more silently while he listened.

"Come on," he whispered.

Heath was in through the driving door before it was properly opened. Charlie followed, switched on, and pressed the self-starter. When the engine was turning over regularly he said to Heath: "Wait here."

He withdrew from the garage and quietly turned the key in the lock of the door.

His full mind was not really doing this experiment deliberately. It was all a sort of beginning to see what would happen; a direction towards experiment, terribly hampered by the fact that his father had absolutely forbidden him to touch the car when he himself was not present. If Nanna came out at that moment and caught him she would tell, and if his father turned on him and thrashed him the whole world would crash to nothing.

"Charlie!" Nanna's voice! While his body stood rigid his brain wondered if he would have time to slip in and switch off. "Charlie!" She was coming his way. In a moment she would be at the corner. He broke out of his stance and ran to meet her so that she would not hear the car.

"Where have you been?"

He was now extremely excited and shouted: "Nowhere!" He rushed into the house, hating her. But she went after him, calling him, and finally took him forcibly from the playroom.

"What way is this to behave?" He resisted her. "What you need," she said in a flash of temper, "is a good sound spanking. And if you're not careful you'll get it, though I get the sack. Now you'll drink that."

But he could not drink his blood warm milk. The sight of it revolted him. Because of the roaring noise his own emotion made within him, he was not even hearing properly what she was saying. "I won't drink it!" he shouted. He turned on her and defied her. He was utterly obstreperous. She did her best with him over a considerable time, ignoring him, stopping his wild rushes. When his voice shrilled in hysteria, she smacked him.

For one moment he stared at her, his eyes wide and glittering; then he attacked her, sobbing and screeching madly, loathing the touch of her, hitting her. When her arm closed on him he bit it.

She dropped him like a snake; called him a demon. Her deepest woman-instinct was revolted, even while it recognised that here there was something tragically wrong. It has the bitter taste of defeat for a normally sound kind woman to be hated by a child.

"Go away!" he was screaming at her. "Leave me alone!"

"All right," she said at last, and left the room.

He listened to her tapping heels ostentatiously dying away; then, before she could steal back, he slipped out of the door and into the drawing room. With the help of a chair he unlatched the french window and was soon rushing on tiptoes for the garage. As the door swung open, the fumes drove him back. Holding his breath, he dashed for the engine-switch, turned it off, and dashed back.

But Heath did not follow. "Heath!" he whispered intensely. "Heath! Heath!"

Nothing came from the garage but the slow, upcurling smoke-coloured fumes.

He found Heath stretched out by the engine exhaust pipe,

overcome no doubt in a whimpering turn-away from the closed door. He dragged him round the off corner of the garage in among some rhododendron bushes, then slipped back, locked the door, and was caught by Nanna as he was re-entering the french window. He gazed at her, swayed giddily and fell, retching a little.

Alarmed, she picked him up and carried him to his bed asking distractedly if he had been eating anything. He did not answer. "Tell me! Tell Nanna!" she implored, kneeling beside him. Then she got a curious, stale odour off his clothes. She knew tobacco more by its stale morning smell than otherwise. Her eyes widened. "Have you been smoking?"

He turned his head away weakly and, without opening his eyes, said "Yes".

Her mouth closed firmly. No wonder he couldn't eat. She nodded to herself. A light of healthy satisfaction dawned firmly upon her countenance. Telling him how much it served him right, she undressed him relentlessly. She had not thought it was in him!

Late that night his father and mother stood looking down on his pale, sleeping face.

"The young rascal, I'll have to give him a hiding, I suppose," said Charles.

"A real good one," nodded Dorothy with a sweet, remote smile.

"I believe", said Charles, "that you are delighted he smoked. I believe you are."

"Hush," she said. "Don't chuckle." Then she stooped and kissed the frail forehead of her son. "Mother's own darling," she murmured.

Charles groaned discreetly.

As they went downstairs, he had his chuckle out. "You feel that he is human having smoked? What a perverted notion for the mother of a coming scientist!"

"Mother of a son, you great donkey!"

He chuckled again. "I wonder where the devil Heath can have gone?"

"Where do dogs go when they don't come home at night?"

"Hush!" He brought his lips to her ear. "That's a question for the scientists."

Love's Dialectic

She walked up the bank of the river trying to have it out with herself. Would she make a stand and risk everything, or would she continue to slide into a relationship. . . . It was difficult to think clearly and connectedly because if she took a stand she might lose him, and at the very thought of that her flesh melted inwards blotting the mind out.

Yet every time she rose again and breasted the question it became a little easier to hold on to it, particularly because now at the back of her mind was the large statement she had read in that letter this morning; not that it had been a long statement, but it seemed large now, like a cloud of light behind her mind, and in this light was encouragement, an aristocratic movement, a high sanction.

This business of censoring letters was a very curious one: the private letters of the public, of the ordinary people and the extraordinary. She had never before realised so clearly the existence of two worlds. She had thought that her own inner world, the secretive world of weakness and desires, the place that lay, intimate and lonely, behind all discussion of sex and morals and politics, was somehow peculiar to herself. Her companions and those she met socially would discuss any conceivable topic sensibly, flagrantly, but always with a bright engaging amusement. She enjoyed the fun, and could toss back words like "complex", "repression", and even "dialectical" with the proper dismissive skill. In this pastime, this certainty of knowledge, her own secretive world would be forgotten, and if a word, an inflection, reminded her of it, it hung far inward like a dark round nut. No more than that. An indigestible core. Until the time came when, alone, she felt an almost horrible power coming out from it that crept through the muscles of her legs, through her chest, leaving her tremulous and weak and fearful.

The two worlds. The revelation of the censor's office had disclosed the surprising fact that they co-existed everywhere. Like light and darkness. Two planes: the one visible, the other hidden. At first the girls (with ancient ones among them) had great fun over some of the letters. Badly worded, misspelt love epistles of an extremely "juicy" nature; heart-broken appeals of a young swain darkly hinting at self-destruction; urgent implorings of a young female who had been "caught". There was no end to them. A dark turbulent river, an underground river, with peephole cracks for the censor girls. Sometimes a letter would be passed under a desk, guaranteed to provide an extra chuckle. Two of the girls got sacked for discussing outside such privately acquired information. Reiteration staled for them somewhat these babblings and idiocies, these dreadful give-aways, these shameless cravings. How girls and fellows could put such stuff in black and white at times quite beat the censor girls. Some of the writers obviously not young at all—probably quite old, over forty—really pretty disgusting. And they stirred their hot forenoon cups.

Light and darkness. Thesis and antithesis. And it did really appear as if you could not apply any dialectical process to them. More light made the darkness deeper. Could you synthesise an object and its shadow? The brighter the sun, the more pronounced the shadow. In matter, in physical fact. Two worlds. Two planes that, however they tilted, kept parallel. She tried to use such engaging ideas in talk, but not very successfully. One had always to be pretty careful of a personal give-away. Eyes would look as much as to say: What's got repressed now?

Is this the dodge of staging an argument to cover—something? Eyes looking *from that other plane*, inquisitive, with an expectancy, a greed, mockingly veiled in good nature.

And her trouble was rather desperate. For she loved her young man as shamelessly as any girl in a letter passed under a desk, and when the letter was ungrammatical and misspelt and unpunctuated, when it achieved in this way the very height of the turbulent and grotesque, did it most closely approximate to a correct expression of her own condition. She realised this, in the moment of the reading, with a mixture of understanding and anguish and shame. He had become for her a complete obsession.

Nor was it any good saying to herself that this was sex rampant. For even if it was, that in no way affected the fact as an experience. For the first time she saw that you could not diminish a natural force by putting a label on it. In any case, she knew with complete certainty that this obsessive emotion was something very different from any sex stirrings she had ever had before. She could not even think of him in that direct way. She could only see his face, the slight wave in his brown hair, the movement of his hands, and the expression of his eyes. She felt a craving, a hunger for these features. She wanted to be near them, looking slightly up at them, and the thought of touching them touched the edge of a happiness like a lovely bright delirium.

But he was cool, with the clean coolness that might have come out of the river beside her, out of its clear water; dressed neatly, with a cool blue stripe in his tie, he sauntered on, the glint of the stream in his eyes. His features were never dull or set in repose. They were always alive, with a smile that sometimes paused just before it came to the surface, paused and contemplated with a flick of the eyelid, with a faint humoured irony, then deepened and was set in motion and passed away as he glanced quickly away, or else broke into a

pleasant laugh while he said something or other that sometimes she could not quite follow but that always penetrated
to the quick.

He was cruel. Often he was deliberately cruel. She knew
that. She was so alive to his most trivial expression, physical
or verbal, that she could feel the satisfaction he got out of
hurting her. But if she tried to act up independently, saying
"That was a sly one!" he laughed, and if she went on the only
other tack, that of hurt silence, he would turn his amusement
into a game, take her arm, chivvy her forward, and ask:
"You're not hurt, are you?" and when she answered: "I am!"
his apparent astonishment broke into a chuckle of delight.

There were times when he was such a complete enigma
that she was frightened to introduce any subject of talk,
frightened even to speak, lest she say the wrong thing. This
could be extremely distressing because at that moment she
lost all faith in herself, even in her instincts, and inwardly went
blank, a nonentity. All she could do then was to hang on,
passive, until the enigmatic state faded in the quick shift of
his mood or interest.

But however she waited, however passive or silent, she
never got hold of him, not even when they kissed, for then he
was quite silent, void of all endearments, and the cruelty of
his nature she felt in the pressure and sting of his teeth.

Yet always she was aware, in terms of the inner woman-
awareness that could so surely assess her own obsession, that
never at any time was he an enigma to her. Quite simply and
certainly she knew that he acted as he did because she did
not satisfy him. To say that he had a sadistic streak explained
nothing. In her blood she knew that the pleasure he got out of
hurting her was a wry thwarted pleasure. There was no final
satisfaction in it for him. He was attracted. He couldn't leave
off. If he did not find anyone who could assuage him better, he
might stick to her. The more she gave in, the more pliant and

passive she was, the less she would satisfy him. And her obsession drove her more and more towards this pliancy and passivity, towards anything that kept him near her.

Blind, but she could not help it. She dared not. To stand up for herself—how at this hour could she do so but primally and horribly?—would be to lose him, to stage a last scene, where he would not turn from her, oh no, he would act kindness, laugh her out of her mood, piercing her with his self-protective lightness to the quick, the glint in his eyes growing harder and the core of his mind growing harder, rallying her while he withdrew from her, evading unpleasantness, being unusually pleasant and tender, insincerely tender—for the last time.

She could not. It was no use. She would go where she wasn't wanted. Deeper and deeper she would sink.

Clearly there was no limit to what a woman would do when she was utterly obsessed. No shamelessness went too far. In swift moments of upsurgence, this roused hate. She hated him as the instrument of shame in sudden writhings, in appalling spasms, inducing a tremulous nausea near to vomit, bringing a clammy death-dew to her forehead, yet all the time knowing that she would not break the cool bright stalk of his body, would not obliterate his eyes, even were the power to do so, now, at this intensest moment, put in her hands; but, on the contrary, that, conscious of her power, she would crawl to him.

She was the victim of extraordinary fantasies of this kind, for she did not think her thoughts so much as see them take human shape, her shape and his. After an hour's tossing in her bed, particularly if she awoke to it, say about two or three in the morning, the figures became thick with life, and her own was then sometimes endowed with the magical power of self-expression, of getting him to see and understand those deeps in her, that, in daylight meeting, she could never disclose; yet from that culmination of superb illusion, while the golden bridge was still spanning the chasm, she would turn over and sink her teeth in the pillow, crying: "If only! Oh, if only!"

She drew her eyes from the river to her watch. She would be five minutes late. She never risked being more and spent a lot of time before her actual departure calculating the matter. That he was never late, that he was on the contrary always careful to be early, did not deceive her. He was of the kind that would never hurt her in *that* way for worlds. Oh, she knew him. When she rounded the next bend, she would find him leaning over the wall, this side of a clump of wild briar, looking into the stream.

She rounded the bend and there he was, his elbows on the wall, which was breast high, looking into the stream. She knew, by a slight movement of his head, that he had seen her, but he kept on looking into the stream. She was too far away for him to sustain without some discomfort an interest that would grow awkward over too long an approach. She knew it as she knew the flavour of a berry. Her knees weakened. The assurance she had had, the new high assurance which had come upon her this morning out of a letter in so strange, so fantastic a manner, began to sink away.

But she kept her head up on the memory of it, though for that matter she always did keep her head up. And she dressed as neatly as he. That she was bright in movement and manner and had a rather subtle sense of style, he had told her, for he would talk about anything and liked to give the personal—it could be an amusing game—an impersonal edge.

So they met, hailing each other cheerfully.

"You are looking rather bright!"

"Am I?" She nearly laughed. "It is pleasant to get away from that office." She had hardly paused as they met. They were walking on. "Oh, I like this—the grass and the trees, and that great bank of broom. Gorgeous, isn't it?"

"And your spirits. What's happened?" he asked.

"Why? Amn't I usually?"

"Sometimes."

And then the accursed little silence, breaking in upon her. But no fear! She was not losing her gaiety, her high indifference. And all at once she heard her voice, high and laughing. It was beginning to tell him about the letter! Out of sheer nervousness, her voice was betraying her. Appalled, she stopped abruptly, smiling, her face suffused, her eyes brilliant.

"Go on," he said. "What was it?"

She remained silent, glancing at trees and golden bank.

"You shouldn't have started, if you're not going on. That's not fair. Out with it!"

"No." She shook her head definitely.

"Oh, come on!" He took her arm and squeezed it, helping her along, companionable, amused.

"I couldn't."

"Why? Feel you shouldn't divulge the public secrets entrusted to your charge?"

"Yes," she answered firmly.

"But," he said, "but—you have told me one or two before."

Her face drew taut and stormy-looking, feeling the touch, as if they were probing fingers, of his eyes.

"Sorry," he said, squeezing her arm and letting it go. "That wasn't fair."

The awful paralysing dumbness descended upon her. He remained silent.

"It wasn't much anyway," she said. "There was no secret. It was not that." She was talking at random.

"No?"

"No."

"All right. Don't tell me if you don't want to. I don't mind. Really."

"I didn't mean to be unfair; to start—and break off."

"Please don't worry about it. It's nothing."

"Thank you," she said. "You sometimes make me feel mean."

"Which is not just a generous thing to say, is it?"

"It's not what you say; it's—it's——"

"Yes?"

But she was dumb. Thought got so tremulous that it would not form.

"Do tell me," he pressed her.

Dumb and stupid.

"You always do flatter me," he went on gaily, "by your delicate implications that I should understand your silences. How's that?"

"Very clever," she said.

He laughed.

This gave her heart. She had been looking over the golden bank at the bright sky in the west; at the enlargement of light wherein she had seen aristocratic movement. The memory of it came back with a slight access of assurance, and all at once she said, with a feeling now of daring rather than of self-betrayal: "He was clever, too, the man in the letter, but in a different way."

This seemed to delight him. "How so?"

But that was the very sort of question, short and penetrating, that, when she was moved, blinded her. However, she now had something to tell, a story, and she hung on to it. "It mightn't be good for your morals," she said, "if I told you."

He threw his head up and swayed on his feet, so delighted he was. He was taking no denial now, not on your life. And before she knew what was happening there was her voice, quite loud, inclined to hesitate, to break, laughing, her face flushed.

She did not know who the man was, she began, but he was very educated and full of fun. He was writing to a woman and her husband and said the most atrocious things very cleverly.

You could see his sly smile, hear him laugh. They must have been telling him that his letters were censored, for this had set him off on the censorship. He said that their mutual friend, Captain Somebody-or-other, had been in the other night and was still interested in literature, seriously. He had been reading, in the original, some old French court memoirs, had the Captain. And very disgusted he was over the way these memoirs—written obviously by the most brilliant men of the period—were concerned altogether with the most trivial gossip and intrigue and above all with sex. You wouldn't believe it, said the Captain. You wouldn't credit it. Do you know, asked the Captain, what these women, these society women, would do? They would undress before their butlers—actually undress before their butlers—as if they were articles of furniture. Well, I mean to say!

She choked. He rolled away, head up, laughing. She was excited all over, but intensely dismayed. What had seemed to her before full of the light of freedom, of aristocratic movement, now, in her re-telling, seemed only a blue story.

"Superb!" he cried.

She waited, dumb, slightly sick, smiling, head up, eyes front.

"I had no idea," he said, babbling on, "forgive me, that your wit could be so searching. But as an attitude to the censorship, as a criticism of it, as—as—a putting of it in its proper place, by God it's superb! Articles of furniture!" He staggered away again. "Less than articles of furniture! For at least the butler did not pry. Lord, I say, isn't there something finally vile in the act of censorship! Prying, not upon the body, which can stand it, which is there to be seen—but into the deeps of the secret individual mind. Watching that, waiting for it as for a treacherous snake, ready to hit it. Vile! Oh, vile!"

She began to breathe again.

He was quite excited, extremely alert, his language more free than she had ever known it, accepting her. He was moved by the whole affair, having obviously seen nothing blue in it at all. Then she felt his eyes coming at her sideways, in a subtle new appraisal.

"Do you smell the broom?" he cried, throwing now his glance in front, towards the short-cropped narrow green alleyways, hidden and scent-laden, between the bushes. "Come on, let us sit down!"

She slowly came to a pause, swallowed, and said, "No, I'm sorry. I must go back."

He swung round and stood still as if he had been struck.

"I have to go out to-night," she explained.

He was looking right into her, searching for the meaning, for the meaning of the possible lie.

She looked at her watch. "I must go." Then she looked up for a moment right at his eyes, with the uncertain but pleasant smile that apparently appreciated his surprise.

"You never said you were going out."

"I didn't know last night. I must."

"Must you?"

"I'm afraid I must. In fact," she added, looking at her watch again, "it's high time I was off."

"Oh, really? That's a pity."

"Yes. I must go." She was swaying, smiling. She backed away a pace. Her head tilted and she gave him a brilliant glance. "Please, you needn't come. But—I must go. Good-bye."

She swayed round, and was off, but at a few paces half-turned, still going, and gave him a small charming salute, swaying downward as she did so, like a branch of a tree, before her head rose upward and went steadily on.

During all this play, he never moved. He still stood looking after her.

She felt him like a pale outraged statue at the back of her

mind; the pallor and the glint. How all her various bits kept together, how her feet kept moving on, she did not know. She had an extreme terror, all through her body, that he would come after her; and when she knew that he was not coming after her, that he was standing still, that he would never come after her, the terror rose up into her head.

By the time she got round the bend her legs were getting out of control, but she managed to reach a wooden seat, conveniently placed for visitors by the riverside. She had hardly been sitting a minute, however, when the pale statue came alive in her mind, striding after her. At any moment it might come round the bend.

From this spectre she got up and fled, and through streets that crossed and wound like the prisoning walls in a maze ultimately got to her lodging, to her bedroom. She threw herself upon her bed, the nightmare flight quivering in her relaxed flesh.

But better that scene than a primal, horrible mess. Better strewn on her bed than strewn on the ground at his feet. She moaned. She would have preferred the mess; preferred the scene, the mess, the end—particularly the end, emptied out, finished, the end. That little bit of silly school-girl acting! She groaned and bit the pillow.

After a time, she came off the bed, feeling more empty than any spectre. She moved slowly; stood at the window. The shades of night are falling, she thought. A smile twisted her pale features as she faced into her room again, seeing it as a strange place, each article of furniture very still, waiting for something to happen. She saw the smooth, hearkening, waiting attitude, characteristic of each piece. She thought: I will look in on Bess's full-moon party. She had said to Bess she was sorry she couldn't go because she had a previous engagement. Bess had looked at her and said: "I am sorry I can't ask you to bring him, seeing it's Ladies."

She took off her jacket and the back of the chair received it. She took off her jumper and laid it across the small reading table. The wooden rail of the bed accepted her skirt like an extended arm. The wardrobe waited her pleasure, creaking a trifle with honourable age and long service as she put forth the necessary effort to open its door. As she took the dress-hanger from its hook and turned towards the tweeds which she had but just removed from her person, she observed the commode. "I regret," she said with calm restraint, in the grand manner, "that I have nothing for you meanwhile."

Whereupon her nostrils closed against a sound that started well down behind them. The sound mounted against great pressure. As it blasted its way through with explosive snort she flung herself face down on the bed.

Hysteria is at first a wild pleasurable madness. It's dark turbulent stream bursts all dams, and as the wreckage is swept forward, bits of it, like arms and legs, rise up and swing over, get fixed for convulsive moments, tremble, and break loose again.

The bed shook under her smothered laughter. Everything was breaking loose. There was no longer any hold anywhere. She couldn't stop. Fear saved itself from the stream by mounting like a monkey into her brain. Pain clung to the banks of her body, its long hands contorting and gripping. Her forehead went bone-cold under a spray of icy spume. After a long time she came into a side eddy, and with the weak fingers of a will that in some miraculous way had not got drowned she held on to herself, floating upon exhaustion; then she let go even so slender a hold and would have fallen asleep had she not hiccupped.

She examined the wreckage of her face in the mirror, lighting two candles to supplement the bulb in the middle of the ceiling. She felt extremely weak and wretched, but the hiccups had not developed, so she was able to bear up before the furniture, and particularly before the two handsome silver-backed brushes which she had inherited along with fifty pounds from her aunt. They were chased, and bore her initials because they were also her aunt's.

Her eyes were the worst, though luckily they never really swole and got red. She murmured with a manner: "Thesis: laughter; antithesis: sobs; synthesis: hysteria." But the slight jest was lost on her aunt. It was lost on herself. Could she face them? Had she the strength to go? Her eyes narrowed. Her face drew taut. She would go, she decided with aristocratic indifference, and refused to haggle. The furniture, impressed, remained suavely silent as she made herself up with languid care. The looking-glass, holding the candles apart, complimented her in bright-eyed silence.

Bess had a real cocktail-shaker and had bought real gin. She welcomed her unexpected guest in a loud cheerful voice.

"What went wrong, Anne?"

"Oh, nothing," said Anne, looking around. "The thought of you shaking that old shaker was too much for me."

"My child!" exclaimed Bess. "Good God, he's not the sort that takes you for a walk?" And she shook vigorously and with concern.

They were simple nice women, offhand and friendly.

After her drink, Anne had some tea and began to revive, feeling at once both very much awake and languid, quite a pleasant state, which left her with assurance and no desire to shine, only a readiness to acknowledge the chance wit of another. This slow motion of her subtle sense of style brought it out rather charmingly, and occasionally a pair of eyes discreetly ran up and down her.

But her turn came when, feeling like a queenly prisoner being led to execution, she told of the French court, the ladies, and the butlers who were furniture.

There was hubbub then. Anne sat silent and saw them

seeing themselves in the censor's office as something less than furniture, something prying and low, if not positively evil. They said things then that should have made tingle the ears of the man who undressed his thought before them. But one girl, a regular tomboy, said, "He's quite right. Woman's emancipation—so that she may become a typist to the boss, if nothing less—or more! No, girls; woman's place is the home. Always was and always will be. For why? Because there she rules——"

"Like Britannia—on a penny," interrupted Bess.

They would have grown sick with laughter but for the natural tendency of woman to consider personal matters as still important.

By the time the last girl said cheero, Anne had not far to go. The full moon shone down on the deserted street, on a city in a stony dream. No other light but the light of the moon as she walked the sky, dark-blue mantle thrown off her shoulders, naked, with aristocratic mien, serene and lovely.

At the corner she all but ran into him, but now he was more astonished than she, for, after all, what had he been mooning about her abode for at this unconscionable hour? She felt this and he knew it. So it was no time for excuses that wouldn't deceive a fly.

"So you thought you would treat me as your butler?" he said.

"No," she answered in a voice gentle as the serene moon; "only as a piece of furniture."

"Ha! ha! ha!" he said, but harshly, not at all in his usual manner. Fortunately he tilted up his head or his breath might have blown her over.

Often she had wished that God had endowed her with a modicum of wit. But she was beyond any such desire now, lost in the miracle of her still upright body. "You are like a wolf baying the moon," she said.

LOVE'S DIALECTIC

From her gentle lips the words came upon him in weird tribute, arresting act and thought.

"Come," he decided masterfully, "let us go for a walk." But she shook her head.

"No?"

"I'm tired," she answered simply.

He looked at her face which reflected the moon.

"Is that the only reason?"

She nodded.

"To-morrow night?"

"Yes."

He gazed at her for so long that she knew at last she was going to fall. In silence he lifted her hand, kissed it like a courtier, turned, and walked away.

The furniture was obviously delighted to see her. Sit here! said the chair. Here! said the bed. "I can talk to him!" she said to herself. "I can talk to him! I shall," she said, as if remembering a marvellous line of poetry, "always be able to talk to him." Pure magic. The bed sighed as she sat on it and stared past the wardrobe which did not intrude. She saw his face as it stooped, and she murmured: "I love him utterly, madly. I adore him." She felt somnambulant, walking in a new world, made out of the union of the old night world and old day world. A new world. "Synthesis!" came a faint ironic breath to seal the cell of honey and keep it from spilling over. Thesis antithesis . . . dialectic. Toys, male toys, under eyebrows and earnest male faces, earnest and adorable creatures. She dared hardly think about him. She thought about him in a wave and threw herself on the bed and wept, she was so deliriously happy.

The Mirror

It came to the point where he saw Glasgow as streets and workshops and yards, baths of multitude with an upper scum of clever people grown faintly green and cynical. So he left it, deciding to strike out for the countryside, for some remote crofting area, where a cottage would stand on an upland and the people would move like peasants in immemorial landscapes, drawing vital life from the soil. From the soil: that was the idea. Glasgow was a machine; even its hideous social problem was impersonal. Not that it was simply soulless: it was in an ultimate spiritual sense lifeless: an infinitely complicated robot animated by a clanging energy and subsisting on the digestive processes of its iron guts.

In the crofting area of Glendun he found a cottage at the foot of an upland, and the ben room with its iron bed of shining brass knobs was given over to his private use. His portable typewriter in its neat black case, his writing blocks, pencils and typing paper, were disposed on and about an old sideboard with peeling veneer.

This old sideboard, surmounted by its oval cracked mirror, at once repelled and attracted him. Sitting with his back to the little window in the two-foot wall, he could see reflected in the mirror the rising hillside. The reflection, in its frame of dark mahogany, gave the hillside a curious, aloof, quiescent quality; lifted it from the realm of realism to the realm of art. The mirror so admirably symbolised his own attitude . . . at any rate to a certain extent, for he had "values" to find that were beneath the surface, human values, drawing vital life from the soil. But the crack in the mirror was a problem, providing speculative moments, not without their humour.

For occasionally the head of his landlady appeared there, or the head of one of her two daughters, or of her husband invited ben for an odd smoke of a night; and afterwards there would appear his own brittle thought running with the flawed glass, particularly if the visitor had been the elder daughter.

She was nineteen, a full-blown woman, clear-eyed, rich-skinned, with a firm busked waist, a quick heavy step, and a ready mirth. In the very colour of her round forearm was red strength. Though he judged that actually he must be as tall as she was, he had the feeling that one of these impulsive jerks of her arm would land him ignominiously on his back.

The first few days he spent looking about him. He was very pleasant to his hosts, very polite, very anxious not to inconvenience them needlessly. Going about in this leisurely way was rather wonderful. No tired home-coming at 2 a.m. with the looming thought of a bolted breakfast and a rush for his police-court copy in the morning. He was in any case due a rest. Moreover, it was essential that he get steeped in the atmosphere of his new environment, which was so much more than merely the place where he was staying. It was going to mean so much more to Scotland, suffering from the incubus of a virulent industrialism, from a complete lapse of any sense of nationhood, from the worshipping of moneyed robots.

As the days went on, however, he began to grow vaguely restless. He found that he could not write. The index finger of a thought did not touch his mind on the quick: it rather sank into it as into a cerebrum of wool.

"You're always at the writing, Mister Craig." His landlady struck him as solidly peasant, with a fat ready smile.

"Ah, but you see, that's my trade."

"You're telling me that?" And the smile paused to look at him, at once credulous and doubtful. "Well, now, isn't that the queer trade!"

"Why?"

"Indeed, then, I don't know," she answered, her smiling wrinkles recovering their humour. "But I never seen anyone who did it before."

Possibly she thought that all books and papers were miraculously conceived! A queer notion enough, worth noting for future use. . . . His eyes shifted to the mirror and he saw her face slant a curious look at him. As she turned away she caught his eyes in the glass. For an arrested moment, they stared at each other. With a warm confusion invading his mind, he heard her stolidly leave the room.

The woolly consciousness grew. He could stare at his mind as at the hump of a sheep's back. He tentatively tried to convince himself that by some malignant mischance he had selected the wrong spot, where the folk he met were absolutely "ordinary" and the soil earthy, clammy, coldly wet. When his boot sank in the mire and he pulled it out, the sound of the suction was a note of sheer negation. In a quite literal and devastating way there was "nothing in it". When he tried to "reflect" it he succeeded too well, for his brain-pan became the clayey, ooze-filling hole itself.

And this dreadful literalness of the soil was also reflected in the people who worked on it. Which might not have been such a great disappointment if only he himself could have reflected them in the mirror of his art. But he couldn't. He could at the most, and then with effort, merely name the things and persons he saw. He could not rationalise or translate them. They would not permit of such a process. Night after night he deliberately sat down to put them into a short story, but at almost every point he found that he was inventing, or idealising, that he was laboriously importing some mental or spiritual or romantic element into his picture in order to make it "go"; was, in short, "making it up" insincerely, was conscious of his insincerity and ashamed; not exactly ashamed of being insincere, but of being unable to compose his picture out of its native elements, as if his original genius had some fatal flaw in it, like the mirror.

The younger daughter was sixteen and very shy of him. But the blown beauty of nineteen was hearty and vivid. The skin of neck and cheek could flush like dogrose petals, palpitant and warm. She began to disturb him secretively. He pursued her in his dreams.

But he could not write about her, much less about imaginary pursuits of her. Apart from the thoughts and emotions aroused being quite unprintable, they were too crude, too actual, too fleshly, for art; in fact he would have burned with an impotent shame had they been capable of being whispered at all. Yet they were at least perfectly real, and were completely in the picture. Indeed he had never experienced any other flame quite like it, in the sense that it was so all-enfolding. It could make him gulp, make him tremble, make him feel like an imaginary devil or a real coward. Yet it was not a thing to be written. Supposing he did set down exactly what he emotionally experienced, painting with a free brush in naked colour? . . . The only printing presses for that sort of thing were in Paris. And even then, how about the "indispensable air of consequence"? Humiliating.

He began to miss a morning's shave; did not put on his collar until the afternoon; refused to have his meals by himself and came into the kitchen for them. Sometimes he gave the crofter a hand about the little steading, or would accompany the elder daughter to the milking of the two cows. The scents of the steading, the byre, the cows, the dung; the life processes of cocks and hens and cattle; the gluttonous gruntings of an only pig quite filled his mind. When he stood in the byre watching her firm pink fists working like pistons into the cow's udder, he could scarcely trust his throat to answer her sound common sense, her cheery sallies.

In the evenings, because as yet he found it impossible to sit with the crofter saying nothing, he always retired to his own room. But he no longer wrote. And being unable to write tortured him almost as acutely as did the flaming roses of Murdina, to whom he was now consciously frightened to disclose himself lest he be repulsed. And to be repulsed by Murdina would certainly be the last word in humiliation . . . not to speak of the difficulties it would raise in his residence.

Out and about, he learned to meet people in the undemonstrative, offhand way that seemed to constitute good form, deliberately suppressing in himself the impulse to sensitive politenesses. At a dance in the village hall he entered into the robust amusement of the evening in sensible style, but was all the time conscious of being not quite in the swim, of being emptily dissatisfied, positively lonely. Nor could he get his tongue to utter their broad humour. Often he felt so witless that he could not get the crease out of his smile. And his natural attentions of courtesy to Murdina were not overlooked. They were made the occasion of sly winks and nods, so that to free her from possible embarrassment he did not go near her for several dances.

During one of these dances he slipped outside for a quiet smoke, but became so lost in his unfortunate thought that he forgot to smoke. He was roused by footsteps mixing near him in the dark, by the audible strife of soft bodies, the sound of a smothered kiss, followed by the rich suppressed giggle of Murdina's protesting voice. The bodies moved on in their amorous combat.

Back in the hall, he watched for their re-entry. He was a big handsome fellow with a moustache, and, yes, his blue eyes were glittering rather self-consciously. So that knocked on the head any half-formed, feverish scheme for seeing Murdina home in the small dark hours.

Yet he clung to the hope . . . until it was finally dissipated, for, after what he had seen—or, rather, heard—he could hardly risk a formal offer. He hung about the dark outskirts of the door until he saw her emerge—and taken possession of. Someone called out something which he did not quite catch. It raised a laugh; and intuitively he knew that the laugh was against himself and in favour of the prowess of the blond cavalier.

On the way back to the croft, walking slowly to his shrinking thought, he was overtaken by timid footsteps which would have passed him by, had he not recognised the younger daughter, Elspeth. He spoke to her chaffingly. "What! no one seeing you home, Elspeth? . . ."

But she was very shy. And presently he found it difficult to keep the talk going. To most of his queries she gave a simple yes or no, occasionally amplified by a "Yes, it was very nice", or "I don't know", or "I couldn't say". Her timid virgin tautness made him feel not unpleasantly cold. If he laid a finger on her, she would bolt. He did actually catch her arm at an awkward ditch and felt the frightened muscle flex and start away from him. She footed the ditch like a young hind. She was only a child of sixteen to his aged twenty-three. And when he had lit the light in the kitchen—there was no sign of Murdina yet—and turned to bid her good night, she replied in a curious voice without looking at him, without even showing her face.

That husky note in her voice disturbed him immediately he had got into his own room, gripped him so that he stood for a time doing nothing, conscious that by some ineptitude he had missed . . . whatever it was . . . but that might have been a certain feeling or passion . . . towards himself. He grinned at that . . . but refrained from breathing, kept listening, excitedly thinking . . . paused in the act of taking off his jacket. . . . He could go through to the kitchen for . . . A sound came from outside. Then silence. Unbroken silence. That would be Murdina and her gallant. . . . He saw them at their amorous game and completely forgot Elspeth. "Damn them!" he muttered with weary spite and took off his clothes. Though he did not feel at all sleepy, yet after a few obstinate minutes he sank into a dog sleep of exhaustion.

Daylight and the earth showed him what was happening: his mind was disintegrating, going to bits . . . or, more clearly, he saw it lapsing into the vacant soil. Nor could he be disturbed about it. He was satisfied now that the crofter never thought, that he carried on for long hours with his mind hypnotised by nothing. It was easy to do this, and anything but unpleasant. He himself drowsed until the possibility of entertaining an original idea and getting excited about it became so remote that its contemplation was burdensome.

He gave up any pretence of writing. One could write in Glasgow, but not here. There was nothing here but a clayey absorption and persistence. Philosophically it had the immutable sameness of the face of Nirvana or God . . . except that it was disturbed by this animal vortex; a warm disturbance, sporadic, whirling downward out of sight, and, when in full career, desperately secretive and cunning. And yet for all its cunning ever ready to egg on the body to its own betrayal. He began to find himself now and then in the barn, on the off chance that Murdina might come in, his heart beating if a footstep came near the door.

Then on the edge of the dark one evening, Elspeth came into the barn. In their surprise, they stared at each other for a naked speechless moment. With the fluttering action of a snake-fascinated bird, Elspeth turned and made her way out. The revelation of their suppressed emotions had been complete.

THE MIRROR

Shame pierced his mind—as a red lance a quivering core of exultation. He sat down. He would have to think this over. He ran his tongue along his lips.

The debate was fevered and sinful and horribly fascinating. Mind and body got caught up in it. He walked miles in the dark, deciding this, and, in tired moments of reckless devilry, deciding that; but finally coming to no conscious decision . . . except that by the hot unconscious urge of things there would probably happen . . . between Elspeth and himself. . . .

Into the slyness of this interminable debate there swept suddenly a note of sheer weary disgust. He cursed the night and the sodden land. He sat down and bowed his head and cursed himself. And crouched there, at bay, he faced at last the thought that was behind all thought, ultimate and annihilating, and it said to him: *You know what's wrong. . . . You're not an artist.*

All of life's meaning and beauty withered in its breath and turned to ash. A grey pitiless face.

And when he let himself go and laughed harshly, obliterating the face, he remembered all the littlenesses that were his too. He could not even do a small thing in the royal way, like an artist. Glasgow . . . he did not simply walk away and leave the damned place. No fear! He had been careful to take his typewriter with him, and writing paper, and all the rest of the paraphernalia. And here to-night now, instead of getting up and walking over the hilltops, no matter what came of it . . . no fear; he would go back, and pack up, and carefully destroy every scrap of paper that he did not take with him. . . .

The following afternoon he did leave. And just as he had thrown his last meditative cigarette stump in the fire and was starting from his armchair, he caught the hillside in the cracked mirror, and in its quiescent quality was a curious aloof mockery, watching him. His face rose into the mirror, pale, tight-lipped, bitter, blotting out the landscape.

THE MIRROR

The crofter accompanied him to the bus, wondering out of curiosity where he might be going to next. But he was not quite sure where he was going. Smiling, he looked about the free world. His mind began to function again; one or two doubtful flashes scintillated from an awakening intellect. As the bus trundled down the glen road, he waved in response to the white hanky at the cottage door. Oh, good-bye, fare ye well! Before the ticket office on the little station platform, he hesitated only a moment, then said, "Third, single, Glasgow."

The Listener's Tale

She knew he was laughing to himself when she kissed him in the lobby and he groped for the peg for his coat and bowler hat. Her own chortle in sympathy was stopped, however, by the smell of drink, the quite distinct smell of drink. The thrill of surprise checked her, and she backed before him into the kitchen as if she could not soon enough see his face, for the lobby was dark. But the three children were now dancing before him, taking his hand and having their hair ruffled, chattering wildly, while he affectionately answered them back.

"Darling," she said, "you've been——" And she sniffed.

"I know," he answered, rubbing his hands and laughing outright. "I know."

"Hurry!" she said. "The soufflé fell—waiting for you."

"It fell, did it? Naughty soufflé!" And he made a solemn face at the children, who mirthfully bumped onto their chairs round the table.

"What happened?" she asked.

He started laughing. "Men are mad," he said. "Quite mad." He shook his head and straightened his knife and fork. "He met me just outside the Bodega, and invited me in, and I had to follow him to tell him I wasn't going in, for he took it for granted, and by that time I was in." He shook softly. "I tried to tell him, but I couldn't get a word in, for he carried on where he'd left off at coffee in the morning, and ordered two glasses of the real Mackay without interrupting himself. What could I do?"

She gave a small chortle. "Who on earth was he?"

"A rare bird—from New Guinea."

"New Guinea?"

"You know—where the Japs have landed."

"Was he?"

"Yes. An extraordinary interesting fellow. And he fairly riled the Freudian at coffee in the morning. What a talk! Old Snozzle gave me a look when I went back. 'A client has been waiting for you for some time,' he said. He just can't understand this habit of going for a coffee in the forenoon. It's the best time of the day, he thinks."

"Do you think it's wise to annoy the old jozzer? Now, Eve, don't gobble—enjoy it, for that's all you're getting."

"Annoy him? I never do. This is a real topper of a soufflé, my dear. Light as a feather. He knows my point of view. This city of ours was in my father's time the most drunken in the world. Now we do our business talk over a coffee."

"Coffee—h'm!"

"And talk—whatho!" He chuckled. "It was rich this morning. The best for a long time. I had no idea that Bill had so much in him. But he knows his Communism all right. Not just the old economic patter. He was jolly good and was giving the Freudian a real hot time."

"Was he? Tell me about it," she said, settling down to enjoy her own food now with the full expectation of being entertained. For her husband, who was a listener at the coffee-room meetings, offering little comment beyond the quick laugh of appreciation when a hit was scored, talked at great length to his wife, often mimicking an action or a tone in a way that never failed to amuse her; for they were so much in accord that they had developed a special humour of their own.

"You know the Freudian line—everything sex—you know?"

"Yes, I know." She nodded brightly. "Here you are, Sam.

And remember the jam is rationed. So take your time with the soufflé."

"It's hot," said Sam. "Can I blow on it?"

"Can he blow on it, Daddy?" asked the mother.

"Just this once," said Daddy.

"You can blow on it this once," she said, and looked up at her husband, her expectant blue eyes alight.

"Evidences of parental affection or similar emotion are", he said, quoting, "a form of sexual love, cheated of fulfilment."

"Cheated?" she repeated. "Who's cheated?"

He put down his knife and fork and tilted his head back. His face suffused with blood. She got a bit red herself and thoroughly enjoyed the conjoint mirth.

"All tenderness is", he began again, and mentally groped until he recalled the words, "inhibited sexuality."

"It is?"

"It is. That's the correct position, you must understand. No snuffy puritanism can veil the truth. You've got to face up to it. Once you face up to it, you're liberated, you're all right. You've got past the censor. At least," he added hesitantly, "I think so."

She had a way of spluttering laughter through her mouth that was sudden and infectious. "It *is* difficult to remember," she said helpfully, "isn't it? I always find difficulty with the id myself, and libido—it somehow gets all fogged with the idea of libidinous. We'll have to read it seriously sometime. It's not really fair to Mr. Freud, is it?"

"And then Bill started in on him—and my word he was pretty good."

"I think Bill is tiresome. He's got such a dry voice. It goes on and on. And he's so cocksure, it's just difficult to want to know anything from him. I think Freud is far more fun—and all that about sex, well, there *are* starved creatures. I met a few of them this afternoon in Moron's tea-rooms."

"I bet you did!" he laughed to himself. "But Bill was good. I never could understand a lot of this business in Freud. It's not that I care a hoot either way. After all, you and I know what's what. Pretty good by us. You bet. What would life be without it? D little. You're a corker at a soufflé." He filled his mouth. "But when it comes to parental affection, or a man's friendship with another man, I always thought it went agley. And that's what Bill proved. The same with 'infantile sexuality'. He was good."

"How?"

"He started off by saying Freud has the bourgeois mind. That astonished every one, for you know how Freud has been the holy terror of the regular church-goer. It put us all into good humour. And to prove that he had the bourgeois——"

"I wish he would give that word a rest."

"—the bourgeois mind, he said look at the words he uses— the id and the censor and the ego and so on, like deities in a new mythology. You see? Mythological—*not* scientific. His whole approach is tainted at the source."

"But they're only names—and jolly good names. You've got to call the thing something."

"But he's made a story of it, just as you make a story of the creation of the world. And there are ever so many stories of the creation of the world. Adler, *he* says the whole thing is not sex, but self-preservation. And his story fits the doings just as well as Freud's. So where are you? You see the point?"

"But, I say, Freud has made a study of the thing all his life. He knows. Bill doesn't. After all, dash it, Freud knows. He has cured people and——"

"Has he? Bill says he knows several people who were cured all right, cured in the way you'd cure a fish—by gutting it."

She could not help spluttering.

"There's a hopeless void left," said her husband, his grey eyes bright above his chewing mouth with its neatly trimmed,

stubby, brown moustache. "Now Bill says that's what's wrong
—that the fish, minus its gut, is left with no outlook. The void
doesn't know even what to ache for."

She put down her knife and fork the better to laugh outright.
The children became noisy. He put his elbows on the table and
elevated his fork, chewing heartily.

"Now if Freud, said Bill, had understood the meaning of
dialectical materialism——"

"Of course!" she said, recovering somewhat, but tremulous
still.

"He would have acted differently thera-peut-peutically."

She started off again. Eve, feeling the need to join in, grew
shrill, and little Sam, having elevated his fork and finding the
gesture wanting, began to beat his plate with it. Mary, aged
nine, midway in the two year intervals that separated the
children, sat smiling and looking from one face to another.

The mother restored order happily.

"And what was Bill's cure?" she asked.

"Quite simple. You must re-integrate the patient into
society. How are you going to do that? By making him understand that social relations are everything, that they are primary,
that we are products of them as the fish is a product of the sea.
In short, you've got to turn the fish back into the sea, not leave
it high and dry, out of its element."

"And what about the gut?"

"Which is what the Freudian asked, without your charm, my
dear."

"Oh yeh?"

"And Bill answered: he will grow a new and better
gut."

She glanced at her husband as she spluttered, a glance of
bright surprise and assessment, as if some new and assured
male element were salting his humour. Very slight—but interesting—and a trifle exciting. The whisky, of course.

"I have heard all that about the social relations. It seems to me vague and so dry," she said.

"But it is possible", he answered, choosing his words, "to conceive of it, after a time, in a wet way."

She shook. "Darling," she asked, "how many had you?"

"Two. I stood the third round, though it was really his, so that I wouldn't have to stand the fourth. In that way I got off."

"So you had three?"

"So I had," he agreed, with some astonishment, and after a glance at her began to laugh in himself.

"And where did this New Guinea man come in?"

"He just came in then, when the argument was at its height. Willie took him in, deliberately, and launched him. He's an anthropologist."

"A what?"

"An anthropologist is, I gathered, one who studies human beings as creatures of society. And he has this advantage over us that he studies societies in different parts of the world, societies that work in quite a different way from ours. He can therefore make comparisons, and some of them stand you on your head, not to mention other parts. Bill was at first very suspicious. I could see his hackle going up when the anthropologist referred to Communism as a culture pattern whose early manifestations he had studied in a primitive tribe in the north part of New Guinea!" He laughed at the memory. "And the Freudian smiled and chipped in helpfully about how the primitive comes out in modern man. Oh, lord, it's funny, too. You've seen three strange dogs, sniffing round one another, with the growl ready, and the teeth, too. It's like that. We're a queer mixture, right enough."

"Now, Sam—no more jam. You've had your share."

"But, Mummy——"

"Never mind, Sam, old boy—I've got something for you—

up my sleeve," and he winked mysteriously to his youngest offspring.

"Do you think that's fair?" she asked, with peace restored.

"Everything depends on the culture pattern," he answered. "That's what the anthropologist said—and went on to prove it. Really remarkable stuff. Sometimes you couldn't help roaring laughing. And not merely at the simple things, like work and dress. Women wear their hair long and men cut it short. Or, in the next tribe, men wear their hair in curls and women shave their heads. Where men wear skirts and women wear trousers, you can see how laughable and effeminate it would be for a man to be seen in trousers. The most extraordinary combinations—and combinations outside in. But more than that. Persons we think great persons, to them would be objects of pity. A man who takes his embroidery about with him, who is submissive and sweet and fond of children, is the male ideal in one tribe, while in the neighbouring tribe it's the morose hefty head hunter, if it's not the cunning leader. But I'll tell you some of the things", he said, with a glance at Eve—who was listening and who, after all, was eleven—"again."

"As bad as that?" she remarked, pouring him another cup.

"Worse," he answered, "but in a new sort of way, really simple and delightful. I told him he must come round some time."

"When?"

"Oh, when the children are in bed."

"Now, Eve," began Mummy, forestalling her daughter.

"Just dry talk," explained Daddy. "On and on. Like culture pattern—a good mouthful, what? For that's where Bill began to see daylight and to agree. We are all products of our culture pattern, based on our economic relations, absolutely, nodded Bill. It was right into his barrow. You could see the pleasure it would have given him to have told Marx about the tribes in New Guinea! For there you could see the whole thing as plain as the nose on your face when you look in a glass. And sometimes you see more than your nose." He chuckled.

"And how about the Freudian?"

"He was getting a bit hot and bothered. Because, you see—take the men business—you know, friendship among men—well, that's a natural behaviour pattern, men go out to hunt or fight or drink or whatnot together. Quite natural and sound. Economic production depends on it. But to confuse that with perversion is worse than ludicrous, much worse."

"How worse?"

"Because it's unscientific. Neat, what?"

"Sounds healthy, anyway," she said.

"That's the word!" he agreed. "Same with parental affection—only more so, because all society depends on that. And that's right into *our* barrow. Grand, isn't it?"

She smiled. "Are you finished?"

"Daddy," said Sam, "want to see what's up your sleeve."

"I told you," said his wife.

"Daddy—want to see——"

He looked up his sleeve and then his face expressed dismay. "They're gone!" he exclaimed.

"They're not!" cried Sam, with the anger that had expected as much.

"But wait!" said Daddy. "I know where they have gone."

"Where?" asked Sam, as if this conversation about unknown quantities presented no difficulty to him.

"They're gone to the Coliseum. That's where they have gone!"

"What's gone?" asked Eve.

"The Seven Dwarfs—and Snow White," answered Daddy, nodding, as if he had half-expected such behaviour from them. "They were at the Coliseum before, long ago, when you didn't see them—and that's how they know their way back."

"Oh, Daddy!" breathed Eve, watching his eyes.

"Andrew," began his wife.

"But," he said, interrupting her and looking at Sam, "if we all went there right off, we might catch them."

"But the Home Guard," began his wife.

"There's no meeting to-night, because we're having a big stunt to-morrow night, street fighting and all. So we'll go. What?"

Sam's voice, despite the pandemonium, was the loudest, because manifestly he had brought all this about.

In their bedroom, while he was brushing his hair, he started laughing to himself again.

"What's the joke?" She threw him a bright glance, ready to splutter.

"It's nothing really—but it took my fancy. I laugh whenever I think of it. It's about a tribe in New Guinea. Most interesting lot they are. They live in the mountains; poorer than church mice; a very hard existence, that you would have said would have ground them all down into ill-temper and worse. But not a bit of it. They are the happiest lot and love laughing. They get far greater fun out of helping their neighbours than helping themselves. You may not believe that, but it's dead right. Going to help in your neighbour's plot is a picnic. They have picnics every day. When it comes to throwing a village party, it's pigs and hind legs and yams an' all, should they starve for it. A laughing happy crowd. But they have one great difficulty. When a spot of bother is brewing amongst neighbouring savages, or when they have to do a bit of big business, they can't get anyone to act as leader. No one likes taking on the job. For anything in the nature of what we call a big shot, they laugh at. To them an aggressive leader, a führer, is just plumb funny. If they saw a fellow like Musso sticking out his jaw they would die laughing."

"And they call them savages," she said.

"Primitives, my dear. A primitive culture."

Seeing the inside of her mouth in the glass as she laughed, she studied her teeth. "So wha'?" she asked.

"So they look around for a couple of likely lads from neighbouring clans and begin training them. They start one cheeking up to the other. You, you softie! Even your pigs won't stay with you, if you had any . . . Pigs, is it? Says the other fellow. If you even saw a pig you'd run. Anyone would know by looking at you that you came out feet first instead of head first."

She spluttered and gave a last poke to her hair.

"And having got power they *don't* become corrupt," he went on. "That's the extraordinary thing. They long for the day when they can retire from this silly play-acting. And when that day arrives they relinquish the chains of office and go back to the normal decent way of living with great relief."

"Well, come along," she said, for now the children were clamorous. "Take Sam's hand, Eve. Off you go!"

"I wish I could understand it," he said feeling for his pocket book.

"Understand what?" she asked, throwing him a glance. There was the oddest worried expression on his face now.

"What makes me laugh," he said wrinkling his brows. "What makes me laugh when I hear them at it."

Her face softened fondly, while her eyes shone in a private assessing humour.

"I know what makes you laugh," she said, and she kissed him. "Come on."

The Clock

As, perfectly satisfied, I caressed my palm with the cool blade my eyes were drawn across my little sitting-room to the clock. The hands lay along each other at midnight. I waited for the striking with a self-deception that was only half-amused. For under its glass dome the clock was noiseless. The minute hand moved silently to an acute angle with the hour hand. I closed my razor and laid it on the table, picked from the oiled hone the split hair with which I had tested the steel, and sat down.

Watching the clock had become for me an absorbing occupation. Indeed, at times and in places the most odd, I could see its round pendulum of burnished brass twist noiselessly through nearly two revolutions, then twist noiselessly back, with always the corresponding twisting of the supporting ribbon of steel, the untwisting, and the twisting back. I understood from it, through long periods of reverie, the sensations that move the hearts of devil worshippers. I became aware of the mockery that is the hidden soul of all perfect mechanism.

I thought again of my morning's conversation with my landlady. It troubled me, because in this matter of the clock I knew that I had, by some malevolent impulse, over-stepped the boundary of good taste. Suddenly, as she smoothed the tea-cosy over the teapot, I had said:

"I was looking at that blessed clock last night till it sent me to sleep in my chair. Then if it didn't come along and sit tight on my chest and refuse to let me wake up. We had a fight and a half, I can tell you."

I stretched for a pat of butter, smiling at the obvious idiocy of all dreams; but at the same time I was acutely aware of tension. She said nothing, and I hurried on:

"The fun of it was that I thought the clock didn't know that I knew that its heart was a coiled spring. I struggled to get at it—till all at once the spring whizzed out and cut my hand off!" I laughed. "I awoke with a jump," I explained, "to find that my hot pipe had merely dropped from my mouth on to the back of my hand!"

But her smile was pale, and she went out without a word.

Before the door was closed I decided that I had been paying far too much attention to that clock. I glared at it, at its silent twisting and glittering in the fresh morning light. Why in the name of the devil didn't she lock it up, and put in its place a decent thing that would tick-tock with cheerful folly?

But all day the little affair had kept cropping up in my mind. Indeed, at moments, with a queer sense of incredulity, I even began to glimpse shapes of something actually sinister: a twist, a flicker, a vanishing expression of something mockingly real; as though the creature of the imagination could take on a life of its own with curious, inimical intent. It was really too much.

Yet its interest was persistent and not without its fascination . . .

No, not without its fascination now that I considered it comfortably, in complete leisure, and without any distractions. The night was so still that the trees in the garden did not even sigh. The tobacco smoke curled lazily, and the light from the shaded oil-lamp had a yellowish tinge. The midnight hour is the hour of inanimate things, the legs and the arms of furniture, for example, or photographs on a wall; at such a moment nothing can be more grotesque than a wedding group, or more persistent than a round knob, or more evilly mesmeric than the toils of an arabesque.

The steel ribbon winked every time it straightened itself, but the upright gleam on the revolving brass was actively constant. My mind began working again, but now in a more direct, human way than the clock had yet prompted.

After all, there was a lot to be said for my landlady's attitude. The facts were in a way tremendous when considered carefully. Here was a woman round about forty, an active woman, finely built, dark hair, dark interesting eyes, and smooth intelligent features, to be credited surely with most mother instincts a woman may possess.

No doubt of it. And because there was no doubt of it I felt I should be able to fathom a few things. Born and brought up as she was in this country parish, capable, for instance, of laying a spotless tea-table to the final butter-knife without my being quite aware of the operation till called to table—surely, I felt, there could be nothing behind these steady eyes, that level brow, savouring of the esoteric, of hidden dark things— in a Scots country parish—and a Scotswoman! My knowledge of landladies between London and Caithness was, I considered, fairly extensive. Yet, in spite of everything, I had to admit to myself there was on her part a curious attitude to the clock, conscious or subconscious, fearful or antagonistic or both, that I could not fathom.

And I knew a lot about the clock, positive facts about its material history, that is—not mere fanciful projections of midnight thought. Shortly after coming, I had asked her one day, quite idly, where in the world she had got the marvellous piece of mechanism. And in a few appalling words, uttered more quietly than any observation about the weather, she told me the manner of its arrival. Exactly what could have prompted her to tell it in the way she did, what incredible simplicity— or perversity—I failed utterly to grasp.

THE CLOCK

Just after her marriage, I learned, her husband had contracted double pneumonia by diving off the pier of the little harbour to save the life of a man who was three parts drunk. One afternoon, round about the crisis of his illness, the doctor, having just left the sick-room after expressing the comforting hope that the turn appeared to have been successfully negotiated, she was called downstairs by a quiet knocking at the front door. She was handed a box. It was the clock—a marriage present. When she went upstairs again she found her husband dead.

The recital in her simple, direct language was so short and stark that I must positively have gaped at her. It certainly left me without a single word.

The incident haunted me for a long time, so much so that almost unconsciously I began groping around for more facts, but this time not of my landlady. And in time stray bits of information seemed to gather almost on their own and to group themselves into a sort of intelligible pattern that more than hinted at a story human enough.

But the process of collation, of gradual perception, need not be elaborated, for like most stories of human happenings the outline can be given simply enough. In the first place, then, it was the man her husband had saved from drowning who had made a gift of the clock. It was thus both a marriage present and a token of gratitude for having saved a life, even though, with life's neatest irony, it had been presented at the door of death. In the next place, it appeared she had at one time been "in service" in the house of this man who had given the clock, a man who was the last of a line of big farmers whose family name had been established a sufficient number of generations to ensure parochial respect. In the third place, between this man and my landlady (whilst still in his service) there had been some clashing of wills. So much was clear.

Then the outline gets blurred. Throughout the countryside it was inevitable that this farmer's character should get known more or less in its main features, and certainly his drunken bouts were notorious. A hard-living hard-riding type of man, and, in his cups, imperious to a degree that was not only over-bearing but frequently verging on a momentary madness, yet always, to those around him, with a certain insolent, aristocratic sanction. When added to this imperiousness were a personal fearlessness and generosity, almost a spendthrift prodigality, the total compound may be understood to have struck the more timid parish souls with a royal air. Further, a few months after the heroic incident of the pier, his drowned body was discovered one morning in the little harbour. On how the fatality had occurred, what had attracted him to the pier during a night of storm when no other living soul was abroad, what his possible state of mind, no one would hazard an opinion, however many heads might be shaken.

As has been said, between my landlady and this man there had been a clashing of wills, and though nothing definite appeared to be known concerning whatever incidents there may have been, it is certain that she suddenly fled from his house.

I have always been attracted by the kind of Continental literature which finds in the mere obscurity of motive an under-world of enthralling interest, and which in the matter of style provides a satisfaction not unlike that derived from putting a perfect edge on a razor. Let me confess, further, that the Highland scene had for me, in this sense, a certain foreignness.

So I deliberately let myself come under the full sway of that noiseless, mesmeric pendulum, while I searched for motives to my landlady's pale smile. . . . Presently I found myself visualising possible scenes in her past, and from the scenes I went to what must have followed. Has not every life had the awful flash that lights up the inmost place? Did that hard-drinking, fearless type of man pierce through her country upbringing, through the barriers of convention and conscience? Did he pursue her. . . .

Fantastic scenes of pursuit began to enter my mind. I saw him chasing her along a narrow corridor in his house, his shoulders hitting from wall to wall, his dark features drawn in a mad excitement from which his eyes gleamed, a ruthless drunken sobriety . . . a half-clutch from which she breaks away, sending him crashing . . . while she runs on, not screaming, panting. . . .

The visualisations became so intense, so worked me up, that I had to stop them.

Panting, not screaming, because of the horrible treacherous appeal, the evil which she must deny if she was not to be destroyed . . . the beam of unholy temptation into her darkness. . . .

I switched off again. If something like that had happened, something of it might have remained, to be dismissed with relief when she married the countryman she loved, who gave her security and peace and decency.

But never to be forgotten. And the clock . . . I saw the meaning of the clock at once. While in his service she must, with the simple country woman's love of novelty, have admired the clock on the large drawing-room mantelpiece (I could see the room). The farmer's generosity was known, and the clock was his wedding gift, his sober smile, his tribute, his *amende honorable*.

That it should have come at such a moment, when he had, however indirectly, just been the cause of her husband's death. . . .

I suddenly experienced the extraordinary feeling that I had been rousing into action the whole horror of the business, calling it up, bringing it to life in this cottage on the outskirts of the village. . . .

THE CLOCK

My heart leapt. The midnight silence had been touched by the slightest of sounds. I smiled while my ears listened. I had noticed this peculiarity about my midnight education before that it left a sensitiveness that was extreme to such material intrusions—the creaking of a chair, for instance, or the sudden tapping of a swaying twig on a window pane. But one mastered these things by an effort of clear common sense . . . .

And now the sound came like a slow, regular padding of bare feet descending the stairs. Now in the passage-way. A coldness crept over my skin. There were fingers against the door. The knob turned visibly, and slowly the door opened. First an arm, then gradually the whole body. I ceased to breathe. Her white nightdress fell straight from the curves of her breast, her head was erect, her face wide-eyed and terribly calm. In a moment I saw she was asleep.

She looked across the room directly at the clock and moved towards it. As she came to the table her fingers crept lightly over its corner surface as though to guide her around it, came in contact with my razor, hesitated, and slowly closed over it.

She lifted the razor, and, without looking at it, opened it. I saw the blade suddenly gleam against the lamplight. In the slow, automatic manner in which this action was accomplished there was something indescribably horrible. Her gaze never strayed from the clock. As she moved towards it I had an agonising desire to cry out, to stop her, that merely left me more rigid, paralysed.

As she came near the clock something sinister, imperceptibly crouching, moved in her, and I think without knowing it I must have risen in my chair. For a few seconds she stood motionless, taut, and I felt that she was speaking terrible words in an agony of intensity. Then of a sudden a violent energy swept over her body, and the arm with the razor swung up—and in that instant somehow I managed to close with her.

Two impressions remain vividly: the astonishing and unexpected looseness of her body so that I could get no firm hold of it, and her incredible strength. But I hung on desperately to the razor arm. Altogether the struggle was probably over in half a minute, for I was presently swung against the sideboard with a terrific crash that swept the clock, glass dome and all, smashing to the floor.

And instantly she was still, like a figure of victorious doom. The razor dropped from her fingers. Instinctively I glanced for it and became aware of my left wrist gushing blood. Cunning made me hide the wound. Her breast heaved with each gasping breath, but already the fever of intensity was dying in her eyes. The fear that she would awake, which had frightened me ever since she had entered the room, now became acute, but the expression on her face was gradually becoming more remote, fixed. Something of fate was there, a deep consciousness of a secret purpose, or of some unsearchable process of the mind, at last fulfilled.

She turned and walked slowly round the table and out at the door. I heard the soft padding of her feet on the stairs. Against an overpowering weariness and exhaustion I fought till I had stanched the gash on my wrist, then I dragged myself to my armchair.

Such Stuff As Dreams

To the woman who sat by his bedside he was delirious, but to himself he was preternaturally sane. His vision was clear and fine and penetrating, and entirely untroubled by the burning sheath that was his body. Indeed, it was as though the burning sheath had dissolved away the dross of the mind, the clogged pores, the stupid obfuscations of everyday.

Thus he was aware of his illness as of something a little apart, as far apart, say, as the burning sheath from this inner central certainty of the mind, which was his real self, his thinking self, with its inexhaustible power of precise imagery. His illness was an objective thing, like a pack on a man's back. And, as with the pack, he knew it could be got rid of.

But not, of course, exactly as one would drop a pack. It could be dropped certainly, but in its own way. There was a way for dropping it, and he knew the way. Only, no one would believe him if he told them.

He turned over in his bed and muttered, so that the woman in the dim shaded light lifted her weary eyes to his haggard face. From side to side slowly his head rolled on the pillow, then suddenly became still as the eyes opened wide and stared fixedly before them. Involuntarily her hand started out over the coverlet to soothe the demon of delirium. It closed gently on his hand.

A small tremor went over his face, followed by a lessening of tension in the pallor, as a man's face will soften at a vision that touches the heart. The eyelids fell and from between the lips came a long quivering sigh, with a curious break in the end of it, like a wonder-catch of the breath.

She noticed that he seemed to quieten after that, breathing so lightly that the movement of the bedclothes above his chest was scarcely perceptible. If only he would sleep for a little! If only she could give him the tiniest fraction of this great weight of sleep and tiredness that weighed on her eyelids like lead and went through her body every now and then in warm weakening flushes of exhaustion. Resting her elbows on the little table, she could support her forehead with her palms and let her eyelids meet for a little to relieve the weight. He was so quiet now. He must be so weak. Odds and ends of the day's work about the house, about the steading, came back of their own accord, with odds and ends of thought for the morrow. Days and nights, twisting and turning . . . fitful, terrible. . . .

But the man was not asleep. He was pondering so deeply that his breathing almost stopped. Hitherto he had merely known how the burden could be dropped, but at the same time had been conscious that the ordinary human forces around him would not allow him to drop it in this way of his. There was also a something somewhere in his own mind warning him to be careful, a secret caution from some far level of his normal life. . . . But a point had been reached, a point—where he must go. He must! . . . His head had rolled from side to side in the urgency of his indecision. His eyes had opened wide. He must get there—to that place!

The vision of the place had risen before him clear in every detail. He had felt the cool water of the small loch caress a hand. Ah! . . . A quivering sigh, and the urgency relaxed, the body sank, while he lay pondering each wild beautiful feature of this place he wanted to go to.

The sheep-track to it was so easy to follow, the peaty track that went twisting on like a black heather snake. It was a sheep-track so lonely, so lost, that its loneliness induced laughter, a gaiety of companionship; notwithstanding that the black peat and the great breasts of the hills and the austere peaks held a certain sombre quality as an eternal mood. For that sombre brooding was known to him, too, known as intimately as were the hill birds. Let the heather-tops whip the ankles. Here was a freedom that sent the feet lightly; and the austerity, the brooding—one enters at the door with the fearful expectancy of the long-wandered child.

And his was surely a case of the long-wandered child. For this little loch in the hills, whither the sheep-track took him, he had visited only twice in his life, and on both occasions as a grown lad on a fishing ploy. He had caught brown red-spotted trout there; had tucked up his trousers and waded in, had whipped off all his clothes and bathed. Even that first glimmer of it in the distance, with the forenoon sun at his back turning the rippled surface to a molten richness of dark blue—ah, he had never seen such a blue again, it had glowed, a great jewel. Nearer, the colour had faded into that mysterious darkness of the hill loch. With the afternoon a blessed tiredness had come on his body and he had lain down and felt the place about him and merged in its stillness and secrecy and remoteness, one with it, bemused, drunk with it.

Yes, drunk with it, for what was an experience at the time was clarified and intensified afterwards. The gathering in of the hills, the shape and colour of the loch, the grey faces of the boulders, heather and reeds and hill grass, silence and listening and sound, moor bird and spotted trout, a brooding, a watching—a grouping more choice, more interpretive of the essential Highlander in him, than any chance place he had ever struck, a grouping that lingered like a memory of some magical place known to the heart with an absolute intimacy, with a sense of healing and rejuvenation in its very look.

Healing; that was the word. There the burning body could slip its burden, be purged of its fever. The hill wind would play coolly; he could see it in a dark wave coming round the slope, along the heather tops, into his clothes, through his clothes, and feel its caress on his skin, its clean honey flavour in his mouth. His mind would slip and sink and merge, and out of that mortal sleep would come surely an immortal health.

But he had to get there. He must get there. The forces that kept him back—they didn't understand this imperative need, the absolute certainty of the healing.

And then suddenly all urgency of doubt, of argument, was dissolved like a mist, and in a swift clear light of the mind he knew that he was going. Immediately a thin excitement flickered along his burning flesh, his body tossed restlessly, his eyes opened wide. But no hand came over the coverlet this time, for the head and arms of the woman now pressed down on the little table in the sleep of utter exhaustion.

Yes, he would go; he would go now. It was many hours' walk, but he would manage it, manage it all the more easily because of this lightness of the body that was on him. Yes, he would go, he would go! How the old heart beat at that and caught the breath! Let him swing his legs out. . . .

He stood on the floor, a gaunt figure in white nightshirt, swaying lightly. The eyes glittered, the cheeks were sunken each to a crease that was a sharp, dark gash, the breath came quickly, audibly, in and out. Without bending the head, without looking, he began to move round the little table with its pool of black hair, between it and the dim-shaded lamp on the mantelpiece, onward to the door. Soft-padding, tall, unbending, he passed out of the room.

The passage-way to the front door was black dark, but that did not inconvenience him; and the dog he did not see at all. The brute had come out from the mirk of the kitchen beyond, uncertain yet expectant, till at last the hair stiffened a little above the neck and a strange whimpering started and choked in its throat. He opened the front door and the greyness in the night smote the eyes that watched him a burning blue-green; but, cowering now, the brute made no familiar rush at the opening, and the man passed out and the door closed behind him.

So much for all that, for the tricks of time between boyhood and this. Now he knew exactly where he was, and already the great black shadow of Ben Fitheich towered yonder, austere, but known with a curious elation to the immemorial in him, to the ineradicable. Human intimacies, human relationships, were well, but there is a last intimacy beyond all others, a last relationship.

It was a long journey, and twice he awoke from a sort of reverie to find himself resting. The second time, that first moon-darkness in which he had started out had given place to daylight, but to a daylight screened by the filmiest veil of shadow, like a twilight of dawn or evening, yet more like evening, because of an imponderable air of dreaming in it, of memories exquisitely saddened, as they might be saddened by the limpid song of a robin as it drips into the hollow of an autumn evening. Only, it wasn't evening, but merely the hill mood playing on the still, yellow daylight.

And all the time a something more than a sense of dreamy peace at his heart, in his vision: a subtle rejuvenescence, a lightness of thistledown to his feet, a freedom exquisite and exhilarating as wine, only rarer, cleaner, less sensuous. Like a dark vein, the sheep-track wound on and on round the great curved breasts of the hills. The heather-sifted wind fanned coolly his face and sent a shiver of cleanliness in among the hair-roots and crinkling along the scalp. Long vistas at once opened out the mountains and closed them in. He was withdrawing from the ever-twisting roots and entanglements of human interdependencies. He was *getting back*.

There was an excitement in it of held laughter and alert eyes. An adventuring back to the lost places, to the ultimate source, with its grey faces of boulders and black clefts of hag, with its watching and waiting and listening, in the loneliness, in the remoteness, where a footfall might well sound like an echo of legend.

Yet in all this there was no inspiration of half-forgotten poetry for him. Of poetry as a bookish lore, a half-remembering of forgotten things, he had none.

If the shadow of reflection touched his mood it did certainly no more. He rounded the last curve, and there the little scene lay before him, so that his heart beat and an exaltation pulsed chokingly, till a strange weakening took his body, so that the flesh on his legs trembled and a strong desire came over him to lie down. But no, not yet! He would sit down there by the lochan, he would sink down into fathomless peace, and round about him would lap healingly all this from which the ultimate rhythm of him had been taken.

He stumbled on now hurriedly, details of the scene, altogether forgotten, coming before his eyes as so many little glad surprises: tiny headlands in the lochan, a twisted vein of white quartz in a rock face, a short steep scree on the off side that ended in a mound like an odd flattened cairn. . . . How dear these little things! Lord, how splendid the welcoming things! The laughter gurgled in his throat. "I'm coming!" he cried to them. "I'm coming! Hold on!" . . .

An hour of the night came when the dog got up from his crouching attitude behind the door. He got up suddenly and began to twist and twine on himself, whining, whining and trying to choke the whine. But the whine, the surge in the throat, became too great for him, overwhelmed him, drowning altogether the careful tricks of training. Throwing his head up, he bayed full-throated.

The mournful howl penetrated the woman's consciousness, and with a sudden jerk her whole body was nervously awake. . . .The bed! The bed was empty. She glared at it, the flesh on her face stiffening. Again the dog howled. She cried out at the awful sound, the awful portent, not knowing what she cried, and in another instant was stumbling blindly for the kitchen.

"Allan! Allan!" she called, her purpose gathering; but there was no answer, except the whining of the dog round her skirts.

She got out, rushed wildly round the steading. She woke the three men who slept in the hut. The oldest man had a grey-whiskered, weatherbitten face with steady, kindly eyes. The prime of his manhood had been spent in the mining camps and wastes of Alaska.

"Where's Luath?" he called to her, stretching for his clothes. Then softly, "The lanterns, boys!"

Meanwhile the woman had whirled from the door, and "Luath! Luath!" she called, "Luath! Luath!" But there was no sign of the dog now.

And presently the lanterns moved about the steading, and from a little distance looked like restless, disembodied eyes in a dream more phantasmagoric than any clear visioning of heather and lochan and hill. But they were conscious, these shadows with the lanterns, of no heather or lochan or hill about them; only of the illimitable prairie, the starlit illimitable sky, and a Canadian homestead lost in the vast expanse.

Suddenly a whistle rang out as the old man put his fingers between his lips, and in a little while there were the short excited whimperings of the dog, doubling on himself, yelping, leading them away. The lanterns gathered now, and in a group started out from the steading. Half a mile across the flat they came on the water-hole, which was a drinking-pool no bigger than the floor of a room, and by the edge of it they found the white-sheeted body of the man, stone dead.

Pure Chance

Have you ever thrown a stone at a weasel in an old dry-stone dike? The stone knocks smoke off the edges of the hole. With a thrill you think, That's given him the fright of his life!

Then you begin to wonder if you really did hit him, if, after all, the brown marauder was a tiny fraction of a second too late. So you go across and examine the hole and get the faint smell of brimstone. But the hole is empty and clean. More absolutely than if you had hit it, the weasel has vanished.

However, as you are walking away, something makes you turn your head over your shoulder. There is no movement in the dike, but your eye is at once held by the weasel's head. It has come out of another hole. It is perfectly still, watching you.

For a time you stare at it. Then, without moving, you stealthily scan the ground at hand. But there is no suitable stone within reach. Raucous primitive sounds suddenly burst from your mouth in an unaccountable fury.

The weasel is not affected. So profound an insult is this that you hurl yourself forward. The weasel vanishes. The old grey dike remains still as a mask.

My mind has grown expert at drawing pictures of the sort, at creating little allegories of this kind. I find a certain comfort in them. The weasel may appear to bob out by a kind of magic, but actually, of course, its procedure is perfectly understandable and natural. The dike has its myriad of little dark tunnels to which the conscious eye remains blind.

But how subtle the game! For I find that I am thinking like this, slipping from one picture to another, in order to give a certain weasel no time to appear. Not that I remain unconscious of it. To-night, obviously, I can think of nothing else. But I am perfectly calm. And I won't admit that this calm is fatalistic. I can argue too well for that. I could wish indeed for the appearance of the most cunning metaphysician so that I could argue him off his feet. Indeed I think of him as I write this. I create him suddenly for my own purpose. I make another picture.

So it goes on.

For I am alone to-night. I left to get certain things ready for the wedding. But I did not let my own people here know that I was coming back to town. The flat is all prepared. It is a modest place. I really had, and have, nothing much to do. This is where Morag and I are going to live.

I liked the sound of the key in the lock and the empty swing of the door as I came in. I had a premonition of extraordinary happiness, of a stillness of happiness—to which, however, I did not listen very long.

There is something in having a place of one's own. Its very emptiness creates the illusion of marvellous things to come. Never before had I understood this properly. Although I am at last a qualified architect in a good firm, never before had the human aspect of house-hunger struck me in this way. I see why a couple hunt with such desperation for a place of their very own.

I'll sleep here to-night, in the spare bed, like a guest. How rare the inexplicable mirth that thrusts its face out of the wild!

Donald MacBain has a curious face. Perhaps I think so because he is fair. Only dark men, I feel, should have his kind of mind. It was when I first heard him play the violin that I looked at him twice. He did not play with force and power.

The strings did not hiss harshly. There was no scrape. The tone came away clear and somehow extraordinarily sweet. Yet it was not lost in the shouts and stamping feet of the merriest reel. The violin looked like a toy in his hands, and he used only the upper part of the bow, as if he were not playing so much as trying a thing over, quietly, to himself.

He had been abroad, and, in India, had won fame, it was said, in some memorable tug-of-war contest.

The first time I ever set eyes on Arduan was from the cockpit of the *Kittiwake*. The four of us had sailed her from the Clyde. By the distance we adventured north you can see we had been lucky with the weather on that, to me, first and ever memorable trip. There were other cruises before the owner got married. But of all the places that we visited, never again did a spot come upon me with the brightness, the charm, of Arduan. A year ago I went there overland, for the second time, for a holiday. I did not stay in the hotel, which is very expensive anyhow, but in the white house with the slated roof, belonging to Mrs. Mackenzie, at the off end of the village.

Long narrow cultivated crofts behind; open fishing boats and the sea in front. Being a west coast sea, there are skerries and islands. Lobster pots and tangle and wettings. All the things I thrive amongst. I can feel the cold, the wet discomfort, the shudder; I can walk down the beach and get the sun on my neck and listen to the low hissing of the brimming sea on a divine morning—now, as I write this.

So they got to know me pretty well, the folk in Arduan. And I liked them so much that I don't think I could even unconsciously intrude, though I was always about with some of them, on the sea, or squatting by the barnacled stone jetty or stirring a pot of paint. My name, Stewart, is a familiar enough one to Highland folk.

There are little gatherings of an evening in one house or another in Arduan. They don't like going to bed. The children play about till all hours. You talk, or listen to a song, and if there is space and young spirits are running high, a boy will race off to Donald MacBain's house for his fiddle. A fast reel sends the spirits through the roof.

I am very fond of some of the old traditional Gaelic songs. They affect me in a way that I cannot analyse. I must make some effort to tell about this. I have never heard it discussed or seen it written about, but what happens is always surprising. A certain song will affect me in the profoundest way. With no knowledge of the Gaelic words, I yet seem to understand their emotional content so overwhelmingly that, as it were, they take on an imagery which has the attributes of fate itself, ultimate expressions of the instincts and emotions, and they deploy before me, vaguely perhaps, but with tremendous power and significance.

The first time this happened strongly I bided my time until I got the schoolmaster, a pleasant, friendly fellow, to give me a translation of the words. When I had finally satisfied myself that they were just the words of an ordinary love song which you may find in any language, I was secretly dismayed, experienced a distinct sensation of being let down!

I did not show anything of this to the schoolmaster, of course, and he agreed that it was a fine song. But he knew better songs, he said. I found, however, that his better songs were for the most part better because of their words. In this way, through experience, I began to realise that I had within me a sort of absolute capacity for appreciating this particular kind of melody. Call it my ancestral illusion if you like—sometimes I could wish it were. . . .

I haul myself back from these dark runways in the ancient dike. I have the usual uncomfortable reaction to them.

Though we travelled up on the same train, I did not see Morag until we were leaving the little country station. She got into the bus, two seats in front of me. The freshness of her fair skin was very attractive, as full of light as my own mind of its holiday. She was gay, too, talking and laughing and really good-looking, not in any "distinguished" way, but just as life looks good. She was full of life, and her brown hair glistened.

Every time the bus stopped so did my thought. The last stop but one she got up. But it was only tc say goodbye. Off went the bus again, carrying us to Arduan.

So I knew quite a lot about her—what Mrs. Mackenzie doesn't know about folk isn't worth the asking—when a mixture of us gathered one evening in Sandy Munro's house. Sandy clips his whiskers with his own blunt scissors and is fond of fun as a boy. I have never known a man so naturally at home in a boat. I suspect him of dodging work on the croft in ways too devious for even himself to follow. In bleak moments the care-free thought of him does the heart good.

It must have been pretty late that night when Morag sang. I don't mean late for Arduan. Whether the afterglow or the dawn, the light was in that still, ghostly phase, which I swear no man ever gets used to. I remembered it as I went home, and looked along the shore for Donald MacBain without appearing to look, and heard a wader crying on the edge of the tide. And I thought, beneath the wonder and delight, in a strange, sombre way, "God knows why she sang like that."

I refuse to analyse these irrational words, even now; they go too deep for me. I can't understand them.

If Morag has nothing very exceptional in the way of a singing voice—for I can discount my own prejudice in its favour—she does have the good sense to sing well within its compass. But that's just it; she sings much as Donald MacBain plays the fiddle. He is, in fact, her uncle.

There is that intimacy, that singing of the song to the inner mind, that terrible, dreadful process of evoking the ele-mental. I shall never lightly ask her to sing, not until I'm ready, with the inner forces secretly gathered—I was going to say "for the contest".

Not that I should write like this if I thought my words were utterly meaningless. But, after all, Donald MacBain did get up when she had finished singing, did get up and walk out into the night without a word.

The drama of that moment is utterly beyond telling. Plainly he could not have been overcome, as I was overcome, for I couldn't move. Besides, it was quite natural to be profoundly affected now and then. One merely kept silent for a little. An eye might glisten here or there, a girl sigh. Then expression came through in softness, in laughter, in a rare chattering friendliness, and a girl did not look back at one—or did. But the thought of separation, of leaving, was the last of all.

Something went with him that absolutely drained the room. His bulk going out seemed terrific. We held our breaths and strained our ears to listen, as though we might overhear him meeting what he had to meet. We broke up after that.

We talk of a "conspiracy of silence". That was not the kind of silence at all. It wasn't a conspiracy; it was a taboo. Anyway, it was the first time in my life that I got a glimmering of the meaning, the queer potency, of that word. As men, we didn't speak of Donald's behaviour next day.

I suspect the girls, in twos or threes, didn't speak of anything else. But I am equally certain they instinctively dropped the subject as men drew near. I cannot tell you quite how I know this, but I know it. In this region of the mind you seem to know things without evidence. That's the appalling thing about it. The weasel's head is suddenly looking at you.

In this same hopelessly unscientific way I became aware, as if told it explicitly, of a certain relationship between Donald and Morag, a curious *rapport*. They were of the same kind. Need I say that in their behaviour they were completely different. Morag's gay, bright ways were in perfect contrast to her uncle's quiet presence. But somewhere, somewhere below all that, they were of a kind, and you apprehended this in a stillness, the stillness that was the silence in which they became conscious of each other and walked away from you.

Not that they ever so walked. My mind is merely at its maddening game of making pictures. Outside pictures, I don't know how we are going to apprehend the truth. I wish someone could tell me about this. Logic is no use. It has no pictures. And without pictures how are we going to grasp, to understand, human relationships? I suppose this has something to do with the function of art. God, it wearies me.

Meg—she helps Mrs. Mackenzie in the house and is distantly related to her—was tentative as a bird with a doubtful morsel.

"You enjoyed the ceilidh last night," I suggested.

"Yes." Her hands were very busy setting the tablecloth dead straight.

"That was a new one to me—Morag's song."

"Yes."

"You knew it?"

"No. At least, I never heard it before."

"What was it all about?"

"What?"

"The song."

"It was a very nice song. Didn't you like it?"

"I did."

I deliberately waited. "There's Mrs. Mackenzie," she said with a fluster, and out she went for some dishes.

Mrs. Mackenzie could stand talking for an hour on end. But she hadn't been to the ceilidh—and clearly Meg had told her nothing about the incident. I didn't say anything about it myself.

"Morag sang very well," I ventured.

"Why wouldn't she? She would always be listening to that uncle of hers when she was a little girl."

A series of pictures followed. The note in Mrs. Mackenzie's voice was not exactly one of condemnation. She didn't slight Donald MacBain. But she did convey the idea that "it was a pity he hadn't made more of it considering all his chances"—meaning more of his life. I glimpsed Meg's face in the passage beyond. It held a brighter innocence than any bird's—and wasn't missing much.

I sensed the change in Donald, for you could hardly observe it. This grew on me. Days of it. And there was Morag. Then I got the fantastic notion that Morag was avoiding her uncle. This worked on me like a diluted acid. I was beginning to understand what avoidance meant. I watched her, without looking.

She was, I must admit, very friendly to me. You don't just run after a girl in Arduan. A small place is all eyes. You do your best in secret or delicate ways, and then nature, thriving on this kind of game, arranges the chance that throws you together naturally. This happens, and can be very exciting.

One day chance did its job perfectly. We were out of sight of houses when we met, among some close-cropped green slopes, with steep sheep-paths to shingly beaches and little caves.

She was really entrancing, something the wind blows on from the sea. At that moment, emotion got me by the throat. I felt reckless, so I laughed, for words were difficult.

However, I managed a few, but she would not come. No, she said, billowing like a sail you can't get hold of. Really, she said, she must go home.

I don't suppose she backed a step from me or billowed much either, for the wind was nothing out of the way. But suddenly I saw she wasn't going to come, and in an instant I felt: this is a test.

The usual kind of jesting followed, the sort of idiotic "Oh well, if you don't want to come!" meant to be meaningful. Suiting the action to the word, I turned my head away—and saw Donald MacBain appearing above the grassy crest below us.

Don't misunderstand me. They hadn't been together—though, of course, it would have been perfectly natural had they been. He was her uncle, a man of forty-seven. She was twenty-three and, as a child, had played at his knee. I had seen Morag coming along the path from Cromag.

She left, and I didn't offer to go with her. I had the feeling she didn't want me to go with her *then*. So I sat down, for there was a tremor in my legs, and waited for Donald Mac-Bain. He was carrying a batten of timber which he had obviously picked up on the shore. My voice was ready, even over-loud with greeting. What was he going to do with that, I cried.

For the first time I felt something deliberately distant in him. He did not answer until he was beside me, then spoke quietly, telling what he hoped to do with the batten. It was his normal manner. But after that first direct glance, he did not look at me. He started walking home.

I tried to make conversation, and that exhausts a fellow. He left me at the proper spot with a nod. I went on in complete turmoil, in a state of frustration that made me laugh. I mean I actually did make laughing sounds, though I did not hear them until I saw old Kirsty Munro looking at me, her head lifted from an old tub. I cried a respectful greeting and passed on, making sounds that might imply I had been attempting to sing. A red heat went over my flesh.

Irritation, anger—I became mentally unsteady. My mind could watch for signs and signals like a sick hawk. Shameful. I avoided Morag; and that I should *have* to do this made me wretched. Why did I *have* to do it? Heaven alone knows. Not that it was obvious, I hoped, for I did not want others to see—

except, perhaps, Morag, and I merely wanted her to be uncertain—and wretched, too.

Strange as it may seem, this set up some perverse current of attraction between Donald and me. In sea terms, a sort of dangerous undertow. I felt my body being sucked towards him—but with some dark intent of its own. And I was not afraid, though he could have killed me with one straight punch.

A friendship developed, a deep reticence being its wordless mode, almost uncanny at times, as when his voice went gentle.

I knew what folk on land—say, Morag—would think when they saw us pulling out and then setting sail for the haddock ground. It was not the kind of evening to go sea-fishing, but the smash of the wooden shell on the waves was invigorating. Cleansing and good. Sandy Munro had come out from his cottage and was watching us. "You can almost see him shaking his head," I said.

But trying to hold the boat up over the fishing ground was impossible, though it showed me Donald's enormous strength. When, with half a dozen haddock in the boat, I insisted on taking the oars, Donald shook his head. As he lay back on the pull, I saw the veins in his neck.

"Dry work," he said. "Would you like a drink?" The light smile was deep in his eyes as they steadied on me.

I got the sail ready, while he kept her head to the weather, then smartly—he could move with an extraordinary purposeful swiftness—he shipped the oars and had her underway before she had time to fall off. But he was not making back for Arduan with its "Bar" tucked discreetly away at the back of the expensive hotel.

He acknowledged my surprise with a silent humour, and I knew a sudden relief, a pleasure, in the thought that we were getting away from it. It was an exhilarating bit of sailing. Wonderful what some of these open inshore fishing boats can do, how near they can stand to the wind with a sail as tight as a board.

We made Melnavreckan long before closing time, wet a bit from inlashings and spray, but not enough to notice, and the sea-fight left peace in the flesh and anticipation in the mind.

As a pub it is nearly half human, but we got thrown out in due course, though not before I had bought a bottle of whisky. The place had been rather crowded, and this had eased talk and continued, as it were, the exhilaration of the sea.

Meanwhile the wind had risen. You could hear the roar outside. There was much talk with three men who told us we shouldn't risk it. They became very confidential about this. We went round a corner and had a drink from a bottle. They had "signs". One of the signs was the way the water spouted from an outer skerry. There were those who had ignored that sign. (I gathered they had been drowned, though this was not explicitly stated.)

Dark and enigmatic grew the talk, but warm, warm and friendly, full of strange portents mixed with soft laughter and earnestness. I produced my bottle.

The three good fellows wet their feet (for she had grounded by this time) in helping to set us afloat. I can still see Callum's face in the faint gloom as he kept a hand on her bow. As if only now realising what was happening, he said with gentle incredulity: "Gode, Donnie boy, you're no' going?" They stood there watching us until we passed from sight.

I had not the least fear. On the contrary, I was enjoying an easy recklessness, a fine excitement. Then we were hit, and then we were thrown. I got a crack on the back of the head and had a complete vision of disaster, of everything breaking up, scattered and sinking.

Wild turmoil, a whistling wind, and now Donald's voice crying near my ear: "We stopped too long. Tide has turned against wind. Going to be dirty."

I am bailing. Hanging on and bailing, with the perfected sensation of being hurled into eternity. Take it from me, that sea was eternity. Not the sea itself and only, but something in it—as the spirit is in the flesh. (There is, however, no mortal picture for it.)

The sail was reefed to a peak, and she sat at times so low that you could see the hunger in the grey-green beast as it reared behind with smoking crest, gathering itself for the drowning smash. Beasts beyond beasts, heaving backs of endless herds, racing on their primordial hunt in the twilight of the world. So will the earth itself go under them at the end, under just such a ravening seeking and smothering.

We fought them out. We preserved the mortal tune. But we did not make Arduan. We could not. By grace and Donald's seamanship we made the sheltered side of Shag Island. In the cove there we found some driftwood, and by doctoring damp matches we got one to strike. I had stuck the half-full bottle of whisky in a coil of rope. It was unbroken.

Raw fire, raw whisky, and a cave. You won't get much nearer the core of what you may mean than that. Not the cave-man core. Just the core of all meaning for you at that moment. The social reticences cease to have point. Reticence itself is seen as a force, the force of restraint. There is a loneliness without meaning. The heart knows its only glow of warmth in giving and receiving, in telling and being told. Thus have things happened to man, and made him the strange social beast he is, the beast who tells and is told.

"God knows," answered Donald, the flames red on his face and hands, in that cave with midnight roaring darkly from its mouth. He sat still for a long time. At last he said: "I may as well tell you." Then his head drooped a little, and if I hadn't been able to see his eyeballs, I might have thought he had fallen asleep.

"We are all affected like that. Some more than others. One

of these old songs can at times get the better of a person. I have noticed now and then how they get a grip on you." He turned his head and looked at me objectively. A piece of wood hissed intensely.

"It's natural enough," he continued. "That's what they're for." The hiss died down and a jet of black smoke volleyed toward me. He stared into the core of the heat.

"I don't remember its beginnings. It was like something before me, that I guided. Perhaps something I had heard from some old woman, heard once as a child, and forgotten. God knows. Sometimes you seem to get things out of the air. The past is always around somewhere. Anyway, I didn't deliberately make the tune. It grew in my head. I can remember trying bits of it on the fiddle and getting lost. But mostly it just kept me company. And there were a few words it fitted. The words added to themselves, without much meaning. Then one day it got an end. It finished itself off. I suddenly saw it was all there, so I deliberately thought of words for it. I had made a song. I was only about twenty at the time, or twenty-two. I couldn't make up all the words myself—didn't think of trying anyway. There was an old poem, very old, of which I knew bits. It had always seemed a bit queer to me. It fitted as if made for the tune. I had only to change it a very little, though I had to keep one line of words—the words that had formed in my own head and hadn't very much meaning. There were four verses—not enough for a song—not enough to tell a story. However, there it was, and no more could be done with it. It was finished for me."

He was speaking in his quiet way, without emphasis, and sometimes, you might think, with an arid humour, but that only made his attitude somehow more objective.

Now something like a bleak but friendly humour did touch him. "You see, if we make a song to-day up here, it must be a comic song, a long rigmarole taking someone off or making a cod of a place. That goes down fine. I enjoy it myself. . . . The deep things—must be left to the old songs.

"So naturally I kept the song I had made to myself. I wasn't going to have anyone making a cod of me. However, I had a sister. She was in Glasgow. She was older than me and married. She had always been very good to me—always. It was out of her first few earnings that she sent me an old fiddle—the one I still have. Before then, it was the mouth-organ or a chance at the boxie (the melodeon), or a scrape occasionally at hairy Alastair's fiddle. She had a grand ear and the loveliest voice I ever heard. She had always been good to me. A boy has to keep his independence. She knew that, too. In her own way, she could get me to do anything.

"Well, there wasn't much doing here. The herring fishing on the east coast had been bad for two years running. She wrote saying her husband could get me a job in his brewery, where he worked as a foreman on the malting side. I could come and have a trial at it, and if I didn't like it there would be no harm done.

"Her husband was a good chap, and everything went all right. I stayed with them for a time, but after that went into lodgings. You know how things can be. My sister was very Highland and clannish. Nothing could be good enough for me. He was, as I say, quite a decent fellow—and is still, for all I know, but he took a sort of pick against me. Nothing that you need notice. But there it was. I suppose sometimes my sister got a little homesick for Arduan and may have moped a bit. But not much, I should say. Anyway, I played her the song, for I would take my fiddle round with me—the little one, her own child, liked it. We would play and sing for long enough. At last I had to sing the song. I never could sing. So I sang it over quietly. I can see her face yet, the air of surprise, and then the eyes—and the tears running down. The little one began to cry next. But it didn't last long. My sister snatched her up and the tears were swept away. She could be extraordinarily happy, my sister. Well, of course, there was no rest for me until she had got that song. She was foolish about it. I told her not to be a fool, and whatever she did, never to tell it was me that made it.

"You'll know the Highland Associations they have in Glasgow, with the grand annual concert, Gaelic songs, speeches and so on. My sister always had to sing at our county one. This song of mine was going to be her great surprise. But one night—some little time before the concert—she couldn't help trying it out on one or two of us. I mean, she sang it. She sang it in her full voice. It had a queer effect on me. I felt—the song —being born. Two nights before the concert, she died."

He sat there, staring into the glow, then slowly leaned forward and pushed a balk of tarry timber into the fire. Ashes and smoke leapt up, tongues of flame and a fierce crackling. Leaning away from a swither of smoke, I saw gleaming points in the back-end of the cave. They vanished instantly. The solid rock trembled under the pounding sea.

"I got another job," Donald went on in the same light, remorseless voice. "It was a job on the docks, heavy lifting work, but I was strong, and there was good money in it. I knew my way about now. Besides, I was thinking of getting married. There was a girl used to come round to see my sister on her night out. She was in domestic service—as my sister had been before her marriage. I got to know her night out. Perhaps, at first, my sister saw to that. This girl came from Melnavreckan. Callum, who wasn't for letting us go home by sea to-night, was her brother—is still, I suppose. Anyway, I have no doubt my sister thought she had got the very girl for me. She had, as it happened. She had been at the try-out of the song in my sister's house. And she was just as mad as my sister on the old music. She hadn't my sister's voice. Her voice was smaller—but it was very sweet. It was also very true, for she had won a gold medal with it at a competition. However, nothing would do now but she must get my song for the next annual concert. I wasn't on for this at all, and as the time drew near we had a few words about it. By now we were engaged to be married. In fact, the date was fixed—for about a fortnight after the concert. But though I stood out—she got round me. And she sang the song at the concert. I was in the audience—and she came on, on to the platform. She was there, and she sang the song. They say that she never sang as she did that night. The cheering sort of started—then grew—till it was a storm. She was dressed in white. Two days before the date fixed for our wedding, she died."

He sat for a long time staring into the fire. His face, clean-shaven and full, was expressionless, a natural mask.

I could not move. I had felt the death coming, and when it came it was the sea falling on me. My body thinned to a shiver, rising up. I was becoming physically aware of the intense cold of the cave in my back when I heard him going out.

But I won't pretend to remember his third story. I think I lost bits of it in my own terrible preoccupation. He got a berth on a steamer going out East. He told me where she was going, told me everything about her. He was in no hurry and made each detail clear. There was something appallingly inexorable in this story-telling. He was not doing it in order to draw out the torture, to build up the simple, hellish climax. He was telling it as he had told the other stories, as anyone should tell a story, to make it clear. He had to remember not only carefully, but absolutely. The events were speaking through him—but he controlled them. And behind all that, behind everything—this man himself, sitting there, in his unthinkable relationship to Morag and me, and to his song which Morag had sung.

There was a "twist" in this third story, a "surprise". O God! It happened in India. This time it was a man who got the song out of him. I could not begin to tell of the psychological intricacies, the beginnings, of the enmity that grew up between this man and himself. Yet as I write this, I see and understand it all. I actually see the scenery. Donald left his ship. "I felt I needed a change," was the way he put it. And when he added "I struck inland", I knew he was going into the hinterlands of his mind. He was going as far as any road could take him. But not in an obsessive way. He noticed everything, with the extraordinary clarity of a person who stands outside himself. He was *interested* in things about him. He told me of bullocks and ploughing, or rice and poverty. I had read about it all before, no doubt, but now I saw the people moving about. I think they mistook him for a holy man. He could not speak to them, not knowing their tongue, so he just did not speak. He sat in the shade, watching them, interested in what they were doing. He described minutely the face of the first old woman who brought him a bowl of rice. I could see his eyes on her, the quiet detachment of his regard. And detachment is something which the poor in that land understand.

Then again, he already knew about the poor, the poor folk of land and sea, and something of this may have come through, in understanding.

But I am not beginning on that. News of him inevitably got about. There is a man on a horse, the owner or manager of a tea estate. He comes riding along and looks at Donald. He looks him over from the saddle. Sees the beard on the young face. (Donald, remember, was still in his twenties.) Sees the eyes that never waver, and explodes: "What the bloody hell are you doing here?"

This was very interesting to Donald for two reasons: it completely explained the attitude to a white man who "goes native", who "lets down" the horseman of his own race; but the second reason was more interesting—for all his "sahib" accent, the man had a Highland voice.

And then Donald said something of which I am not too

sure: "When I did not answer, he did not continue to curse me from the saddle: he dismounted. That made his Highland origin certain."

The man wanted to know if Donald was trying to be a "bloody fakir" or what, but in that early stage the conversation went on between their eyes. It came, however, to words, and when Donald answered quietly that he *would* take a job, the man looked at him long and piercingly—and laughed.

He got the job and was there over a year. Now that I think of it, how extraordinarily revealing would be an absolute account of that period from Donald's standpoint. No political theories, no intellectual assessments. Naked life in its relationships, its beliefs, its labour. Donald did not say he was happy, but I got that feeling, a feeling of his detachment that was yet alive and curious, that learned the language, that caught at the heart of the musical rhythm, that moved about sensibly, strongly, doing its job.

And all the time there was the "White" background. It would not, it could not, leave him alone. Particularly in the shape of "the boss"—a tormented man, whom Donald's detachment drew fatally. Things somewhere in the past had gone wrong with him, and he was having an affaire with a young married woman on a neighbouring estate. He drank at night, and now and then got Donald to drink with him. When he drank too much, instead of getting drunk, he got that awful white sobriety with its craze to penetrate mercilessly. He came at one, feeling for the last fibres of the mind. Perhaps ultimately and in essence he was destructive. Not that Donald said so. To Donald, he was simply like that there, at that time, and something in this was intimately known to him. Towards an end of a bout, there might be a challenging, annihilating intimacy between their minds. One night, goaded to sing "one of these old damned Highland songs", Donald sang his own song.

At such a moment, the man jeered at the Highlands more than at most things. Perhaps jeering at origins, his own origin, ultimately himself. Donald seemed to understand it all. And the song had an effect.

Then a conspiracy started, the sort of intricate business that suited the fellow's perverse mind. The woman was a southern English woman, but her people had had "a place" in the Highlands, had been tenants of a small sporting estate in the wild north-west. To ride forth with Donald and casually meet the woman and her husband was easy. Everyone of the whites within many days' travel had heard of Donald, of course. It was the sort of gossip titbit they could let go on. And the woman made it clear at once to Donald that she "adored" the Highlands.

"You should hear him sing," suggested his boss.

And that was the peg on which he hung his scheme.

There was a big social function in the offing, about a month ahead, complete with field sports, then songs, costume pieces and what not. Originality the keynote. This woman was due to sing, because of her really fine English voice, and a song in Gaelic just suited her mood down to the ground. Italian or French might have been a bit arty. But in Gaelic—she was entitled to that! And it gave the distinction of her own social origins with its Highland estate, its "place for the season". She could say: "Darling, I have often heard the natives sing these songs." And in truth she had.

Donald rode over to teach her the music and the Gaelic sounds. All perfectly straightforward. Secretly he carried his boss's letters and brought back hers.

Why did he do this, help this rotten intrigue? He admitted he liked the girl—the married woman—and thought her husband a simple, decent fellow, not exciting, but reliably sound.

I don't know. Was he trying to test the song? To rid his own mind? Had he really reached the stage where he didn't care, yet was interested, curious? Or was he moved in some fatal, irrational way, himself against his boss?

As I say, I don't know. Two nights before the show, they were having a final bout. It was then his boss told Donald of the plan that he, Donald, had helped so admirably to mature. Donald was to stay on and run the estate, after his boss had cleared out with the woman. The authority, in writing, was pushed across the table to Donald. Two nights thereafter, Donald would be in sole charge.

Well, the affair came off. First, the field sports. Then the concert party. She did her piece; she sang Donald's song. She was excited a bit, and in her effort at restraint showed too much feeling. The applause was of the restrained kind that made this clear. She hadn't quite achieved the air of being superior to the native piece. The song had "got" her. Perhaps no wonder, because "the boss" hadn't turned up, and by this time she may have burnt a boat or two. Anyway, his absence had made things a bit awkward all round, for he was on the field committee, and there had been subdued curses from some of the men. On a pony he was a star performer.

"I had been watching for him all day," said Donald to me; then, without the slightest change in tone, continued, "and I was still watching for him. There was a little disturbance behind, and some of my own boys came up to me in the hall. They had found him with a broken neck. His horse had come down and thrown him. I had to destroy the beast."

In the silence his eyes broke their stare and moved over the fire. Unhurriedly, he stuck his left leg out, the toe flexing like a footballer's as it caught the end of a log and persuaded it unerringly into the heart of the fire. I leaned back from the crackling thrust of flame and smoke and saw the gleaming points again—I was going to say in the wall, but it wasn't a wall, it was a blackness, and there was no face.

He must have seen my expression, for he followed my look. The gleaming eyes vanished. I was now carried beyond myself, rooted for a stone, yelled "Eyes! Eyes!" and let go. The stone exploded in the blackness.

Donald's body slowly swayed and held. Then he said: "They're not living eyes." Swaying back, I saw two glittering points. I could not stop my muscles from trembling. I was desperately cold. I drank the whisky like water and was violently sick. Then I really thought I was going to die. I did experience absolutely, for a little time, the death coldness. But death was not meant for me.

I won't tell of his unobtrusive kindness to me, of the rest of the night; but one final question I did ask. He answered that he had never heard the song again.

Neither of us referred to Morag and her singing of the song. Why? It is one of the innumerable questions I ask myself. Donald must have known I would ask myself. Could he not bring himself to talk of it? Had he had a horrible premonition, that time he had walked out? Was he warning me—in order to save Morag?

Morag, of course, had been the little one, his sister's child, in Glasgow. Now, at last, I understood what was between them. I understood it all.

But I could not, in the following days or later, mention it to her. How could I, without going too far into that death region? She had a job as a typist in a big drapery store here in Glasgow. She has, of course, given it up, because in three days we are going to be married.

You will not be so crass, I hope, as to imagine I have not thought all this out, have not penetrated the more appalling implications of superstition to their miserable core. Of course I know that the fatality attending the singing of the song was a matter of sheer coincidence. I even took steps to make certain of it. For example, Donald's own girl, who had died two days before their wedding, had caught a chill through her thin white dress in the shivering ante-room to the concert platform. The chill had "fastened on her lungs".

Coincidence. Chance. . . . We use the words with an appalling, an idiotic complacency. They drive me at this moment to a cold fury. The gambler gets a hunch, he stakes on this colour or that, this number or the other. The ball stops at his colour, his number. He breaks the bank. Pure chance, of course. Quite! Quite! But it *happens*!

I feel exhausted. This intolerable business of writing has drained me. I had hoped it would. I am going to stretch myself in the guest's bedroom.

Down to the Sea

"Poor Lachie," said the precentor to me, "it 'id hev been better for him, mebbe, if they hed pit him to the poorhoose." We were on the way home from Lachie's funeral, and as the precentor spoke he meditatively rubbed his shoulder-blade, for he was a tall, gaunt, grey-whiskered man, difficult to "pair" when it came to a "change over" at the four handles of the black bier.

But I felt the instinctive humanity in the reservation of that "mebbe"; it struck darkly, dumbly, for it boded forth a levelling sense of fellow-mortality, with a something else of inscrutable, kindly fellow-feeling. Lachie's body had been found just awash on the shingly strip of beach that lies between the off end of the quay-wall of the little harbour and the first precipice of the "braeheads". "Poor ould doddering mannie," he had no doubt, "slippit in." For though nobody had seen the way of it, hardly even the one or two ribald spirits of the fishing village had suggested anything darker. All the same, it was one of the many meanings implicit in Rob the precentor's words that it would have been more respectable, both for himself and the general feelings of the place, if the old man had died decently in his bed, maybe even in a poorhouse bed, God help him. . . .

At a certain season there moves in the breasts of all migrant things a strong beating urge. Man is not immune, but his season is uncertain, the call at once more ordinary and more mysterious.

DOWN TO THE SEA

In the two-roomed, squat cottage down at the straggling tail-end of the grey fishing village the shadows were gathering. By the peat fire the old man sat as though awaiting quietly his summons. The shadows gathered body all the more quickly because of the piece of "barked" sail-canvas that stretched across most of the window. Only the coming of the darkness did not excite the old man, for its call ran smoothly along the ways of a long-ingrained, powerful habit, a habit that could be indulged without conscious waste of thought or effort, a habit, too, that called minor supporting habits into being.

Thus, presently taking his knife from the cross-pocket of his thick, black-cloth, fisherman's trousers, shrunken round the thin legs and shredded over the "ould bachles o' boots", he started slicing very methodically a twist of bogie-roll tobacco into the palm of his left hand. When he thought he had sliced enough, he rolled the flakes between his palms, occasionally pausing to tease them out with gnarled fingers; then, taking his cutty from a waist-coat pocket, he removed the lid, scraped out the "dottle" beside the new tobacco, blew through the short stem, and, carefully recharging, saw that the old dottle, as good kindling, would be first to meet the light. This done to his satisfaction, and having blown the remnants of dottle dust from his grooved palm, he cast about him for a bit of paper. He found it in the table drawer, which held most of his valuables, from the four or so dented pieces of cutlery to his Old Age Pension book.

As he set light to the black-seasoned bowl his whiskered face and screwed-up eyes glimmered in a sort of wrinkled phantasy. His hair, excepting an occasional silver-white thread, was almost jet-black, and covered head and face generously. His eyes were dark and sharp (though not invariably, for when sitting before the fire in the hour before the darkness, they became lack-lustred, filmed, or, in the local phrase, "far away" —the "far-awayness" of the old, that is, not of the young). His lips made a sucking, smacking sound as they pulled at the cutty, and the blue-grey smoke gathered in his whiskers and round his head in a cloud.

Lifting his old-style fisherman's hat, or cheese-cutter, from the smoke-yellowed cover of the old wooden bed, he gave an instinctive look about him, to make sure that all was ship-shape, then with a slow, doddering gait made for the door, which he did not think of locking behind him as he passed out.

The north-east coast-line of the Moray Firth is wild and forbidding, its grim inhospitality welcome only to gull and peregrine falcon, to cormorant and diver. But wherever a "fault" occurs in its stretch of tall sea-cliff and low tidal-rock there will be found the little fishing village, straw-thatched or slate-roofed, home of a notably hardy breed of seamen. Small, often picturesque creeks and harbours, too often now with a grey silence about them, intensified, perhaps, by the presence of two or three small boats and a salmon cobble or so, that are as the spent backwash of a once virile storm of fishing life.

Along the side-path, with its dockans and grass, round the end of a black shed, once storehouse of herring nets and baskets, and so by a short-cut to the "shore road", went the old man. The stillness of the twilight was in the quiet air and on the grass, a silence that was a listening to one's own thoughts— or memories. Yet as he trudged along he was not possessed by memories; his mind lay fallow awaiting the finger of awakening, the thing he would respond to effortlessly, as to some old rhyme to which his marrow was attuned.

It came just as he turned the "look-out" and entered the valley cleft; it came like a crying from the ends of life, a surging and a long-drawn breath—the noise of the sea. Life and death in it, and eternity. He paused a little, and mumbled something that he himself did not hear. But there came a quickening to the eyes, and they looked out on the grey waste with a darkling intelligence; the seaman's eyes, steady, self-reliant, used to far horizons. He took his cutty from his mouth and spat. Was there pride in the eyes—pride of the sea, to which he had been, to which he was, so wedded, body and soul? An uncertain, momentary glimmer of the face, and the cutty went back between his gums.

He moved on now, as it seemed, more easily, much as the pipes give renewed lightness to leaden feet. It is conceivable that one may be proud of the sound of the sea. Never in all his long life had he known it without a murmur, never had its green lips been tired of the rocks. Never. For those who are finished with terror, and whose mistress the sea is, there may be a sharp pride in the thought and a last flicker of human defiance.

Down the grey track to the harbour he plodded on, the evening air about him and the intense glowing of yellow wild-flowers. His skin was too insensitive to feel the air's fingers, but his eyes did see one little patch of wild flowers. Lately, indeed, he had been in the habit of pausing in the descent and gazing at that grassy patch, yellow with dandelions and buttercups. Flowers on a grave have a respectable decency, and that women should be interested in them is characteristic and as it should be. But that wild flowers should be growing there, on that little level stretch, was, for a man, a thought full of desolation, more full of desolation than the gaping, roofless curing-shed which sagged stricken beside it. For in the prime of his manhood no grass nor yellow weed had grown there—because of the salt and the herring-brine.

On down the grey track, glancing at the one or two haddie-boats motionless in the shadow of the long stone-wall, at the one or two bigger boats "hauled" and rotting at their moorings, past the cooperages, with their boarded windows like blind eyes, past the tall, grey, salmon-net poles, and so towards the pier-head. Usually his walk ended there, with a long, indefinite look out to sea, a slow scanning of sky and cloud, an indistinct mumbling as to weather prospects, and so meditatively back to his solitary cottage. But of late he had got into the habit of climbing on to the top of the quay-wall that faced the sea, and of sitting down to rest himself, feet dangling above the restless water.

Perhaps the spell of warm weather had made the old man feel unusually tired. The morning had been heavy, with thunder threatening; the early afternoon sultry and oppressive; and not until about six o'clock had the change come and the atmosphere lightened. It was his own observation that the weather usually came to "wan thing or anither" round about either noon or six o'clock. He sat down with a pech of relief on the cool stone and let his feet hang in comfort. The heavy weather put one "clean throughither", he muttered, feeling a certain lightness of the head. But the cool stone revived him and the slight lightness of the head was not unpleasant. He had noticed as much before, noticed, in fact, that the lightness gave a sort of incorporeal feel to the body. Fancy gained a little freedom then; could roam backwards more easily; catch faces of boyhood; could certainly tell with far more accuracy and vivid detail what happened sixty years ago than what happened that day, or the day before, or last year, or twenty years ago.

Hunched and motionless on the quay-wall, with the darkness settling about him. No sound but the sea's and the intermittent, cavernous crying of the gulls. Weird the crying of these birds against the deep, reverberant precipices at night-time. Once the old man, troubled, perhaps, by some memory of the Castlebay and Stornoway days, had thought to himself that they might well be the keening souls of drowned bodies. Some such thought came to him now, but affected him hardly at all. In the ultimate quietism nothing is all-important, not death itself. To the hunched figure on the wall the living reality of things shone and glimmered, rather, in the magical days long dead, the enchanted days where not a face that he could now see but was touched by a light that the carnal eyes had, somehow, missed then. Boys together, bare-legged, racing the braes through endlessly sunny days; fishing for "peltags"; grouped round the cooper with his mysterious fire issuing fearfully from barrel mouth to clank, clank of resounding hammer; playing old four-corner games in the wooden gutting stations, where presently, when the boats came in, the cran baskets of herring would be "teemed". . . .

Ah, the boats! There they were, with their brown sails, magical sails. Hear the Gaelic chant of the "hired men" as mast left crutch and halyards creaked rhythmically, as mains'l went aloft. A fleet of them, dozens and scores, making out of this same harbour-basin to court the sea, that passionate, fickle mistress of theirs.

Morning and the boats coming back, racing with feather of foam at the forefoot for a good berth and an early discharge. Then the gutters in their black oilskins, stiff *rustle-rustle*, their gaiety, their wit deft as their incredibly deft fingers should a man dare a sally. . . . And suddenly glowing there before him, like a still flame darkening the grey waste behind, blotting it out, a face and eyes, and a light on the face that somehow he had never missed. . . .

Something stirred, twisting a little and knotting in his breast, as though heart and flesh held a trace of the excitement of youth's red blood. Straightening a little . . . he saw only the grey upheave of the sea and the brooding precipices.

Ay, the sea, always the sea, restless, full of infinite variety— yet ever the same, eternally changeless; and the dark, gull-haunted rocks, carven, brooding—yet ever changing, wasting. The old man had no metaphors to shield him from the direct reality of things, no movement of poetic words to bear away the starkness on a bier of flowers.

Time writes no wrinkle on thine azure brow—
Such as Creation's dawn beheld, thou rollest now.

The personal gesture of one standing on the surf edge with raised arm and a godlike, booming intonation. The old man knew nothing of that. Direct the rhythm of the grey water, direct and wordless and quite stark. Stark because of its power, its sheer, destroying power, that a man could respect, and love, too, as one could love, not a god, but a passionate, variable woman. With smell and feel and nearness in the way of it, salty to the lips and stinging, wild laughter and peace, indifference, death. . . .

More mysteriously the night gathered in, and now where waves swirled into one another were born curling eddies of blackness that bobbed on like drowned, black-haired heads. A tidal rock, just awash, assumed the appearance of a monstrous sea-animal that moved about voraciously as the waves covered and uncovered and washed lickingly about it. Movement of hypnotic waves like refluent arms, monotony of ever-varying sound ever the same, green fingers searching the interstices, green lips choking and suffocating, all gathered into one slow elemental spell, aeons old, irresistible. The old man begins to sway a little, his eyes round and fixed, his shoulders ever drooping forward. A last flicker of earth-born anxiety, wherein bits of old visions flash uncertainly—a face like a flame, with wistful, smiling eyes, threading its way mysteriously, like a moon of the soul, through swift, fragmentary passing of brown sails and voices and human gestures and old, old yellow sunlight—and the flicker goes out. Colour dies finally. The hypnotic sea, catching utterly within its rhythm that swaying figure drooping forward, forward. . . . A suddenly shocked gull sets up a cavernous crying, and the dim line of the quay-wall against the grey sea is unbroken once more.

I was startled a little when the old precentor came to a standstill by the little path that left the road for his own cottage. We had walked the better part of a mile in silence.

"Ay, he wis a bit queer," he said; "in the end he wis a bit queer, mebbe."

For a moment I could not bring myself directly to search his expression, and when curiosity did empower me it was but to find that he had turned his shoulder in leave-taking. Already he was moving off, his face to the heavens. "There's wind in that sky, and it's rain they need," he said. For Rob himself had followed the sea, but he spoke for the crofters.

The Ghost's Story

I was never a fighting man, said the ghost; yet for seventeen years I fought in the wars over the broad back of Scotland, from the glens and the moors to the low lands that spread themselves out far south of the waters of the Forth. But in all that great country there was no land so bonnie to me as my own land, the Laigh of Moray. My forefathers had been on that land for generations going far back beyond the coming of the Danes, and sometimes indeed my blood told me that they had been there for ever.

It was the year 1297, for that was the year I got married. The name of the girl I married was Janet Gordon, and she could have married anyone in all that countryside, but for some reason of her own she married me. We had our cottage and our bit of land, our small head of stock, and the outrun on the moor. She was nineteen and I was twenty-two. It was like being at the beginning of the world.

Now often enough there were wars, and chiefs would raise their men and march away with them on some wild foray. There were lads in my land who were fond of adventure. But the great bulk of us did not care for fighting. That's the way it always was. But now something strange began to happen to that land, and because it happened to that land it happened to us.

Our country had been conquered by the English. They had marched through the length and breadth of it, through all the bonnie lands of Moray, and had put garrisons in the strong castles and fortified places. Sir Andrew de Moray, who was the overlord of our land, was shut up in an English prison.

Well—so it was. But what, at the end of the day, had that to do with us? Some of our cattle had been lifted and some damage done; but far more damage had been done many a time in a clan fight, as the tales told. The lords of the castles fought, and their fighting always boded ill for us. Let them fight.

But now, as I say, something strange began to happen in that land. The name of Sir Andrew's son, young Andrew, was whispered from one mouth to another, from one tree to another; you heard it in the sound of the river water, it lay in the throat like a salmon in the throat of a pool. I fell silent, thinking of that name. And all the time like a voice in the night it called: Come!

It was not the beauty of my wife Janet that had troubled the minds of men, it was her spirit, the way she bore herself under her bracken-bronze hair: it was her eyes. And she hated war.

"This is different," I said to her.

"Ay, it's always different," she answered. "And it's always the same. The great lairds call you to their private tulzies and you go like sheep, and like sheep are killed."

"No," I said, "it's not the same. The greatest lairds in Scotland, the highest nobles, side with the English and sit fast in their lands. Moray could do the same. By rising now against the English, he is risking everything, including his own father's life. Like you and me, he is newly wed; and maybe he loves his wife as I love mine."

At that her anger against me increased. She drew her own picture of the state of Scotland in the grip of the English, with Scottish war lords supporting the English rule, and, behind that, the whole might of England herself. What chance did we think we had—we, a handful of simple Moray loons, against such powers? But though the flame of her scorn irked me a little, I replied as truthfully as I could, saying, "I think we have nearly as good a chance as the snowflake has in hell."

After that, for two days we hardly spoke a word. During the seventeen years that followed I never again experienced so hard a time as that time. Moray's voice spoke now not from the trees and the river and the wind, but up out of the land I walked on, until I knew it was no longer Moray's voice that called me, but the voice of the land itself. I looked at the land, this land of ours, this land. Then . . . I found . . . I could not look at it.

That night suddenly, and for no reason I could see, Janet gave way, and buried her face against me, and wept.

"You will go," she said at last, "you will go, and I will go with you."

All through the night we talked of it and I tried to persuade her to wait for me, to wait at home. But now that the hard wall of her anger had been swept away, she was full of a light fun, and teased me, and mocked me, and did many a queer thing besides. It was no unusual thing for women to follow their men to war. Women were the camp-makers. They cooked the food and attended to the wounded, and left the men free to forage and to fight. And Janet had always been curious about herbs and growing things, for her grandmother had great skill amongst them.

So it came about that one fine evening in the middle of May, Janet and I walked into the camp of the men of Moray. I smile sometimes to myself when I think of that odd gathering of country lads with little but a bow and a bunch of arrows to their back, and the handful of women who were sometimes with them and sometimes not. For their aim was not to defend their simple homes against a gang of freebooters, but to go forth and take great castles and reduce strong garrisons, to turn aside thundering cavalry charges, to defeat armies, and finally to smash the mail-clad chivalry of all England and drive the English from our Scottish lands. One might well say, looking at the matter calmly, that the snowflake had the better chance.

Yet one new thing there was in that little camp, perhaps for the first time in all Europe. And it was this: it was a meeting of the common people, a rising of the folk themselves, determined to win back freedom from the hand of the conqueror, to win back the freedom, not of Moray, not of Galloway, not of any one place, but of all Scotland—of Scotland, their own native land. It was a strange, fitful thing, this spirit, but it would not let us rest; a haunting, powerless thing that drove us on. Yet nameless as it was, time proved that in the end only one force could defeat it, and that force was death.

Now, because of this spirit among us, we in that company were often a happy band. In fighting for the freedom of our own land we found freedom in ourselves. From Moray we passed to Inverness. Our band grew. Young Andrew raised the standard at Avoch. The English nobles met in the castle of Inverness to see how best to destroy us. With Andrew at our head, and an Inverness burgess as next in command, we ambushed Fitzwarine of Castle Urquhart on his way home from the meeting with his escort of troops. It was my first fight. In Inverness I had gotten a long spear. Never before had I encountered a mail-clad man, but many a horse had I ridden. I made the horse rear so suddenly on that broken ground that he heaved right over and pinned his rider to the ground. Fitzwarine and a few of his escort were lucky to get away. It was our first fight, and we had won! We laid siege to the castle itself. In the dark we tackled its walls. But it was too strong for us. The Countess of Ross, who was on the side of the English, managed to send provisions to the garrison. We lifted the siege and turned our attentions to the Countess. And so the war for freedom started.

If I harp on this word freedom, it was because we soon found that the spirit that had moved us was everywhere wakening in Scotland. In July we were back in Moray, but not yet strong enough to meet an armed force sent against us from Aberdeen. We let it pass. But now, behind it, Aberdeen rose. And down in the forests of Selkirk, Wallace was waiting with his men. There were risings and there were capitulations. But ever and always Moray in the north and Wallace in the south held on. Their power grew. Castles fell before them. Within six weeks from that same July the men of Moray looked down from the Rock of Stirling upon an English army that was ten thousand strong. The moment had come at last. The fights and the skirmishes were over.

You know how the battle went: how the Scots won, and how Wallace followed the fleeing enemy to the border. But not Andrew of Moray, for he had led the way into the heart of the battle. I had seen him go down. Oh, desperately we fought, a little ring of us, over his body. Janet, running, met us as we bore him from the field. She said he was not dead, and she made us lay him down, and there and then she dealt with him according to her skill.

He lived long enough to know that Scotland was free. His name first, and Wallace's next, were put in documents of State; and then he died.

Back in the Laigh of Moray, we thought the wars were over. They had hardly yet begun. England gathered all her strength, set her intrigues going at home and abroad, and marched her forces north once more. Wallace was defeated at Falkirk and became a fugitive, hiding in his woods of the south.

Edward came again, and came to Moray, and near and far he laid our bonnie lands waste. For six weeks he sat between Kinloss and Lochindorb when the birches were turning yellow, and from there sent his armies to the taking of all the great castles in the north.

For seven bloody years after our victory at Stirling Bridge, Scotland suffered as surely she had never suffered before. She was so beaten down, with all her great lords Edward's men once more, so trampled upon and overcome, that it seemed never in the history of the world could she breathe the word freedom again. I looked at Janet and wondered, but she said no word. Our first son was now six years old, and our second son was three. She had won back from the hunted woods to our little place, and I had joined her there. Was it the end of fighting now for me? She said no word. That was in the month of September in the year 1305. I can remember the evening, for a lovely quiet evening it was. My care for Janet had grown with the years. I should stay with her, for a new birth was near to her; and the bonnie woods and the land. . . . It was in the quiet of the evening the man came to our door. I looked at his desperate face. "Wallace," he said, "Wallace—has been beheaded in London town as a traitor—and his body torn asunder."

The news froze our hearts and all the outside world, so that for a time everything was still as death. So still the birch trees were, you would think they grew in eternity. Never in my mortal life did I know so stricken a moment as that moment.

We spoke little. The man went on his way. And that night, out of a great quietness, Janet said to me: "To-morrow you will go, but this time I cannot go with you."

And on the morrow I went, slipping through the woods to join with the hunted men. And as I went I knew why Edward had murdered Wallace and torn his body apart with the bloody hatred that no wolf knows. He had done it because of this thing, this new thing, which had been in Wallace's heart, which was in the hearts of all the hunted men and women of

Scotland. Great lords he could buy and sell according to the rules of that chivalry of which he was the head. But this new thing, this love of our land, this love in the heart of the common folk, this love of freedom, this thing he could neither buy nor sell, and so he feared it.

As I went on my way, I saw Wallace again as I saw him before Stirling, and I called his name, and I wept. There in that wood I made my vow to myself—to hold by the struggle till Scotland's freedom was won, or to die.

There followed years of such adventure that the telling would take nights without end. You will have heard how Bruce was hunted by man and by beast, and how often his escape seemed half a miracle. His wife and daughter were torn from holy sanctuary at Tain by the Earl of Ross and sent prisoners to Edward; just as the son that had been born to the widow of young Andrew of Moray, a few months after his death at Stirling, had been caught and sent to England, too.

But through all these terrible years the thing that Edward feared did not die. Watered by tears and blood, it grew. It grew, and grew stronger; and at last, seventeen long years after the battle of Stirling Bridge, I was once again a spearman in an army, gazing down on the might of England, this time at that place where the Bannock Burn runs into the Forth.

In men they outnumbered us by three to one, and in wararms they outdid us still more. On the first day I was one of Randolph's men, one of that schiltrom of spears against which the cavalry of Clifford and Beaumont broke as great waves break on rocks. The spears that could not be broken, until the schiltrom broke of itself to pursue the flying horsemen.

But the main armies did not engage that day, and at night Bruce left it with our leaders whether we should fight on the morrow or, against such desperate odds, more prudently retire. But all the leaders and all the army cried out to fight, and fight they did.

It was a sunny daybreak in the middle of June in the year 1314 when the Scots went forward to the attack. Before we reached the English lines, we kneeled for a moment. At that, there was a shout from the English, who thought we were kneeling to them. I was in the centre, under Randolph, and after our right had been engaged under Edward Bruce, we held steadily against the main body.

It was a desperate battle, that battle, and we fought on grimly without a word, without a cry. But what drove the battle in our favour, rising like a slow tide, was just that simple thing which we had and which they had not, the thing which I have called the love of freedom. And it beat them in the end. It broke them. As we saw them break, the warm flood of emotion at last mounted in us, and from our ranks rose the great cry: "On them! On them! They fail!"

At that immortal moment, as they broke in rout and victory was certain, a horseman leaned over towards me. There was a soft, sickly movement in my body and I lay down for ease; and then over me came a great desire for sleep. As I fell asleep, I cried on Janet in a loud voice. . . .

My boy, Andrew, who was named after me, was cleaning a piece of ground in front of our cottage as I drew near. I went up to him with a strange excitement for there had always been an affection between us. He was a fine lad of sixteen years and working in my absence as head of the house. I stood before him and waited for his cry of welcome, but no cry came. It was as though he could not see me.

Then Janet was in the door. Her face looked scared. She took a step or two towards us and stopped. "Andrew," she said to her son, "did you hear anyone crying?"

"No, Mother," answered my son and as he glanced about him his eyes went through me.

"I thought," she said, "I heard your father crying my name."

"Nonsense, Mother," he said, but gently. She went inside. After a moment he heard her weeping, and took a step or two towards the door, but thought better of it and came back to his work.

Montrose Rides By

"There's Meg," said Dunbar to himself, "—the auld warrior." But he smothered the smile in his beard before he came opposite the door of Meg's grand lodging-house.

"Ay, Bailie," called Meg, "you'll be on affairs of state?"

"Well, Mistress, the town maun be governed."

"Ay, it's being governed. It's being tight governed as a piper's bag. And the tune you haven't called—you'll be paying for steady, Bailie!"

"Well, Mistress"—she had a biting tongue, the Hieland besom—"ye can't expect to get without giving."

"Who's getting—without giving?"

"Nothing personal intended. Ye ken that. Though come to think on't, your house hasna suffered since the military cam' to Inverness." His sly chuckle was good-natured. They often had a bout, and occasionally she said something that provided illustrative comment for the Council board. These days they had to laugh out of some corner of their mouths. But he could see she was bitter to-day.

"What I get I have to work for. That was aye the way, military or no military. But it seems the sole governing the Town Council does now is to take from its decent citizens what they honestly make—in order to hand it over to their military masters. It's an easy way to govern, Bailie, if a bit feckless."

"May be. How do ye suggest we change it?"

"That was, I thought, your business."

"Ye expect us—to stand up to them?"

"No." She shook her head. "I would never expect you to do that. That would need what your Lallan tongue calls smeddum."

He laughed. "Ye were up early this morning."

"Most mornings I see a worm about, for that matter. That's not what's worrying me now."

"Gode, you're keen, woman! What's gane wrang?"

"What's gane wrang! Here's our decent law-abiding town turned into a trooper's warren, with its earth walls and ramparts and trenches and pallisades, a port at the east, a port at the south, a port at the kirk, a port at the bridge, Kerr's whole regiment and a military governor to order the bailies to his bidding and skin us all alive. What's gane wrang! And last night they said they were going to lift my six horses and the red bull."

"Did they, faith? I hadn't heard tell o' that." It rather staggered him. "What did ye say to them?"

"I asked them if they were quite sure there was nothing else they wanted. They said yes, they wanted two pewter tankards of my best ale—at once."

Bailie Dunbar smiled grimly. He knew the humorous ways of the officers of the garrison.

"But I gave them something to think on."

"Did ye now?" He looked at her expectantly.

"I asked them whether I should pray to be saved from Montrose or from them. For at least so far Montrose has taken neither our money nor our gear, nor our horses, nor our oxen. If we were to be beggared before Montrose came, what matter whether he came or not?"

The Bailie whistled. "That was direct. Fine! And how did they take it?"

"They took two more tankards, and then the big fellow with the black moustaches and the stoop on him—the Campbell one—says he, 'There is still your house. And that's a problem. For it's a good house and you run it well. Your ale is really excellent.' "

There was a short silence in which their eyes, hard and glistening, held.

"That would fair shut ye up," said the Bailie, thoughtfully removing his eyes. "It's difficult times we live in and un-certain."

"Answer me. Face to it, man! What did they mean?"

"I have heard folk jeer, Mistress, that the town is mostly run by Lowlanders. How can they be expected to under-stand the subtle intentions of the military mind?"

"Parish after parish have been forced in to build your earthworks and your pallisades, to make you safe. But what of us bewest your bridge, outside your ports? What's going to happen to me—or what's left of me when you've had your utmost will? What's going to happen to my property?"

Only now did he really see how deadly her humour was. There were threads in her eyes. Doubtless she hadn't slept much last night.

"My property is a problem!" she cried. "Ay, a fine problem. A problem that will be left to be mucked and destroyed by the Montrose riff-raff. It's ruin, stark and staring. It's the end of me!"

The Bailie was aware of heads at windows. He heard foot-steps behind him and, turning, saw Polson, the farmer of the Bucht, drawing near. "Don't let us meet the trouble——"

"No, let it catch us up!" she cut him short. "What we want with all your governing, it's God Himself knows—but it's the folk pays; the defenceless, decent folk, who take no part or parcel in covenants or kings. That's the truth, and I don't care who hears me!"

"Good day," said the Bailie, smiling wryly to Polson. "We're having a small talk on current affairs of state."

"They have a certain interest, I allow," acknowledged Polson drily. "Any news?"

"Nothing definite, I believe—but rumour has the enemy beyond the gate."

"Which gate?" asked Polson.

Meg laughed grim appreciation of the point through her nostrils. For the Bucht, lying west of her property, was also beyond the gates. And the Bucht was a farming township in itself, heavily stocked and well run, for John Polson was not only a burgess of Inverness and a large farmer, but also a man who chartered ships from Leith to run his cargoes of salted salmon, plaiding, and deer skins to France. He was of the merchant class who had everything to lose and nothing to gain by war, who in their secret hearts cared little for Kerr's regiment and less for Montrose's—a great deal less. But he did not openly show this—though there was something more than derisive humour in his appreciation of Meg's renewed attack. Meg, of course, was famed for her tongue and her sallies. But she had all of a working woman's practical sense, and property besides. The house they stood against was three stories high. She had a score of standing beds, many of them guest beds of luxury. She had other dwellings, barns, kilns, brewing vats, pewter, brass, and fine plenishing. Her establishment was justly celebrated, and her sharp wit and love of good gossip were equalled only by her native kindness when her heart was touched.

And she could be enthusiastic over her sport of baiting the fighting animal, whom she reckoned she knew in all his guises, drinking, boasting, whispering, scheming, sticking a sprig in his bonnet and off to the wars, leaving bairns and women-folk to starve or be fondled by the tender hands of his enemies.

As they left her on her doorstep, the Bailie remarked to Polson, "She hasna altogether got a grip o' the situation, and that is remarkable, for whiles I think she kens things afore they happen."

"What's your meaning?"

"I wouldna repeat it, for I gathered it from no definite source. But if it comes to the enemy actually giving siege, then buildings bewest the river may well be burned down *before* Montrose comes, lest he occupy them as cover for his attack."

"By orders of the Governor?"

"Ye've heard as much?" The Bailie glanced at him.

"I may have jaloused as much," replied Polson grimly. "Doubtless everything must be sacrificed for the salvation of the town."

"I wish I could see more salvation in it. It didna take Montrose long to snaffle Aberdeen. The folk in the country may be despoiled, but the folk in the town may be butchered forbye. It's no a matter o' great choice, despite Meg's clishma-clavers." His tone was suddenly as bitter as Meg's.

The soldiers at the bridge saw them pass, Polson going down the riverside to his wharf sheds, and the Bailie giving good-day to Councillor Abraham and proceeding with him up Bridge Street to the Council Chamber.

Then Montrose came.

Meg put up a roaring fight for her household goods, but the soldiers of the garrison were ruthless. In recent years the town of Inverness had been spreading out on the west side of the river, from the Merkinch as far as the Bucht, and there was no time for parley with any householder. A whirlwind drive by Montrose and they would all be caught.

The scene became one of stormy confusion, oaths, shoutings, firetorches, driven animals, screaming children, men and women begging the soldiery—and daring them in the struggle to save what they could from the flames.

Outside Meg's big house her laden domestics were gathered together, whimpering and crying, for Meg herself had made a final sally into the building and had not come back, and now the joists were crackling and the windows belching smoke.

"She's gone!" The hysterical cry was taken up. Those running past paused to throw a look at the roaring scene of her doom. A couple of swine, screaming as if their throats were cut, rooted in among the domestics, who scattered in panic and set valuable articles trundling along the ground.

At that moment a faceless being appeared in the smoke of the doorway cluttered around with pewter and brass and holding in the crook of one arm a chamber-pot charged with brass candlesticks. The figure lurched over the doorstep; the apron fell from the head, and Meg's face took in the rout of her staff.

"Ye feckless, wanton, daumt hussies!" she rasped, reeled over towards them and came heavily to the ground, where she sat coughing as if she would have her lungs up, while holding to her gear. She was in no hurry now.

"Come away, Mistress," pleaded the girls, plucking at her.

She turned her baleful eyes upon them. "Where?" She coughed harshly again, then slowly got to her feet, and, leading the women, crossed the bridge amongst the rout into the fortified town.

But she was now in no haste to go to her friend's house in Kirk Street. Once beyond the port, she turned to survey the scene of destruction. The flames from a two-storied house of hers shot sky-high as its thatched roof fell in. She moaned. Tongues of fire licked out now through the smoke from the windows of her three-storied house. She felt them lick her breast. Every article she could see, from her iron pots to her feather beds, her pint stoups to her girnels, her clothes to the gold ring with her turgie stone which she specially treasured and which she had nearly perished in hunting.

She was perishing now, the fire eating up her own vitals. When the roof of the great house caved in, she felt her chest cave in, and groaned and staggered.

She held what was in her arms like a demented mother, whimpering and moaning. But through the loosened strands of greying hair that fell over her soot-smirched face, her reddened eyes gleamed steadily on the burning ruins of all that had given purpose and grace to life.

When the whole west bank was on fire, she turned away. As she went up Bridge Street a ribald voice cried, "More gifts for the Governor!" The reference was to the pot with its candlesticks, for the town had to supply the military, *inter alia*, "with coal and candle during their abode". Meg looked at the man. He wiped his mouth and slid by.

For five days Montrose laid hot siege to the town. It was known that Huntly had agreed at last to support him; that many of the northern clans who had previously been for the Covenant were wavering; that in fact some of Seaforth's men and a band of Macdonalds were already with him. The river was low, and his troopers could be seen splashing across the shallows on their foraging expeditions. May had come in, but all the scents of summer were lost in the smell of burning and destruction.

Montrose had fixed two brass cannons under a hawthorn tree on the Castle Hill, but fear of the hurtling shot did not keep Meg indoors. With grim humour, she saw the Bucht township go up in flames. In Merkinch, Rose's property went the same way. What the Governor had not burnt, Montrose did. And now it was known in the town that the countryside as far as Guizachan, twenty-six miles distant, was laid waste. "Not a sheep is left to bleat nor a cock to crow the day," as the saying went.

This is what the whispering and scheming and sprigs in the bonnets came to! Chiefs like Huntly—the daumt fox— played the game for their own profit; but the common folk— poor deluded gomerils—lost their all whoever won!

And Huntly proved the fox again. He did not come to

support Montrose. He would have as excuse, if Montrose still won out, that General Middleton had come pushing through his country to the relief of Inverness, and it would have been bad for him—and little better for Montrose—if he had intervened then.

Middleton, in fact, came so quickly upon Inverness that the first Montrose heard of him was the blowing of his bugles a couple of miles away. At that there was as great consternation in the Montrose camp as in Meg's camp when the burning had started, and Montrose saved about as little. The two valuable brass cannons were abandoned where they stood under the hawthorn tree. The shallow waters of the Ness frothed more ardently than on any foraging raid as Montrose and his men headed for Beauly.

Nor did Middleton press upon them. He was taking no chances with a man whose victories had already gathered the quality of legend. His immediate job was to relieve Inverness; and relieve it he did, entering in triumph to the huzzas of the populace. Then he left it to follow Montrose, passing on the high road to Tomnahurich the post where Captain Drummond had been shot for treachery after the battle of Auldearn. Drummond had been in command of the cavalry, but those who had played traitor, it was said, were more important men. There was the post, and, remembering Auldearn, Middleton sat for two days facing Montrose at Beauly. This was no rash general risking all on a throw. On the morning of the third day, Montrose gave him the slip and went by Spey to the Continent.

And then Meg's private war began. Her war was for her goods and chattels, her houses and barns and kilns, her six horses and her red ox. By the end of July a Commission was set up for "trying the losses of the Burgh of Inverness". Meg had all her losses by heart. She recited them like one of the ancient epics of her people. When written down, they filled pages, from the "well roofed joisted and lofted" buildings to the bolls of "ready malt", nor did she forget the gold ring with the turgie stone. She could talk about nothing else, discuss nothing else. Shamelessly she would waylay bailie or councillor. She got to know their business better than they did themselves. With the thousands of pounds Scots due her, she would build again and brew, and dispense the mercies of land and sea and vat from her generous boards.

But bailies and councillors were growing glum. The garrison had been a desperate enough burden before; now it was becoming a nightmare. The soldiery, grown insolent, walked down plots and gardens into mire. The officers demanded *aqua-vitae*, horses, and money, and when they were not forthcoming, took them by force. They robbed a Beauly chapman, and the country people would no longer come and trade in the town. Business passed to Dingwall and Chanonry. Petitions by the Town Council bore the one burden: ". . . our daily crosses are so many, which we sustain through this overburdening garrison, that almost anent our sufferings we are turned senseless . . ."

But Meg dreamed on. All these afflictions had been brought on them by the accursed Montrose. But when the money would come and the garrison be taken away . . . .

But the money did not come and the garrison was not taken away. Parliament sat and Parliament rose. Two years passed. Three years passed. Until, by way of diversion, the town was infested by Mackenzies and Mackays, demanding the surrender of the garrison. And the garrison mutinied. Nor could the governor now trust the magistrates. So Governor and troops fled. Regiments got once more on the march. March and counter march. And then King Charles was beheaded, and the honest townsfolk knew that at long last they could look out for trouble.

When Meg heard the old rumours, the tavern whisperings, that Montrose was coming again, her voice grew harsh and piercing. Bailie Dunbar avoided her now. His own mood was bitter enough.

And Montrose came. But no longer as a warrior. Meg crossed the bridge with the townsfolk to meet him, there to make her short dramatic entrance into recorded history.

It was May again, four years to the day since Montrose had given Middleton the slip at Beauly. "To win or lose it all." Assuredly now he had lost it all. He appeared riding upon a little sheltie horse, a bundle of rags and straw for saddle, his feet tied under the horse's belly, a cap on his head, and a dark old reddish plaid in rags about him. A musketeer was on each side of him, and his fellow prisoners came on foot behind. His face was pale, for he was in the first throes of a fever, and he gazed before him with the high mien that, despite his condition, made the onlookers see in him "the great Montrose".

It was the quiet countenance, the far-seeing level eyes, the complete detachment from all the winnings and losses of men, that was too much for Meg. Too much for her to bear. She broke from the throng, thinned and aged in those four years, grey wisps about her face, her eyes demented. "Look there, Montrose!" she cried, thrusting her hand at the blackened ruins of her home. "Look there, and see what you have done! Look there!" Montrose regarded the wild, screeching, witch-like figure, gazed over her, his face losing none of its calm, its weary serenity. Then he passed on over the bridge and up Bridge street to the Cross, where the magistrates had prepared a table with wines. But Montrose asked for water, and was given it; while his officers, standing under a forestair, drank heartily of the town's hospitality and glanced at the two brass cannons.

At the town's end, the Provost, taking leave of the distinguished captive, said, "My Lord, I am sorry for your circumstances." And the great Montrose lowered his eyes upon him and replied, "I am sorry for being the object of your pity." And so rode on.

The passing of Montrose affected the townspeople and the magistrates. Duncan Forbes of Culloden, the Provost, spoke to some of the council on the bearing of a great gentleman. Bailie Dunbar left the cross and went bewest the water on business. His heart was troubled. That morning they had been drafting a letter: " . . . for the burden here is so great, that we are all ready to scatter through the world where we may best . . . " The town was dead. Great men like Montrose marched in the great ways of history. The bearing of a great gentleman. Ay, ay. But the figure of Inverness . . . .

As he came against the doorway of Meg's ruin, he heard a strange sound within. Thrusting his head round the blackened jamb, he saw Meg sitting by the stone neuk of the hearth of the eating hall, her chin on her breast. At long intervals her breath came from her on a quivering sob. There was blood on her chin and her mouth was bloody and swollen.

He could see she had been struck. Because he was greatly moved, he could not go in to her. But neither could he go away. So at last he went in, and when she did not answer him, he put his hands under her oxters and lifted her up.

"Come wi' me, Meg," he said. "Like this town of ours, ye're in low estate; but it's no' the end. You inspire me to fight, woman. Lean ye on me, and wi' God's grace, I'll hand ye across the brig to your dwelling like a queen."

And this he did quietly and without spectacle.

Henry Drake Goes Home

He's like a man in a story, the country folk said. They also said he had a face like a ripe apple and eyes as blue as the sky. His appearance, at seventy, prompted such figures of speech quite naturally. There was that freshness about him, with his straight shoulders and courteous manner. The children of the Highland village would hang about a shop-door to hear his English tongue. They did not cry words after him, but stood silently and watched him go. When he was out of sight they would sometimes indulge in mimicry by giving a Devonshire twist to their "best English".

All this the Official remembered as he stared through his office window, the letter which he had just read lying on his desk before him. He remembered in particular the first visit to the small thatched cottage fairly high on the side of the glen that went inland and westward from the village. It was rough ground, steep in places, with clumps of broom exhaling a heady fragrance in the calm noonday. There was an occasional rabbit scut and a spilling over of notes from a sleepy warbler. Once he had rested, half in pleasure and half in protest, for with a day's work on hand there is always the urge to get on and get finished. However, the present "case" would not take very long, because on the claim form for "the pension" the applicant had described himself as a trapper, with income "nil".

At last the Official came over the brow, saw the cottage before him, and, at the same moment, a man walking towards the door, a bunch of yellow rabbit snares, with brown cords and small stakes, dangling from one hand. At sight of his visitor, the man turned and waited.

"Uh," said the Official, drawing forth a folded blue form and glancing at it, "uh—you are Mr. Henry Drake?"

"I am, sir—at your service."

"I have come to see you about the pension. I have a form here which you filled up at the post office."

"I hope, sir, that you have found it all correct?"

"Well, I have a few questions to ask, if you don't mind. Perhaps . . .?"

Mr. Drake nodded, and after courteous invitation, ushered the Official into his living-room.

The Official was used to all kinds of humble interiors, from the polished brightness surrounding an old maid to the last stages of decrepitude and dirt on and around an old bachelor. This was, however, by no means a noisome interior. If it had a dull bareness, at least it had order, and there was nothing smeared over the edge of the table upon which the Official proceeded to lay out his blue and his buff forms.

From long experience the Official could tell at a glance whether a woman lived in a house, not so much from the absence of feminine things, such as clothes or scalloped edges or little curtains, as from the absence of a something quite intangible but admitting of no doubt. Actually, there was many a bachelor kept a house like a new pin, complete with polished grate, scrubbed table, and even a white—not dingy—slip of window curtain, kept it with as much finikin taste as any old maid who had been housekeeper to a banker; yet with a difference, always with a difference, even with a different smell. On the present occasion, the Official had hardly even to glance at the fire, which was a mess of dust and ashes. It was stale and smelt of male death. Yes, there was the distinction: not feminine warmness and living, dirt or no dirt; but male hardness and staleness and furniture like old bones.

To be able to appreciate such a distinction was of some value to the Official. For example, the present applicant had described himself on the form as "married". Had he been a "widower" he would, as instructed, have written the word "widower" on the given line. At least, the post-mistress would have done so, for it was she who had filled up the form, all except the signature, and on such a matter it could be taken as more certain than either life or death that she had assured herself in full "as to the validity" of the descriptive epithet "married".

Accordingly, the Official assumed a pleasant manner. With possible awkward questions in the offing, it is always as well to begin by putting the applicant at his ease. So the Official jocosely asked, as he unscrewed the cap of his fountain-pen: "And what brought you all the way to this far part of the world?"

"Because there is no justice in England," answered Henry Drake.

"I beg your pardon?"

The eyes of the old man never wavered. They indeed filled with a strong light as the mouth repeated the charge against his country.

The Official glanced down at his papers with a smile. Sometimes he had to humour old men who lived alone. They got wasps in their bonnets. "Really!" he murmured.

"Yes," answered Henry Drake. "There is no justice in that land, from which I was persecuted and driven forth."

This sounded bad. The Official squared the folded buff form in front of him and, as he prepared himself to write, said lightly, "Come, now, Mr. Drake, that is surely a bit strong. However, we had better——"

"It's the truth," answered Henry Drake firmly. "There is no justice to be had in England, as I can prove to you." With that, he got up and went to a wooden chest, took a key out of his waistcoat pocket, and presently returned to the table with a mass of manuscript contained by a piece of string.

His features, which had been rosy and gracious, were now stern. The Official saw that he would have to get over this particular foible before he could hope to proceed to business. "I haven't a great deal of time," he suggested.

"It is all there," answered Henry Drake. "All my petitions are there—to the magistrates, to the Lord Chief Justice of England, to the King himself. You can read them for yourself." As he laid the bundle on the table, it shoved the buff form a little to one side.

The Official glanced at the top sheet. It was grimy to the extent of almost obscuring the writing. The writing itself, however, was firm and fluent, with flourishes at capitals. The phraseology was sustained in the legal manner, and charged with such words as "whereas" and "the aforesaid". The Official was trained to pick out from verbiage the words that mattered. "This", he murmured, "seems to refer to your wife?"

"It does," said Henry Drake.

"Is she still alive?" asked the Official, unobtrusively.

"I do not know whether she is alive or dead. She was in league with them. They listened to her. She was a liar. She was a liar born," added Henry Drake, even more firmly, "as this will show." He undid the string of the bundle with fingers that now for the first time shook a little. He exposed a document. "Read that," he commanded, and, with hand open, palm upward, he hit the document with the tips of his nails.

The Official's eye, ignoring the introductory matter, ran over a curious statistical list: 7 eggs, 2 loaves, 3 quarts of milk, 2 rabbits. . . . It was quite a long list. "Uh—this refers to . . . "

"That's what she got every week," answered Henry Drake. "Every week. And yet she sued me for maintenance. I laid these facts before the magistrates. They would not believe me. No one would believe me. At that time I still thought there was justice to be had in England. My first appeal, which I carefully drew up . . ."

And so Henry Drake got going. The Official listened with the remote interest that does not touch sympathy. He knew the woman would have her side of the case. Yet the pattern that formed itself in that remote cottage interior was curiously fantastic. The fight with the woman through months, through years, was gradually transformed into a fight with the forces of justice, until in the end this fight became a complete obsession. When Henry Drake called the woman a liar, he was no longer thinking of a living woman but only of the chief material factor in this fight. As a living woman she had quite died out of his mind.

"And so", concluded Henry Drake, "I saw that there was no justice in all England. I saw it was the one country in the whole world where justice could not be got. It was like living all your days in a bad dream. I could stand it no more. So one day I got up and left it, and took my papers with me."

He was courteous in his manner at all times, but now he had a grave strong dignity. The sky-blue eyes had gone a shade darker. There was a tracery of lines, as if the appley texture of the face, still fresh, was yet slightly wizened. He was a judge before whom his native England stood condemned. He had shaken her dust from off his shoes for evermore.

The Official bowed over his form. All this had taken a long time. There would be the usual small domestic trouble over a cold lunch. Quickly now, yet without the appearance of haste, he found out that all this had happened thirty-five years ago, that the applicant might be regarded as permanently separated from his wife, that there were folk in the neighbourhood who could vouch for his having resided in the district for the last twenty years, together with other necessary details that had to be inserted on the various forms. The question of means presented no difficulty. Although there were some three acres of land attached to the cottage, Henry Drake kept no stock. Neighbours were kind in the matter of milk and potatoes, and there were seasons when he made a few pounds out of rabbit trapping. The Official could see, however, that he was not at all of the begging kind. Quite the contrary. In the end, he entered his total means from all sources as, on an average, eight shillings a week from trapping, and this placed the applicant well within the limit for the full Old Age Pension. There remained only the question of his age. He had no birth certificate, but in due course the Official, who was now genuinely anxious to get him the pension, traced his family in the 1861 Census, where Henry Drake, a son, was shown as three years old.

Each year after that the Official paid Henry Drake a visit, handing him a new book of ten-shilling orders, and getting him to sign a small document to the effect that his living conditions had not changed. As he was himself fond of hill sport and interested in wild life, he would chat for a little while before taking his leave, careful at the same time never to give the old man a chance to introduce his obsession. And in fairness it must be said that, on his part, the old man never again attempted to bring the matter up. With his pension, he seemed to have settled happily and finally into his background, his health good, his cheeks fresh, his step firm, his eyes blue.

Time went on until a certain day in September, when, as the Official sat in his office, there was a knock at his door. "Come in!" he called, and Henry Drake entered, white hair neatly combed and cap in hand.

"Ah, Mr. Drake, come in!" the Official welcomed him, getting up at the same time and offering his visitor a chair.

"Thank you, sir," answered Henry Drake. "I hope I do not intrude?"

"By no means. Take a seat. And how are you keeping?"

"I am very well, thank you, sir, and I hope I see you the same."

These courtesies over, the Official asked: "Well, now, and what can I do for you to-day?" And then he saw a look come into the blue eyes that he had never seen before. They stared past him in a hazed way.

"I was thinking", said Henry Drake, "of going on a journey, and I was wondering about my pension. I would need my pension."

"Well, I think we could arrange that," answered the Official pleasantly. "Where were you thinking of going?"

"I was thinking," said Henry Drake, in a voice vague and strange as the look in his eyes, "I was thinking of going home."

"Home!" echoed the Official.

"Yes," answered Henry Drake. "I was thinking I would like to go to my own county of Devon."

The Official looked closely at his visitor, then nodded slowly. "I see," he said. "It's a long way, Mr. Drake, and, as you know, war has broken out. You must remember you have been a long time out of Devon. The people you knew there—may not be there now. Let me see—how old are you?"

"I am eighty-two," replied Henry Drake.

It was a great age. Still, something in the demeanour of the old man made the Official hesitate to suggest directly that, for the time being, in any case, it might be wiser for him to stay where he was. "It's a long long journey," he said, "and you would have to get out at many railway stations and change."

"I am going to walk it," said Henry Drake simply. "I walked here on my own feet and I can walk back."

"Walk it!" echoed the Official.

"Yes, sir," said Henry Drake.

And so it finally was arranged. Nothing could move the old man from his decision. It was clear, of course, that he had not enough money to pay for his railway ticket. He had not sufficient shillings to keep him going on the road. Yet he was too independent to accept even the suggestion of help. He would manage all right with his Old Age Pension, he declared, if only an arrangement could be made whereby he could cash an order from time to time. That was why he had come to the Official.

The Official did all he could for him, as if, indeed, the old man were his own father setting out on a perilous but fated journey. As they shook hands, Henry Drake said, "Thank you very much, sir. You have been kind to me. All the people in this land have been just and kind to me. But it has come over me that I must go back to my own country."

"I understand," replied the Official gravely, aware now that the outbreak of war had touched a profound instinct in the old man. "If ever you are in difficulties, you will remember to refer the authorities to me."

That piece of advice, certainly, Henry Drake did not forget. The Official was able to follow the old man's journey by the letters he received from the police. But in spite of detentions, in spite of what appeared to be temporary illness or exhaustion, Henry Drake went on. Through the Perthshire Highlands, through the Lowlands, he tramped his way. A letter came from Carlisle. He had crossed the Border.

The year was wearing on. Cars and lorries would overtake him, hurtling past along the great south road. But his head would not turn round. To expect a lift would not occur to him. The Official now understood Henry Drake better than ever before. That solitary forsaken figure plodding along the edge of the great road assumed lines of a mythical simplicity. The ways of a wife, injustice among men, were no more than the accidents of life. Henry Drake was going back to something deep in him as life itself. Indeed, the spirit had already gone back. The body was struggling to follow.

When he had got beyond the Lake country, on past Lancaster, the Official began to have hope. He took out his car map, studied the route, and thought that if Henry got through the Manchester area, he might in truth reach his journey's end.

Then came a long silence—broken this very morning by a letter from the local authorities in Manchester, requesting all possible information concerning one Henry Drake, a vagrant, who had died in a poor-law institution. "Deceased", said the letter, "was in possession of a Pension Order Book, No. 1413, issued at your office, of which six orders are due but uncashed."

The Official sat quite still in his chair for some time. Then he got up and removed from the Register of Pensioners the loose-leaf containing the short life-story of the dead man. For a minute he toyed with the idea of adding to his report that the deceased had expressed a strong wish to be buried in Devon. As if that, he thought, with a small ironic smile, would make any difference.

And then, in a moment, he saw that in truth it would make no difference, one way or the other. They could deal with the body as he himself would now deal with this loose-leaf. The spirit eluded all bureaucratic forms. And the spirit of Henry Drake had gone home to Devon.

The Telegram

" I am now an old woman. The years have been going over me that fast I hardly noticed them—until this came, and now time stands in the houses and on the shore, ay, and on the little field you will be looking at from the door, hearkening."

She spoke like that, not exactly sadly, but with a rhythm in 'it that evoked a queer feeling, something that seemed familiar far back in time but had got suspended or lost somewhere, and I raised my eyes, too, and stared over the little fields at the sea, a dark-blue sea that went flat to a remote horizon. Had the sea been really flat and my sight good enough, I could have seen the coast of my home State of Maine.

"For five months now we have been waiting," she said, "for five months."

Only the Atlantic lay between the shore I had played on as a boy and this island in the Scottish Hebrides where my mother's grandfather had been born. I began thinking of my mother, about a certain softness in her voice when she used to tell us stories as children.

"Sometimes word would be coming that seamen had been rescued in some distant place of the world," the old voice went on, "and then there was no rest for us until we found out. But always the men were never our men, never our men, and so the waiting would begin over again. Sometimes Shiela down there would be listening on the wireless at certain times to hear if the enemy had any names they would be giving of men they had taken on the sea, but though often enough they have been heard to give the names, they never gave our names, not our names."

From the small green mound on which we sat I could see Shiela's cottage. She was a pleasant, good-looking girl and had been showing me how they work their primitive looms. It's a small loom for one person, operated by the feet, with the hands free to attend to the shuttles, and the cloth it produces is called Harris Tweed. Since coming to Scotland I had learned that there is a considerable export of it to our country, so I had plenty of questions to ask Shiela. I liked her voice very much, liked listening to her, but I find it difficult to describe her smile; it sort of waited, as light waits, and then her eyes flashed on you.

Now a thought struck me and I contrived to ask the old lady if Shiela had a particular interest in anyone aboard the missing vessel.

"She has that," came the answer quite simply. "He was a clever lad—and indeed it's herself that's clever too—and he learned to be a wireless operator, and that's what he was on the ship, on the *Batamor*. Perhaps that's why she keeps on thinking that news will come to her on the air."

"Has she said that?"

"No. She would not say that to anyone. But I know fine she thinks it, for the young have life before them and they cannot believe they will be cheated of it; even though that has been happening. . . . Nowhere in Great Britain has there been such loss of life as we have had in this land you have come to visit, for here the men were men of the sea and all of them who were able-bodied were in the Naval Reserve. They went at the beginning, the beginning. The sea took them."

I waited, looking upon that sea so quietly blue under the harvest sun.

"But our place was spared. It was spared because the *Batamor* was spared, for no less than eleven men out of this small township were on her. All on her. Eleven of them. And now for five months she has been missing."

The township consisted mostly of straw-thatched cottages with curved roofs scattered here and there, and the small fields were like oddments of coloured squares in a bed-quilt. Grey-haired men swung a double-handed scythe and women and children gathered the grain as it fell and bound it with straw bands they twisted deftly.

"The news she was lost came first from Australia. The Navy Minister there said that one of his warships, which was out searching for survivors from a boat that had gone down, came on a lifeboat. It was drifting all by itself on the Indian Ocean. That was the way we first heard the news. We waited, and we waited, but no more news came. Then tidings reached us that British seamen had been rescued from an island far in these distant seas, and our hopes went up, for the school-master has all the maps of the world, and he said that it could very well have been the crew of the *Batamor*. But it was not the crew of the *Batamor*. So our hopes now went down lower than before. A long time passed, and then word came that British seamen had been rescued from the coast of Africa. The name of the place, I remember well, was Mogadishu. And they all said that it would suit the circumstances and the time, for they worked it out, them who know such things, and they said it would be a very likely place for a German raider to land any crews she had taken on board. And this time there was truth in the story, for men were rescued from Mogadishu. Yes, they were rescued, but among them was no one from the *Batamor*, no one."

All the oceans came lapping about this remote island, and I realised that here was no primitive spot but a place that ex-tended to the utmost corners of the earth, to all places where seamen wandered and men and women lived. My own coast of Maine and the coasts of Africa; winds over Indian and Eastern seas; empty boats and death, and the strangeness that gathers all into one old woman's voice, with the rhythm in it of the sea itself.

I was caught now in a curious spell, and I know that that is the thing I really cannot communicate. I know, because I have read over what I have written and had to stop at that mention of my mother. If it seems that my mind had gone soft there, just a little sentimental, that's not what happened, for I saw her distantly. I saw her as if I were looking on at what she was doing, at her movements, her pale smooth neck, the expression on the clear skin of her face and the light in her eyes, and I saw the three faces of her listening children, of whom I was the youngest.

Here, again, I was listening to a woman telling a story, and over me there came the old reluctance to speak, to ask any question, as though everything would unfold itself if no voice interfered.

It was the same kind of listening, though my mother was telling a simple story to three small children and this woman was telling the story of all humanity to a man in a soldier's uniform, who had got a short leave and had been moved by an amused or (as it had seemed) absurd curiosity to find out what this little lost spot on the map was like.

One thing more—for I may as well give myself away properly when I'm at it: there was born in me, as I sat on that green mound, a new conception of woman, and I was aware, even as I listened to the old voice with its haunted rhythm, that I should never forget it.

They had had no more news of the lost *Batamor*. But hope was not entirely gone. Not until the war would be over and every port of the seven oceans searched, would hope wander away from these little fields and from the strand where the small fishing boats were hauled up. In the meantime the figure of hope was invisible and somehow dark as it stopped on a threshold or moved silently behind a woman reaping in the bright autumn sunshine.

My time, however, was up, for I had to get to the east side of the island to catch the mailboat which would call that evening on its way to the Scottish mainland. I think everyone in the township shook my hand—and Shiela's hand I won't forget—and as I got to the crest of the slope and turned round, they waved to me, the old and the young, pausing in their harvest work to give a last farewell to the stranger. I was laughing and waving back and indeed was so blindly moved that I all but got run over by a mad boy on a cycle. The small pebbles of the road shot from his wheels as he whizzed by me on his rattling piece of old iron. But I had seen his eyes.

All the others saw him, too, and each stood rooted in the ground. The machine went down that slope like a young tornado. But it must have had some sort of primitive brakes, for when the boy parted from it he was only brought to his knees.

And there was Shiela, not going over to the road to meet him, but waiting by the cottage wall, and she waited until the boy went across to her with the yellow telegram in his hand.

She took it and looked at it, but she did not open it. She had a short talk with the boy first, while the world stood still. Then she opened it.

She started running out into the fields, and her high cry released all those whose feet had been held by the earth.

It was the most extraordinary sight I have ever seen, for of course their feet had been gripped not by the earth but by death, and now they were released and they came running. The old women wore loose wide skirts to the tops of their boots, and they pulled them up a little and, waddling like strange dark birds, converged on Shiela and old Maria, my story teller. The old men were slower, some of them continuing to stand with the scythes in their hands, like figures of time in a story book. Then they dropped their scythes and began to come too, but with a solid purposefulness, as though to a strange rite or to repel enemies. The young went like the arrows their cries shot in the air. The sunlight caught the cries and threw them far and wide over the silent potato flowers and the standing grain. There were glad cries, but also there were high sounds of weeping, but somehow in my bones I knew that the weeping came from some of the women who could hardly bear the knowledge that what they had created was not yet destroyed.

I watched them for some time, terribly curious to know exactly what had happened, yet strangely reluctant to go down. I sat on the roadside and thought I would wait for the boy who had brought the telegram. But only when I was beginning to get anxious about my own time, did he at last appear, driving the cycle up that slope, for they had fed him cream and honey.

I stood right in the middle of the narrow road and he jumped off. I had hardly begun to ask my question when he answered with a shy breathless earnestness: "Yes, they're all saved!"

I shook hands with him and let out a cheer. I asked him who saved them and where they were.

When he told me, the news itself might have acted as a slight damper, for though the eleven men were alive they were actually prisoners in German territory, but it didn't affect me like that at all. For some reason, it was a spur to my spirit. It heightened the fun of being alive, made the thought of action wonderful.

"Do you think", came the boy's voice, "that we will take that territory and set them free soon?"

"Think?" I cried. "I don't have to think—I know."

He walked with me for three miles.

Half-Light

I

'Where the half-sphered scabious nod in a purple mist." The words were pencilled on a scrap of an old envelope as though jotted down hastily or in semi-darkness, and represented the only writing of any sort found in his clothes. But to me the words represented—what?

I could not answer. They haunted me. Haunted me more uneasily than ever, when, after an absence of some years, I got caught again in the half-light which comes to that grey northern land when the sun has died finally beyond the headland that crouches like a beast on the sea, shutting out half the western world. There is a quality in this half-light that is at once a closing in and an awareness. Colour intensifies, "runs", so that the ditchside of kingcups at hand becomes a sheet of gold, and the field of "half-sphered scabious" beyond the bank a veritable ravishment of "purple mist". Into the silence creeps a listening stillness. The bleating of a sheep or far barking of a dog dies out in ears that continue to hear the echoing forlornness. Upon the body itself, squatting stiffly, steals that subconscious alertness which, if a sudden hand were to descend on a shoulder, would cause a jump with the heart in the mouth. A bathing, a physical brooding. It is the hour of the earth spirit.

But not alone of the earth spirit. All that has been bred of the human spirit for untold generations is interwoven in this web, so that vision loses focus in a sense of human things forgone, of heroic days leaving ghosts to an unearthly half-light. . . .

And thereupon, as though waiting its chance, through from the back of the mind comes the thought that possibly he saw it like this, and, having seen, was driven to jotting down "notes" like any conscious, deliberate artist. That was the uncomfortable thing. I *should* have been prepared to accept the tragic circumstances as they were plainly accepted by the village or township. The young headmaster had taken to the practice of bathing down by the rocks in the evening after school hours. Then one night he didn't come back, and later a little heap of clothes was found in Breac Cove.

Deep, green water licks about the black barnacled rocks by the entrance to Breac Cove, the speckled cave, with its astonishing walls of purple and yellows and greens, with its great flattish roof curving to the droop of a gashed upper lip and thick with tiny stalactites, which can draw no answering forms from the multi-coloured pebbles that slither uneasily beneath a foot. Wrack of sea-ware here, too, going inward in parallel lines of high-tidal storm, till all is swallowed up in a threatening gloom. Regarded steadily, this gloom seems pierced sometimes by the beady eyes of monstrous tusked sea-animals lying in wait.

That, and the disturbing scabious "note"—together with my most vivid memories of his attitude to this same grey sea-board when we "digged" together in Edinburgh. His vehemence had startled me. "I tell you I wouldn't go back there—no, not though it meant a fortune; not though it meant——" Wordless, he waved an arm and laughed harshly. "The place is dead, man! It's done! Good God, it's full of ghosts! The little harbours are silting up, the curing sheds are roofless, the boats are gone. And what else is there? What else was there ever there but life in the heyday of the old mad fishings? What are the few crofts but crouching, squatting brute things—dead, too, by heavens!" He walked up and down, while I continued to stare at him. The face, normally pale, had whitened to a lip-twisted intensity; the eyes, normally lazy, blazed with light. "No, not likely! We've been starved enough! When I get my degree I'm going out East. I'm going to get warm with colour and sun and snakes!" Then he became conscious of himself and sat down; but somehow his throaty laugh died abruptly into a long silence.

That was his first real outbreak. But once he had thus shown his mind, it appeared much easier for him thereafter to refer to the matter. Any desolate scene, any description of grey wastes, would draw a sort of commenting undertone. "Just so!" He understood all about it. Not much could be told him. The most fearsome and ungodly places could at best draw a nod. "Quite. I follow. But——" "But what?" "To be the finished article it just lacks that something of decay——" "Look here, Iain, you're getting positively distorted, a bally decadent——" "My dear chap, who's the decadent? Do I go reading all that sort of stuff you do? Do I have anything to do with Celtic Twilights or quattrocentists or any life-at-second-hand business of that sort? You enjoy that; I don't—no more than I do the grey wastes—yonder!" "Well, dammit, why can't you leave the blessed wastes alone?" "I'm going to, I assure you. Don't worry about that!"

I didn't exactly worry about it. Yet like a poison his tormented visioning of our birthland must have got some sort of hold on me, for a chance occurring to spend a protracted period in Italy I jumped at it. Free of his influence, in that land of colour and sun, my memories by degrees so softened that I was guilty once or twice (the stifling heat and the flies of high summer!) of writing verses to that birthland, each line drenched, indeed, in the cool dews of the northern twilights. If only old Iain had been able to look through his eyelashes. . .
Then came chance word that he had accepted the old Oulster

school. I was shocked. I should have been infinitely less shocked, I think, if I had heard he had proceeded to the South Sea Islands and gone native.

No one else appeared to be shocked, however. A stray home paper reached me, commenting on how happy the appointment, how fitting indeed that an Honours graduate should return to shed lustre on the places of his boyhood, and (they doubted not) be instrumental in equipping many a bare-legged laddie for future high appointments in Church and State. I laughed. So much for these old proud college-day ideas. How quickly, how smoothly, the world puts them in their place, oftenest without even the sentimental paragraph of the local reporter! In truth, I didn't quite know whether to be sorry or pleased about it; for I am willing to confess that Iain's sensitiveness to seaboard "atmosphere" had not been lost on me. I had always been jealous of justifying the artist, the literary spirit; and how disturbing had been that elusive atmosphere to him then, how real! I had understood intimately—even while I may have wished that the old homeland had not been the subject of it. Still, in this new twentieth century, with its wonderful promise for humanity, its clear vision of progress, the very troubling of Iain's spirit was hopeful and stirring. Yet now here he was apparently, having sloughed this sensitive skin, settling down to the daily round, much in the style of hard-fisted business men who have had what they regard as their callow Tennyson or Browning days. And that I didn't like.

However, there was plenty material of assurance for me in Italy, inexhaustible assurance, and it was not until the succeeding autumn that I visited the homeland—to find Oulster hush-voiced in gloom. Breac Cove with that little heap of clothes, the scabious "note", and my Edinburgh memories. . . . I got up from the ditchside. Could I accept the "accident"? Would there not be some more "notes" somewhere among his papers? . . . But the northern chill must have crept to my bones, for I shivered again.

2

To come into the presence of Iain's mother is instinctively to perform some act of courtesy. A welcoming, a mysterious something of the spirit, a living hand. Your mind hesitates; words, conventional words of sympathy, wither away in this air of steadfastness, of natural dignity.

"The sea is cruel," she admits. "I've always been frightened of the sea, though we've always belonged to it. We managed to send him away—but he didn't escape it." The eyes moisten, the lips grow tremulous, the worn fingers make a pleat of the black silk dress. "He always had a word for you."

She nods. I turn away.

"He was a good boy to come home—because of me. But I should—I should have left him."

In the end as I prepare to go, it is with the utmost sincerity I manage:

"I thought I might be of some little help. All his books and papers—I could arrange and pack them—anything like that."

My hand receives a quick pressure. It is very kind of me. I mumble something, to find that the tears are in my throat, that they sting my eyes. I turn quickly up the little path from the schoolhouse.

Next day she left the schoolhouse to return to the old fishing cottage, her brave adventure over; back to the old walls, the old memories, to sit through the half-light till the fulfilment of the promise of a final Dawn.

Her going gave me a whole evening, a whole night, alone with his books. I locked the front door, I drew the blinds of his study. My legs trembled with excitement. There was just this about it: I felt that were there anything unusual in the manner of his disappearance, then the information were better in my hands than in those, perhaps, of any other. Whether I could understand better or not was an argument that did not arise: I knew definitely I could so keep the information to myself that his mother, having made her renunciation, should not be aroused by the black iniquity of bowelless gossip.

The first superficial survey of his study astonished me. Yes, he had very decidedly started reading. I skim over the bindings. Fancy gets struck by the prevailing note of green, from the lengthy row of old Bohn's Classical Library to quite a number of books on the sea. Sea-green, I think, and pause to look more closely at obviously new backs. As title follows title I hear the sea's surge, on tropical reef, on grey rock of the Hebrides. The grey note is actually interspersed, too, with an early Yeats and, yes, a grey-covered Fiona Macleod.

Of course! I pluck out the Fiona Macleod. . . . Ah, I expected it, I knew it! The volume is pencil-annotated into a criss-cross jigsaw puzzle. Here on a double sheet of notepaper are something like the beginnings of a considered essay— on the Celtic Twilight! The opening satire is good, if a trifle bitter, sweeping. He finds it difficult to be patient. Then my smile dies. A short paragraph, and our seaboard lives before me. Gathering one or two choice Celtic blooms he tosses them into the seaboard atmosphere, and immediately they shrivel up like flowers in a grey frost. "Here's the Celtic Twilight for you if you like!" he says. I rebel in the first words that come: "Ah, but you forget that you are looking at an old literature with a modern, agnostic eye. That makes a difference!" And suddenly his face is before me, his mouth twisting. "And wasn't Fiona Macleod a modern?" I snap the book shut.

I have got to make a pathway through this jungle of reading and annotating: he has got to put the weapon in my hand. Promiscuous quotation would be like cutting round and round. Let me take a poem of his, both because it hints at the real significance of that scabious "note" and because verse-making does necessitate some thought-refining, a certain quintessential treatment of idea. It is the only completed poem I find—

whatever else of verse there is being fragmentary. It is also interesting as carrying on the Edinburgh attitude, so that there is a certain mental continuity—with this addition: that he is now attempting to give concise expression to his physical desire for the seaboard's opposite.

It is headed "The Croft", and the opening verses run:

> The dark wind up the braes
> From the cold sea
> Comes whining its barren ways
> Through the grey tufts, days on days,
> Mercilessly,
>
> Combing each withered mass
> Of wilted hair;
> Between the tufts there pass
> The lean kine cropping the grass,
> Grey-green and bare.
>
> No more colour nor sound
> Than that. The stern
> Lean years are all around,
> Grey boulders that abound
> For death's grey cairn.

The poem is called "The Croft" as though instinctively the mind of the writer felt that it is the earth spirit that is the dominant thing—not the dominated human spirit of the old crofter. For from this point it is the old crofter of the poem who speaks.

> Here from this sheltered lair
> Of blaeberry
> And withy stems I stare
> At the dead years and dare
> My blasphemy.

And so he is off. As the whole runs to very many verses only the trend need be shown. There is, for example, youth's visioning of the "colour and sun and snakes", the seduction of the East:

> *Days out of mind did the beat*
> *Of my heart rhyme*
> *The pulse of illicit fleet*
> *Passing of sandall'd feet,*
> *Days out of time.*
>
> *As Chinese lamps come aglow*
> *To a piping flute*
> *Did my secret dream-flowers blow*
> *Into colour and luscious sweet flow*
> *Of forbidden fruit.*

Luscious and rich enough, but savage, too, where

> *Vast scorching noons held sway*
> *Over naked flesh*
> *That trampled down the desert's way. . . .*

The realities are envisaged to the sweat-blinding and the "miraged mesh". Nothing "twilight" about it. On the contrary, a savagery—sometimes more concealed than may appear. For these things have been denied by the grey years that lie about him like inescapable grey houlders. And he misses nothing, as though every forbidden, sensuous thing had to be savoured. Colour cannot be left alone, till in one verse it is positively—or sardonically—cloying:

> *And colour that ached on the eyes,*
> *From snake-lustred gleam*
> *To scarlet of poisonous lies;*
> *And colour more soft than the sighs*
> *From passion's hareem.*

The temptation to quote is strong. I realise, however, that the appeal of the verses to me may be bound up in the personal element, and that to the normal reader they may be quite unexceptional. But the concluding three verses I should like to quote in order that the Edinburgh attitude may be given its due Scots metaphysical twist, and a seal set to his whole thought up to this stage. Here is the croft, here his denial of it, his rebellion against it and its "grey creed"—his "blasphemy", as he calls it. Then:

> *Sin? And my dried lips twist*
> *On this childish name*
> *For the fire and the knotted fist,*
> *The dream-woven gossamer mist,*
> *The flame upon flame.*
>
> *Colour and passion and sun,*
> *These three my gods*
> *Over all—and these three were one—*
> *Painting with sundering vision*
> *The very peat sods.*
>
> *Sin? Till wild laughter shook*
> *When the word it saith:*
> *Till old laughter—stares at the Book*
> *That stares back with Jehovah's look*
> *And His grey breath.*

3

In the absence of anything more forceful than "The Croft", I found myself compelled to adjust my premonitions. That the theme should have been a croft and a crofter rather than the sea and a fisherman pointed to one possible interpretation of everything; namely, that he had found in such literary outlet for his feelings some sort of relief; more, that the very "complex" which the seaboard stood for became, through the literary channel, an original unifying theme for essay and verse. I know only too well how scarce original themes are for the modern writer, how he has to hunt for one and quarry in it. Here, on the contrary, was clearly an obsession, instinct with qualities, awaiting a virile development that would be a most realistic counterblast to the Fiona Macleod twilights, from the land of Gaeldom, and using, to begin with anyhow—as will have been seen—the old poetic rhythms that he might one day destroy.

Quite. It explained everything. I became conscious of the loss of a fellow-worker who might have set our seaboard on fire. At that moment I tasted the bitterest sorrow of his passing. Yes, it surely explained everything. The scabious business was just the colour line of some contemplated poem; the bathing no more than a purging of the day's petty toils before the compositions of the night. That he should have been plucked away like that. . . .

I took a turn up and down the study. The small hours were upon the deserted schoolhouse. A sense of stillness and empty rooms surrounded me. In an involuntary vision I saw some of the doors of these rooms standing agape, others blindly closed. Tenantless; their emptiness crowding round this ghostly brain of a room I walked in. What was I doing here? . . .

I lifted my mind from this trivial by-play. "Yes, it explains everything," I said. And by the very sound of my words in the silence I suddenly knew it explained nothing. There was a "feel" for life in him, for naked life, that no creative artistry could ever satisfy. Life itself was what mattered, was the blinding thing: not its expression, its "life-at-second-hand business". . . .

What was I doing here? The question became insistent. The backs of the books regarded me in a certain way. The very swirl in the air I made as I walked was, as it were, populous with the question. I stopped dead.

I had no fear of Iain Mackay. I had no fear even of the appearance of his naked spirit. Whatever of mere curiosity there may have been in the original twist of my thought, there was certainly nothing now but that curiosity actuated by a sense of service. I should like to be the discoverer of knowledge so that his mother might be safe. . . . Safe from what? For the first time I really faced the question. The books watched, particularly Fiona Macleod, which I hadn't pushed right flush with the others. Safe from—from—I dismissed the halting horror. Iain Mackay, I thought, deliberately, epitomised in himself this particular sea-coast. He knew with an intimacy of the marrow its uttermost essence. He merged again with that essence willingly or unwillingly, but in some way *wittingly*.

I paused, listening, on edge. There was Fiona Macleod. In an instant I had gone up and smashed the book flush. On a level with my face on the top shelf of the bookcase was a tobacco smoker's cabinet, and as the bookcase shook under the impact of my fist the little wooden door of the cabinet swung noiselessly open, revealing to my staring eyes a blue tobacco jar and a black-covered, thick notebook leaning against it.

A notebook! Presently my hand reached out for it; then restraining a desire to look around, I went deliberately to the oak knee-desk and sat down.

4

It was a diary of sorts, at least an irregularly-kept record of evening excursions and midnight thought. It starts with the Edinburgh attitude, toned down, as theory must be toned down, in face of actualities. He notes things, names them, severs the thought from the fact in many a raw local phrase. This impression of coming into contact with things physically is very vivid, the visual sense being curiously abetted by the tactile. You can not only see the grey rock his hands touch, but feel its roughness with his finger-tips; and not only the tactile but the auditory as well, so that when sand is rubbed by his bare soles on a dry ledge of the rock the sound sets your teeth on edge.

And you sense the same old aim in it all. He is at his game of purposely stripping things bare, tearing ruthlessly the films and the fancies, so that the essential starkness may be laid open like a dry fibrous wound. For there is no blood in the body of this land of his, only a greyness and unheeding expanse. There may be a skeleton—of kirkyard bones. He wants to make sure he has no illusions about that, no "Celtic Twilight hallucinations".

And then the change comes.

It comes gradually, almost furtively. A few leaves of the notebook escape under the fingers and it is more pronounced. Little by little he is slipping into the habit of identifying himself with things, at first with the apparent excuse of gaining more graphic force in the phrasing, but then, as it seems, without his always being aware of it. Keats said he could be the sparrow picking about the gravel; but the old woman of Tiree said:

> "*It is the grey rock I am,*
> *And the grey rain on the rock.*"

Iain was losing his destroying, logical objectiveness and occasionally identifying himself with the outer forces, the surrounding elemental forces. Not yet at the stage of the old woman of Tiree by any means, but rendered occasionally reflective, subjective, in a new momentarily quiescent way. The process goes on, subtly but persistently, begins to eat into him with a certain secretiveness which he plainly hides even from himself; then less plainly hides; until at last even the human figures he encounters become slightly more significant than spent automata.

Slipping some more pages, I find this entry:

"Went out on the edge of the dark and came on ould Sanny at the Look-out. His grey whiskers were to the sea and he spoke to me without turning round. I wonder what moves in his head? I'll tackle him one of these nights, when I've more time. I know definitely he thinks now and then of the old fishing days, and *sees* them, too. He draws in his breath on that wheezy 'Ay', then spits fully. 'Done! Done!' he says. 'It's no' what I remember.' It's not. God knows it's not. The gaping curing sheds in the darkening, the glooming, pervasive greyness, the lonely calling of the wheeling gulls. As I left ould Sanny I felt like laughing at it all, as it twisted and knotted in me. A husk of a place! A place to be laughed at. . . .

"I used to laugh, too, at Fiona Macleod and the like, but now—I'm damned if I'm not becoming fanciful myself. The tall grey salmon-net poles got me to-night. They stand there in that bunch near enough together, so that you could almost spit from one to the other; yet to-night each seemed lonely and thin and wrapped up in a grey self-communing. 'Apart' is the word. Good Lord—'apart'! Yet there it is. These bits of grey weather-cracked poles! And they got me with a sense of kinship, so that I stood among them till my hearing and sight became abnormally acute and my body stiff. From their little green plateau you look down on the harbour basin. It is empty. Look long enough—it fills. Oh, I know it is imagination, that I am allowing my staring eyes to see things. Obviously there is nothing—nothing material. There is merely this much: the place has its 'influence'. By way of experiment, I have given way to this influence once or twice. I give way again. A certain hypnotic, sinking sensation. . . . The harbour basin fills. Boat-decks, rigging, masts slanting to rest in their crutches, figures moving about, at first dimly, then more distinctly; a face, faces; sounds: all coming before the staring eyes through stages, as it were, of imperfect

269

focusing, till the picture lives, moves, throbs. A species of 'movies', if you like—for away from the influence one must joke about it to keep balance. But under the influence—my father's stride, a trifle quicker than the others; the face a trifle more alert; the tongue with its ever ready shaft. And there his men from the Lews—the heave-ho! chant of the voices, the *krik! krik!* of the halyards as mast goes slowly aloft. The brown sails—there they go slipping past the quay-wall to breast the sea: out of the smooth harbour-basin to this restless dipping and rising and gliding of the great brown-winged seabirds they are. The smother of life left behind, the ripe richness of the young women gutters' faces, the smiling wrinkles of the old, the incredibly deft fingers, the talk, the laughter, the work.

"An ache comes to the soul, the lips stir to an old savour, salty, brimful of life. Something here of the marrow. School-keeping, shop-keeping, book-clerking, all the pale, anaemic occupations of landsmen and citymen, dear Lord—how ghostly! their passion a hectic spurting, their contentment a grey haze. Teaching children all day long so that they may 'get on', may be successful in attaining the clerical stool or pulpit, or in measuring, at a profit, so many yards of red flannel for a country woman's needs. Eh? And being polite always: it pays. God!

"I am a throw-back, am I? Sort of quintessential heritage? All this centred in me as the living evocation of the dead sea-board? Perhaps my very hate of this place but a sort of wrong-headed, savage worship? What a damned juggling with perhapses!"

Then farther on and one stage farther on, this:

"With what an exquisite shudder the cold green water twists round body and limbs! It ensheaths you. Gracious and savage in a way less obvious than the East. In its coldness what clean passion! You want to throw caution to the winds and write of it in a choice prose, as of a beautiful woman, un-attainable, but near, so that her eyes are regarding yours with a measured expressionlessness—that at any moment may break and engulf you.

"I struggle to cast off this twilight phrasing, to regard the sea with clear eyes, knowing the Old Man as he is—veritably 'sea-green and incorruptible'. Yet even that leads me to a choosing of images. And when the caress of the water takes the shuddering body, and an exultation grips overhand at the wavetops . . . You can keep going on for ever. Turning back is a shattering. On and on, the under knowledge that you are going too far breeding a warning, an excitement. And how vision riots as doubt of the body's safety increases! In such a position is not one justified in dropping the stark logicalities and rioting, has not one earned the right? On and on, arm cleaving, body cleaving . . .

"Suddenly something pulls you up. You stop, tread water, look back to the shore. Panic forces rush in. You mutter a scattering curse at them—and start back in a long slow stroke. The water grows chilly, gets the back of your neck in a cold grip when you turn over. It is a long way. It is a devilish long way. Limbs begin to drag. A numbing sensation spreads. . . .

"At last the jagged rocks, the dark weeds, the black entrance to Breac Cove. Feet touch. You drag the body a yard or two and let it lie. The round stones press into it softly, the wet weed is velvety. Your head rolls off your arm on to the cold stones and the sea-water is a gurgling and lapping infinitely far off. You realise with a remote, impersonal unconcern that you could not have gone much farther—and come back . . . . "

One more quotation, though it is with reluctance I pass over a description of the twilight hour in Breac Cove, not so much because of the wild beauty and lurking ferocity dwelt on, as of the obvious giving way to its "influence".

"The struggle to-night was the hardest yet, for when the pause came and the panic forces rushed the brain, I continued to tread water and did not immediately start for the shore. In going out a saying had come to my mind from *The little book of the Great Enchantment*, and prefaced, I think, to *The Dirge of the Four Cities*, by Fiona Macleod. Fiona Macleod! There will ever be a grain of bitterness in my acknowledgement of him, or of Yeats, or of any of the modern Celtic twilighters, an irritable impatience of their pale fancies, their posturing sonorities and follies. Yet on a certain side they are 'getting' me, and sometimes a phrase, a thought, has a positively uncanny, mesmeric power over my very flesh.

"This sort of dream poetry is clearly a drug, an insidious drug. Intellect strives and flashes towards some final illumination—till the effort expends itself like a two-penny rocket attempting the work of a sun. And when failure rushes down in a renewed darkness, swamping all meaning and logic, dream poetry is there, a glimmering half-light, beckoning. Not an interpretation of the ultimates: a refuge from them. The man of action, with his raw grip on the realities, ignores it—till he finds the sphere of his activities dissolved, till (for this is the thought) the routh of life that swarmed the seaboard and clothed the very salmon-poles is left a ghostly greyness and a calling of gulls. Then poetry casts its net, its iridescent net, and the silvery fish of the intellect is meshed in the music of lost days and forgotten beauties. My images get mixed, I think—like my thought, and the bitter-raw becomes the bitter-sweet. Such a lovely vagueness is poetry, if one could but admit it! Perhaps the making of all great poetry has involved this fight—and this admission. Perhaps the men who have written greatly of the half-light have known the stark realities of the light. Let me say as much, even if I don't believe it yet, for, after all, what do I know of the ultimates that I should talk of a refuge from them?—There the fading light on the breast of the sea, there the dim-glowing west facing me as arm and body cleave through: and haunting my brain hypnotically the saying: 'And the symbol of Murias is a hollow that is filled with water and fading light'."

I am conscious of a light, a glimmering light. It is the half-light of the dawn on the window blind.

5

"Come away ben," she invited me, after we had sat in the kitchen for a little time; and I followed her to the parlour. It was bare of the gilt china ornaments of the old days; indeed, it was altogether bare.

"This," she said simply, "is going to be his study."

I knew a moment's insecurity. I suppose I was still young enough to think that tragedy is a thing to be swept into the dark places.

"So we'll put the bookcase there," she went on, gently, indicating a wall, "and the desk there—fornent the window."

I nodded, and, looking away through the window, saw the grey sea.

"My time cannot be so long—and the books and things of his will be company for me." Her voice was quiet and natural. A quietening came on me.

At the doorway I turned.

"He loved being here at home with you," I said. "He was happy with you. And he loved the old harbour and the sea."

"Perhaps, perhaps," she answered, her hands pressing my hand in the heart's quick acknowledgement. "I am so glad you think it. It was sometimes—on my mind. But I think he did love it—in the end; and we've always belonged to the sea."

The Moor

A few miles back it had looked like a sea-anemone on a vast tidal ledge, but now, at hand, it rose out of the moor's breast like a monstrous nipple. The scarred rock, heather tufted, threw a shadow to his aching feet, and because he was young enough to love enchantment in words, he savoured slowly, "Like the shadow of a great rock in a weary land". With a shudder of longing he passed his tongue between his sticky lips. The wide Sutherland moor under the August sun was silent as a desert.

At a little pool by the rock-base he drank and then dipped his face.

From the top of the rocky outcrop the rest of his tramp unrolled before him like a painted map. The earth fell away to the far sea, with cottages set here and there upon it like toys, and little cultivated strips, green and brown, and serpentine dark hollows.

He kept gazing until the sandwich in his mouth would not get wet enough to swallow. Then his eyes rested on the nearest cottage of all.

The loneliness of that cottage was a thing to catch the heart. Its green croft was snared in the moor's outflung hand. In the green stood a red cow. Creaming in upon his mind stole the seductive thought of milk. Tasting it made a clacking sound in his mouth and he stopped eating.

As he neared the cottage the red cow stared at him, unmoving save for the lifeless switch of her tail. The cottage itself, with its grey curved thatch and pale gable-end, made no move. The moor's last knuckle shut off the world.

The heather had not yet stirred into bloom and, far as the eye could see, lay dark under the white sun. He listened for a sound . . . and in that moment of suspense it came upon him that the place was bewitched.

A dog barked and every sense leapt. The tawny brute came out at the front door, showing half-laughing teeth, twisting and twining and in no time was at his back. He turned round, but still kept moving towards the door, very careful not to lift his eyes from those eyes, so that he nearly tumbled backwards over the doorstep . . . and was aware, with the beginnings of apologetic laughter, that he was in the presence of a woman. When he looked up, however, the laugh died.

Her eyes were gypsy dark. Perhaps she was twenty. Sunk in the darkness of her eyes were golden sun motes. His confusion stared speechless. A tingling trepidation beset his skin. A tight-drawn bodice just covered and repressed her breasts. Her beauty held the still, deep mesmerism of places at the back of beyond. She was shy, yet gazed at him.

The dry cup of his flesh filled with wine. Then his eyes flickered, shifted quickly; he veiled them, smiling, as though the rudeness of his bared emotion had gone forth unpardonably and touched her skin.

To his stammered request for milk, she smiled faintly, almost automatically, and disappeared.

Then he heard the beating of his heart. Through the warmth of his tired body swept a distinct heat. Excitement broke in spindrift. He smiled to himself, absorbed.

When he caught himself listening at the door, however, he immediately bespoke the dog, inviting his approach with such a sudden snapping hand that the brute leapt back, surprised into a short growl. He awaited her appearance so alive and happy that he was poised in apprehension.

She brought the milk in a coarse tumbler. He barely looked at her face, for good manners could not trust his instinct; his thanks he concentrated in a glance, a word or two, a smile breaking into a laugh. She had covered somewhat the wide V gleam of her breast, had swept back her hair; but the rents, the burst seam under an arm, the whole covering for her rich young body was ragged as ever, ragged and extraordinarily potent. He said he would drink the milk sitting outside if she didn't mind. She murmured, smiled, withdrew.

He ate his lunch excitedly, nibbling at the sandwiches to make them last, throwing crusts to the dog. His mind moved in its bewilderment as in coloured spindrift, but underneath were eyes avid for the image of her body, only he would not let their stare fix. Not yet. Not now. . . . Living here at the back of beyond . . . this secret moor. . . . Extraordinary! . . . But underneath he felt her like a pulse and saw her like a flame—a flame going to waste—in the dark of the moor, this hidden moor. Attraction and denial became a tension of exquisite doubt, of possible cunning, of pain, of desire. His soul wavered like a golden jet.

As the last drop of milk slid over, he heard a sound and turned—and stared.

A withered woman was looking at him, eyes veiled in knowingness. She said, "It's a fine day that's in it."

"Yes, isn't it!" He got to his feet.

She slyly looked away from him to the moor, the better to commune with her subtle thought. A wisp of grey hair fell over an ear. Her neck was sinewy and stretched, her chin tilted level from the stoop of her shoulders. The corners of her eyes returned to him. Just then the girl came to the doorway.

"It's waiting here, mother." Through veiled anxiety, compellingly, she eyed the old woman.

"Are ye telling me?"

"Come on in."

"Oh, I'm coming." She turned to the young man and gave a husky laugh, insanely knowing. The daughter followed her, and he found himself with the thick glass in his hand staring at the empty doorway. A sudden desire to tiptoe away from that place seized him. My God! he thought. The blue of heaven trembled.

But he went to the door and knocked.

"This is the glass——" he began.

She smiled shyly, politely, and, taking the glass from his outstretched hand, withdrew.

His hand fell to his side. He turned away, going quietly.

Down between the cottages, the little cultivated strips green and brown, the serpentine dark hollows, he went jerkily, as though the whole place were indeed not earth but a painted map, and he himself a human toy worked by one spring. Only it was a magic spring that never unwound. Even in the hotel that overlorded the final cluster of cottages, the spring seemed wound up tighter than ever.

For privacy he went up and sat on his bed. "Lord, I cannot get over it!" he cried silently. He got off his bed and walked about the floor. This was the most extraordinary thing that had ever happened to him . . . without quite happening to him.

Inspiration had hitherto thrilled from within. This was from without, and so vast were its implications that he could not feel them all at once in a single spasm of creation. He got lost in them and wandered back to his bed, whereon he lay full length, gazing so steadily that he sank through his body into a profound sleep.

He awoke to a stillness in his room so intense that he held his breath, listening. His eyes slowly turned to the window where the daylight was not so much fading as changing into a glimmer full of a pale life, invisible and watchful. Upon his taut ear the silence began to vibrate with the sound of a small tuning fork struck at an immense distance.

THE MOOR

His staring eyes, aware of a veiled face . . . focused the face of the girl on the moor. The appeal of her sombre regard was so great that he began to tremble; yet far back in him cunningly he willed body and mind to an absolute suspense so that the moment might remain. Footsteps on the corridor outside smashed it, and all at once he was listening acutely to perfectly normal voices.

"Well, Mr. Morrison—you here? What's up now?"

"Nothing much. The old woman up at Albain—been certified."

"So I heard. Poor old woman. When are you lifting her?"

"To-morrow."

"There's no doubt, of course, she is . . . ay, ay, very sad."

"Yes. There's the girl, too—her daughter. You'll know her?"

"Well—yes. But she's right enough. I mean there's nothing —there. A bit shy, maybe . . . like the heather. You know."

"I was wondering what could be done for her."

"Oh, the neighbours will look after her, I'm sure. She'll just have to go into service. We're fixed up for the season here now, or I . . ."

The footsteps died away, and the light in the bedroom withdrew itself still more, like a woman withdrawing her dress, her eyes, but on a lingering watchfulness more critical than ever, and now faintly ironic.

His body snapped into action and began restlessly pacing the floor, irony flicking over the face. Suddenly he paused . . . and breathed aloud—"The auld mither!" As it was also an apostrophe for his country, his eyes gleamed in a profound humour.

The exclamation made him walk as it were more carefully, and presently he came to the surface of himself some distance from the hotel and realised where he was going.

But now he cunningly avoided the other cottages and in a roundabout way came in over the knuckle of moor in the deepening dusk. The cow was gone and the cottage seemed more lonely than ever. Indeed, it crouched to the earth with rounded shoulders drawing its grey thatch about its awful secret. Only the pale gable-end gloomed in furtive watchfulness.

Grey-green oasis, dark moor, and huddled cottage were privy to the tragedy of their human children, and, he felt, inimical to any interference from without. Never before had he caught this living secretive intensity of background, although, as a young painter believing in vision, it had been his business to exploit backgrounds of all sorts.

The girl herself walked out from the end of the house, carrying two empty tin pails. On the soft turf her feet made no sound. Unlike her background she was not inimical but detached. And, as her slave, her background spread itself under her feet.

By the time he joined her at the well she had her buckets full, and as he offered to carry them she lifted one in each hand. He pursued his offer, stooping to take them. The little operation brought their bodies into contact and their hands, so that there was a laughing tremble in his voice as he walked beside her, carrying the water. But at the doorway, which was reached in a moment, he set down the buckets and raised his cap.

As he went on into the moor, still smiling warmly as though she were beside him, he kept saying to himself that to have dallied or hesitated would have been unpardonable . . . yet not quite believing it . . . yet knowing it to be true.

He sat down on the moor, his heart aflame. The moor lost its hostility and became friendly. Night drew about them her dim purple skin. Silence wavered like the evening smoke of a prehistoric fire. The sense of translation grew in him . . . until the girl and himself went walking on the moor, on the purple, the rippled skin, their faces set to mountain crests and far dawns.

He tore his vision with a slow humour and, getting to his feet, shivered. As he returned by the cottage he saw her coming out of the byre door and on a blind impulse went up to her and asked:

"Are you not lonely here?"

"No," she answered, with a smile that scarcely touched her still expression.

"Well—it does seem lonely—a bit?"

Her eyes turned to the moor and only by a troubling of their deeps could he see that his words were difficult. She simply did not speak, and for several seconds they stood perfectly silent.

"I can understand," he broke through, "that it's not lonely either." But his awkwardness rose up and clutched him. If the thickening dusk saved his colour, it heightened her beauty in a necromantic way. Mistrust had not touched her, if tragedy had. A watchfulness, a profound instinct young and artless—yet very old.

The front door opened and her mother came peering on to the doorstep. In low quick tones he said:

"I'll come—to-morrow evening."

Her eyes turned upon his with a faint fear, but found a light deeper than sympathy.

By the time he got back to the hotel, his companion, Douglas Cunningham, had arrived, round about, with the motor-cycle combination.

"Sorry I'm so late. The beastly clutch kept slipping. I had the devil's own time of it."

"Had you?"

"Yes. We'll have to get down to it to-morrow. . . . What happened?" Douglas looked at Evan shrewdly. "Seems to have lit you up a bit, anyhow."

"Does it?"

Then Evan told him.

Douglas met his look steadily.

"You can't see?" probed Evan, finally. "The moor, the lonely cottage, the mad mother, and the daughter . . . . My god, what a grouping! Can't you see—that it transcends chance? It has overwhelmed me."

"My dear chap, if you'd been in the ditch with a burst clutch and umpteen miles from nowhere you would have been, by analogy, completely pulverised. You're the pure romantic."

Their friendly arguments frequently gathered a mocking hostility.

"You show me the clutch of your tinny motor bike," thrust Evan. "I show you the clutch of eternal or infernal life. I'm not proving or improving anything: I'm only showing you. But you can't see. Lord, you are blind. Mechanism, clutch, motor bike . . . these are the planets wheeling about your Cyclops glassy eye. You are the darling of evolution, the hope of your country, the proud son of your race. You are the *thing* we have arrived at! . . . By the great Cuchulain, is it any wonder that your old mother is being taken to a mad-house?"

"By which I gather that you have found the daughter's mechanism—fool-proof?"

Evan took a slow turn about the floor, then with hands in pockets stood glooming satanically. "I suppose," he said, "we have sunk as low as that."

Douglas eyed him warningly. "Easy, Evan."

Evan nodded. "Whatever I do I must not go in off the deep end!" He suddenly sat down and over his closed fist on the table looked Douglas in the face. "Why shouldn't I go in off the deep end?"

Douglas turned from the drawn lips and kicked off his boots. "You can go in off any damned end you like," he said. "If you can't see things as they really are, I can't help you."

THE MOOR

In bed, Evan could not sleep. To the pulse of his excitement parable and symbol danced to a pattern set upon the grey-green oasis of the croft, centring in the cottage . . . fertile matrix of the dark moor.

Vision grew and soon wholly obsessed him. He found in it a reality at once intoxicating and finally illuminating. A pagan freedom and loveliness, a rejuvenation, an immense hope . . . and, following after, the moods of reflection, of beauty, of race . . . to go into the moor not merely to find our souls but to find life itself—and to find it more abundantly.

But the following evening the little cottage presented quite another appearance. He came under its influence at the very first glance from the near moor crest. It had the desolate air of having had its heart torn out, of having been raped. A spiritless shell, its dark-red door pushed back in an imbecile gape. One could hear the wind in its emptiness. A sheer sense of its desolation overcame him. He could not take his eyes off it.

And presently an elderly woman came to the door, followed by the girl herself. They stood on the doorstep for a long time, then began slowly to walk up to the ridge beyond which lay the neighbours' cottages. But before they reached the ridge they stopped and again for a long time stood in talk. At last the elderly woman put out her hand and caught the girl's arm. But the girl would not go with her. She released herself and stepped back a pace, her body bending and swaying sensitively. The elderly woman stood still and straight, making her last appeal. The girl swayed away from that appeal also, turned and retreated. With hooded shawl her elder remained looking after her a moment, then like a woman out of the ages went up over the crest of the moor.

From his lair in the heather, Evan saw the door close, heard, so still the evening was, the clash and rattle of the latch. And with the door closed and the girl inside, the house huddled emptier than ever. His heart listened so intently that it caught

282

the dry sound of her desolate thought . . . she was not weeping
. . . her arms hung so bare that her empty hands kept plucking
down her sleeves . . .

She came at his knock. The pallor of her face deepened the
dark eyes. Their expressionlessness troubled and she stood
aside to let him in. Only when they were by the fire in the
gloom of the small-windowed kitchen did she realise what had
happened.

But Evan did not feel awkward. He knew what he had to do
like a man who might have imaginatively prepared himself for
the test. He placed her chair at the other side of the fire but did
not ask her to sit down. He sat down himself, however, and
looking into the fire began to speak.

Sometimes he half turned with a smile, but for the most part
kept his eyes on the burning peat, with odd silences that were
pauses in his thought. He was not eager nor hurried; yet his
gentleness had something fatal in it like the darkness of her
mood.

She stood so still on the kitchen floor that in the end he
dared not look at her. Nor did his immobility break when he
heard her quietly sit down in the opposite chair, though the
core of the fire quickened before his gaze.

Without moving, he started talking again. He did not
use words that might appeal to a primitive intelligence. He
spoke in the highest—the simplest—way he could to himself.

He looked at himself as a painter desiring to paint the moor.
Why? He found himself dividing the world into spirit and
mechanism. Both might be necessary, but spirit must be
supreme. Why? At twenty years of age he knew the answer.
Spirit drew to spirit in a communion that was the only known
warmth in all the coldness of space. And we needed that
particular warmth; at moments we needed it more than anything else. Man's mechanism was a tiny flawed toy in the vast

flawless mechanism of the universe. But this warmth of his was a thing unique; it was his own special creation . . . and in a way—who could say?—perhaps a more significant, more fertile, thing than even the creation of the whole mechanical universe. . . .

As he thought over this idea, he felt her eyes on his face. The supreme test of spirit would be that while not knowing his words—what did they matter?—it would yet understand him perfectly—*if it was there*.

"I do not know," he said at last, and repeated it monotonously. "Coming in over the moor there I saw you and the woman. Then there was the moor itself. And you in the cottage. The woman could have helped you. Only you didn't want to be helped in her way yet." He paused, then went on slowly: "I can see that. It's when I go beyond that to my sitting here that it becomes difficult. For what I see is you who are the moor, and myself with the moor about me, and in us there is dawn and out of the moor comes more of us. . . . That sounds strange, but perhaps it is truer than if I said it more directly. For you and I know that we cannot speak to each other yet— face to face."

Then he turned his face and looked at her.

Her dark eyes were alight with tears that trickled in slow beads down her cheeks.

It was there.

Quietly he got to his feet. "I'll make a cup of tea."

She also arose. "I'll make it."

It had grown quite dark in the kitchen. They stood very still facing the unexpected darkness. Caught by something in the heart of it, they instinctively drew together. He turned her face from it.

In the morning Douglas arrived at the cottage on the heels of the woman with the shawl. The woman had tried the door and found it locked. But her quick consternation lessened when she found the key under the thatch.

Douglas, grown oddly curious, waited for her to come out. She came, with a face as grey as the wall.

"She hasn't slept in her bed at all."

"Oh!" His lips closed.

The woman looked at him.

"Do you know . . .?"

"Not a thing," said Douglas. "Must have gone over the hills and far away. They've got a fine morning for it." And he turned and left her, his scoffing sanity sticking in his throat like a dry pellet.

AS IT WAS

An Autobiography 1897-1918
Naomi Mitchison

Naomi Mitchison celebrated her ninetieth birthday in 1987 and is considered one of the foremost contributors to the literary scene. In SMALL TALK she plunges us into a child's eye view of Edwardian life. Girl matures to woman in ALL CHANGE HERE and Naomi Mitchison explores her desire for freedom to be and know herself and her own mind.

CHARLES RENNIE MACKINTOSH

1868-1928
Jocelyn Grigg

An indispensable fully illustrated guide to the architect, designer and watercolourist who, for his futuristic vision, was acclaimed father of the modern movement.

BURRELL: PORTRAIT OF A COLLECTOR

1861-1858
Richard Marks

In 1983 the fabulous collections of *objets d'art* built up by Sir William Burrell went on show in its entirety for the first time in a gallery specially designed and built for it.

This is a unique and lavishly illustrated portrait of an extraordinary genius.

Other titles in the SCOTTISH COLLECTION

THE BRAVE WHITE FLAG *James Allan Ford*

THE LAST SUMMER *Iain Crichton Smith*

THE SCOTTISH COLLECTION OF VERSE
VOL 1 to 1800 *Ed Eileen Dunlop & Antony Kamm*

THE FIRST HUNDRED THOUSAND *Ian Hay*

DUST ON THE PAW *Robin Jenkins*

THE MERRY MUSE *Eric Linklater*

MAGNUS *George Mackay Brown*

THE BULL CALVES *Naomi Mitchison*

EARLY IN ORCADIA *Naomi Mitchison*

THE CHINA RUN *Neil Paterson*

WHERE THE SEA BREAKS *John Prebble*

A GREEN TREE IN GEDDE *Alan Sharp*

TIME WILL KNIT *Fred Urquhart*

WALK DON'T WALK *Gordon Williams*

SCOTTISH BIOGRAPHIES

BURRELL: PORTRAIT OF A COLLECTOR *Richard Marks*

AS IT WAS (Autobiography) *Naomi Mitchison*